# T<sup>the</sup>emptation

## *Trap*

# IVY LAYNE

GINGER QUILL PRESS, LLC

**The Temptation Trap**

Written by Ivy Layne as Alexa Wilder, originally published as Alexa Wilder

Copyright © 2016 by Alexa Wilder

All rights reserved.

Find out more about the author and upcoming books online at www.ivylayne.com

# ALSO BY IVY LAYNE

**Don't Miss Out on New Releases, Exclusive Giveaways, and More!!**

Join Ivy's Readers Group @ ivylayne.com/readers-group

## THE HEARTS OF SAWYERS BEND

Stolen Heart

Sweet Heart

Scheming Heart

Rebel Heart

## THE UNTANGLED SERIES

Unraveled

Undone

Uncovered

## THE WINTERS SAGA

The Billionaire's Secret Heart (Novella)

The Billionaire's Secret Love (Novella)

The Billionaire's Pet

The Billionaire's Promise

The Rebel Billionaire

The Billionaire's Secret Kiss (Novella)

The Billionaire's Angel

Engaging the Billionaire

Compromising the Billionaire

The Counterfeit Billionaire

## THE BILLIONAIRE CLUB

The Wedding Rescue

The Courtship Maneuver

The Temptation Trap

# CONTENTS

Chapter One                          1
Chapter Two                          5
Chapter Three                        13
Chapter Four                         21
Chapter Five                         27
Chapter Six                          37
Chapter Seven                        45
Chapter Eight                        55
Chapter Nine                         59
Chapter Ten                          69
Chapter Eleven                       79
Chapter Twelve                       87
Chapter Thirteen                     95
Chapter Fourteen                     105
Chapter Fifteen                      113
Chapter Sixteen                      119
Chapter Seventeen                    123
Chapter Eighteen                     131
Chapter Nineteen                     141
Chapter Twenty                       151
Chapter Twenty-One                   161
Chapter Twenty-Two                   169
Chapter Twenty-Three                 177
Chapter Twenty-Four                  185
Chapter Twenty-Five                  191
Chapter Twenty-Six                   193
Chapter Twenty-Seven                 201
Chapter Twenty-Eight                 209
Chapter Twenty-Nine                  217
Chapter Thirty                       227
Chapter Thirty-One                   237

Chapter Thirty-Two                        245
Chapter Thirty-Three                      251
Chapter Thirty-Four                       257
Chapter Thirty-Five                       267
Chapter Thirty-Six                        275
Chapter Thirty-Seven                      283
Chapter Thirty-Eight                      291
Chapter Thirty-Nine                       299
Chapter Forty                             307
Epilogue                                  317

The Winters Saga                          323
The Billionaire's Secret Heart            325
Sneak Peek: Unraveled (Evers & Summer)    329
Also by Ivy Layne                         341
About Ivy Layne                           343

# CHAPTER ONE
## AXEL

E mma Wright was becoming a problem. She was supposed to be a job. An easy job. Get close to her, find evidence that she was selling confidential data to a competitor. Get paid a ton of money. How hard could it be?

She was the head of Human Resources at a shipping company, not Mata Hari. This kind of thing was the bread and butter of Sinclair Security. I figured I'd take the meeting and pass the case to one of my guys.

Then I got a good look at Emma Wright.

Fiery red hair, creamy skin, abundant curves, and clear blue eyes with a wicked glint. She was irresistible. Luscious, soft, and more than a handful in all the right places. The moment I saw her picture, I knew I'd be handling her myself.

Fucking the suspect wasn't usually my MO, but in this case, I was prepared to make an exception. Normally, my approach was to get the evidence, give it to the client, close the case, and cash the check. Not with Emma.

Getting her into bed wasn't the hard part. Neither was

pretending to be her lover. But Emma was tricky. She was smart. Funny. Gorgeous. And surprisingly kinky. Deliciously kinky. I'd never admit it, but it's possible I was taking my time on the case just to have an excuse to keep fucking her.

That, and it was harder than I'd expected to find what I was looking for. I kept waiting for her to slip. Everyone did, eventually. But so far, nothing. I hadn't caught her in even the tiniest lie. The client was getting restless, and I was starting to wonder if I was losing my touch.

I knew she was guilty. Most people were when it came down to it. I already knew what would happen in the end. Tears. Pleading. Excuses and justifications. None of that would matter to me.

I'd taken the contract, and I would do my job. In the back of my mind, I was hoping it would last just a little longer. I hadn't yet had my fill of that lush body, and once I found the data Emma was smuggling out of Harper Shipping, she'd go to jail and our affair would be over.

Tonight, my plan was to push her off balance, enough so she might make a mistake. Until now, I'd worked it out so that most of our dates were dinner at her house. More intimate and easier to search her place.

When I did take her out somewhere, I chose places that were upscale, expensive, and not my usual style. I didn't need to be recognized as Axel Sinclair when I was pretending to be Adam Stewart. But tonight, I'd picked a quiet, low-key Italian place around the corner from Emma's.

I'd expected her to pout or act annoyed that I wasn't spending a few hundred dollars on her dinner. I should have known better.

Emma was relaxed, drinking her wine and digging into her fettuccine Alfredo. Watching the woman eat pasta was a torturous form of foreplay. When the creamy sauce hit her tongue, she sucked a stray noodle into her mouth with pursed lips, her eyes closed in rapture.

I couldn't help but imagine her sucking me off with that same expression on her face.

She couldn't have cared less if she was in an exclusive restaurant surrounded by the best of Vegas society or a place like this one with paper napkins and a chalkboard menu on the wall. Emma enjoyed life however it came at her. I wondered if that would serve her well when she went to prison.

There was a chance she could avoid going to jail. Either way, I had to remind myself it wasn't my problem. My job was to find proof she was stealing and give that proof to her boss. What happened to her after that was between them.

Most of the time the client didn't press charges. That kind of publicity was worse for business than the crime itself. But the owner and CEO of Harper Shipping had made his intentions clear. As soon as he could prove what she'd done, he was calling the police.

Knowing Emma, she'd get off with probation. She was smart enough to hire a good lawyer, and she'd be able to afford decent counsel. She'd managed to hide the money she was getting for the data she'd stolen. If my hackers couldn't find it, neither would the police. Somewhere out there, Emma had a tidy little nest egg, ready to cushion her when she fell.

Watching her wind pasta around her fork as she laughed over a story a friend had told her, I found it hard to reconcile the woman before me with the liar I knew she was.

I'd been in this game long enough to know that anyone could be a criminal, no matter how innocent they appeared on the surface. But Emma just didn't give me the guilty vibe.

If I hadn't seen surveillance video of her rifling through secured files and copying them, then later handing them off to a competitor in a dark parking lot late at night, I would have sworn she wasn't the one they were looking for.

But I had seen it, seen her face clearly. Even had one of my guys check it. Video could be manufactured. This was real.

On top of that, she treated her briefcase like it held the keys to Fort Knox. And she got jumpy whenever I brought up her job. In fact, it was the only time she acted oddly. Not guilty. Not exactly. But not her usual fun-loving self.

All of it added together was more than enough to convince me. Emma was guilty, and I would bring her down. A voice in the back of my head told me to find the evidence and close the case before I got in any deeper.

Sitting across from her, my eyes glued to her lips as she sipped her wine, I knew it was already too late. I was in deep with Emma. And part of me, a part I'd thought long dead, hoped that somehow I'd find a way to prove her innocent.

## CHAPTER TWO

### EMMA

Adam had that look on his face again. I'd seen it before, and I didn't know what it meant. He stared at me as if I was a puzzle and he needed to figure me out. It didn't make sense. There's not that much to figure out about me.

I'm a basic girl. I have a job I like, good friends, nothing out of the ordinary. In fact, the only unusual thing in my life was Adam.

We'd been dating for more than three weeks, and I still wasn't sure what he was doing with me. Don't get me wrong, I'm a pretty good catch. I'm intelligent, not hard on the eyes, and my friends say I'm fun to be around.

I have a few too many curves for guys who like skinny chicks, but that's okay with me. For every guy who wants a waif, there are two who like a full set of DDs and a round ass.

I hate starving myself, and while I don't mind going to the gym a couple of times a week I'm not spending my life there. I'd never be on a catwalk, and I didn't care. None of the few guys who'd seen me naked had complained. That said, I've never dated much, mostly by choice. No offense to any good guys out there, but most of the guys I'd hooked up with were assholes.

Going out every night and trying to find a good man is a waste of time. I know they say you have to kiss a lot of frogs to find your prince, but seriously, I've had enough frog kissing to last a lifetime.

Maybe I have a low tolerance for bullshit. Or maybe I'm impatient. Either way, I'd rather hang out with my friends, have fun with my hobbies, and live the good life without one more lying, deadbeat guy asking to borrow money before he cheats on me.

I'm not bitter or anything. I don't have some horrible ex in my past. I have a great dad and two fantastic brothers. And I have some girlfriends with amazing husbands. I know there are good guys out there, I just don't seem to attract them.

I attract the dicks who have mommy issues and can't hold down a job or think that having self-confidence makes me a bitch. No thanks.

Adam was different. So far, not an asshole. But also way out of my league. Like I said, I'm a pretty good catch. I've dated men with money. Successful men. Good-looking men. Adam was all three.

He was the kind of man you'd expect to see helping a supermodel out of a Ferrari. Not the kind of man you'd expect to meet in a cooking class at the local community college.

There I'd been, slicing carrots at my first night of learning to cook Thai food, when from beside me I heard a low, deep voice say, "What exactly are we supposed to be doing here? I got in late, and I don't have a partner. Tell me you're not taken."

I'd almost passed out when I got my first look at the new arrival. Tall, at least, 6'4". I've always loved tall men. At 5'10", it was a luxury to look up into a man's eyes.

Short dark hair, eyes so dark brown they were almost black, sharp cheekbones, and full lips. All of that with broad shoulders, lean hips, and no sign of a beer belly. I was ready to swoon.

I immediately forgave my friend Allison for talking me into Thai cooking class and then bailing at the last minute because she got back together with her boyfriend.

"Nope, I'm free," I'd said with a smile. "I signed up with a friend, but she's a no-show."

He let out a relieved breath and said, "Same for me. I thought I was going to have to do this myself." Holding out a hand, he'd said, "I'm Adam Stewart."

That was the beginning of what had become the wildest love affair of my life. That first night we'd eaten the Pad Thai we'd cooked, and Adam had asked me out for a drink.

The class was on Wednesday nights, and I didn't usually go out drinking when I had to work the next day. Especially with all the stress at the office in the last few months. But cooking with him had been a blast. He was fun as well as hot, and I wasn't ready to say good night.

Two glasses of wine and a scorching kiss later I'd left him in the parking lot and driven home wondering what would happen when I saw him in class the following week. If he even showed up.

I didn't want to get my hopes up. After that kiss, I had no doubt he would've preferred to end the night in my bed, but I didn't sleep with guys on the first date. Not even guys as hot as Adam.

Who was I kidding? I'd never been with a guy as hot as

Adam. I still wasn't sure why I hadn't taken him up on his not-so-subtle suggestion that I invite him home.

Maybe I was intimidated. Maybe it just seemed too good to be true that someone as attractive and interesting as Adam Stewart wanted me.

I walked into class the following week to find him waiting at our work table. He looked up and saw me, a welcoming smile spread across his face, bringing light to his intense eyes and melting my caution.

We spent two hours making a green chili curry, and when we were done, I swallowed my nerves and asked him if he wanted to have a glass of wine with me. At my place.

We'd barely made it through the door before we fell on each other, all eager, frantic hands, his mouth hungry and insistent on mine. That first time he overwhelmed me.

He tore the buttons from my blouse, my fingers slipped on the catch of my skirt, and then the rasp of the carpet against my back as we hit the floor. I was lucky he remembered protection. By the time we were naked, I was too far gone, dizzy and blind from the feel of his hard body against mine.

I'd been going through a dry spell for the past few months, and the press of his cock inside me was almost too much. The first orgasm had crashed through me in a tidal wave of sharp, sweet pleasure.

He fucked me in hard, deep thrusts, dragging out my orgasm until he followed me into bliss, his eyes squeezed shut, teeth clenched. We'd laid on the carpet for a few minutes, trying to catch our breath, before Adam rolled to his feet, took my hand, and led me to my bedroom.

And then things got a little crazy. As I've mentioned, I'm a pretty normal girl. Not a virgin, not a slut. I don't break any mirrors, but I'm not gorgeous.

I'd had sex before, a handful of boyfriends and one long-term relationship. So far, the sex had been fairly normal, just like me. Not much worth gossiping about with my girl-friends, but not bad. Just sex.

Sex with Adam was not normal. Not that first time when it was all desperate urgency and crazed desire. And definitely not normal the second time when he carefully removed what was left of my bra and used it to tie me to the bed.

It had never occurred to me that I'd like being tied up. I've been thinking about it since that first time. A lot. Because I didn't just like it, I loved it. When we had our clothes on, Adam treated me like an equal.

I could be loud, and I could be opinionated. That had been a problem with men in the past. My personality attracted them at the beginning, but once we were together, it always seemed that what they really wanted was a quiet woman who agreed with everything they said.

Not Adam. He enjoyed our verbal sparring. He liked my enthusiasm. And while he was pretty much the definition of confident and assertive, he didn't need to control me to feel powerful.

When the clothes came off, everything changed. Adam was in charge, and what he wanted, he got.

In a million years I never would have thought I'd find that attractive. I don't know if I can explain it, because I've always hated it when anyone told me what to do. The easiest way to get me to do something is to tell me to do the opposite.

But when Adam gave me that intent focused look and followed it with an order, I complied immediately, my body heating in anticipation. I think it's safe to say the whole rela-tionship had me spun.

The first time he told me to get on my knees and suck his cock, I'd glared at him in outrage. He'd raised one dark eyebrow and stared me down. By the time I had his belt open, the insides of my thighs were slick with moisture, every cell in my body white-hot with need.

Maybe I would've felt differently if he'd dismissed me afterward, if he treated me like a one-night stand or a booty call. But after the sex, after the orgasms, he was always there.

He never slept over, but he didn't rush out either. He'd lay in bed with me, his long body curled around mine, his hands stroking my skin, soothing and sweet. Sometimes we'd talk, whispered conversations about nothing and everything. Other times I'd fall asleep with him and wake alone.

Adam Stewart seemed like my dream man. For the most part, he was. But still, there were things that didn't add up. He was very, very good at distracting me with his body, but I hadn't missed the fact that I'd never met any of his friends, never been to his place, and never seen where he worked.

We hadn't been together that long, barely a month, but by now he should have at least invited me to see where he lived. I'd asked, and his excuse about renovations could have been the truth.

I didn't want to doubt him. For one thing, I trusted him. At least as much as I could trust anyone I'd only known a month. Maybe I just didn't want to believe he was hiding something.

I'll admit it; I worried that if I got any deeper and found out something I didn't want to know, I'd have to give up the best sex I've ever had.

Maybe I should have broken up with him or demanded he prove he didn't have a wife or girlfriend. Another woman might have tried snooping in his cell phone or his wallet. I didn't do any of that.

My life had gotten very complicated in the past few months, and Adam was a blissful distraction. I was afraid if I peeked behind the curtain I would find out that he had been nothing more than an illusion. I was wary enough to continually remind myself not to fall for him.

Laughing over a shared dinner, mind-blowing kinky sex, and snuggling were all well and good, but I was keeping my heart out of it. At least, I was trying to.

Across the table, Adam broke through my reverie when he put down his fork and pushed his plate away.

"Almost finished?" he asked, his eyes focused on my mouth as he watched me take my last bite of pasta. Adam had a number of looks I couldn't decipher. His intense gaze and heavy eyelids were not one of them. My belly tightened in anticipation.

I had no idea what he was planning for tonight, but I knew whatever it was, I was going to love it.

I put down my fork, finished chewing, and took a sip of wine. "I'm finished," I said. Adam gestured for the check, not bothering to ask if I wanted dessert.

Normally, I always wanted dessert, but with the way Adam was looking at me, I couldn't have cared less. I'd get my after-dinner treat; it just wouldn't be in the form of food. The waiter was at the table a moment later, then walking away a minute after that, cash in hand.

Adam and I rose together, our eyes locked on each other. He helped me into my coat, his gaze leaving a searing path across my skin everywhere it touched.

Standing behind me, settling my coat over my shoulders, he reached around to fasten the top button, his knuckles grazing the bare skin of my upper chest. My nipples tightened at his touch, and I shivered when he whispered into my ear, "I like this dress. I'd hate to damage it. What should we do about that?"

"I guess that depends on how you want to fuck me," I murmured back. "Do you want me naked? Or do you want me to bend over and pull it up out of your way?"

Adam's hands dropped as he fastened the middle button of my coat. I felt the loss of his touch as soon as he stepped away. He took my arm and led me toward the door in silence, my question hanging in the air between us.

# CHAPTER THREE

## EMMA

A dam was silent on the ride home. So was I, though the sounds of my fidgeting filled the car. I couldn't sit still or stop thinking about being naked, Adam's skin on mine.

I had an image stuck in my head of me bending over, braced on the couch or the kitchen table or the side of my bed, the skirt of my dress pulled up over my back while Adam took me rough and fast. Or slow and sweet. It didn't matter.

Every time I put my body in his hands, he paid me back in pleasure. I was willing to follow his lead wherever it took us.

He parked the car in front of my building and came around to my door. It still felt odd to wait for him to let me out of the car.

I'd never dated a man who insisted on opening my car door, or any door, really. Adam refused to have it any other way. The first time I'd preceded him through a door, he'd grasped my shoulders and set me firmly behind him.

I'd made a comment about his wanting the 'little woman'

to take second place, annoyed at being treated like a second-class citizen. He'd scowled at me and told me it was a matter of safety, and by going first out of the door, I was leaving myself exposed.

Which was a weird thing for an app developer to think about, but he'd said he'd been in the military when he was younger, so maybe something stuck.

I humored him and let him open doors because I liked it. The downside of being a tall, smart, and outgoing female is that very few people worry about protecting you. It was undeniably nice to have a big, strong man looking out for me, and I planned to enjoy it for however long it lasted.

He led me through the parking garage, his strong hand pressing against my lower back, the heat of his palm making my knees weak. By the time we were up the elevator and walking down the hallway to my apartment door, my heart was racing.

I pulled my keys from my purse, and, as he always did, Adam took them and unlocked the door, using his tall body to herd me into my foyer. My hands reached up to unbutton my coat when he stopped me.

"Don't move," he said. "Close your eyes. Don't open them until I tell you to. Do you understand?"

At the sound of his deep, intense voice, I trembled and squeezed my thighs together, my body swaying back towards him slightly, as if the timbre of his words was a magnet.

In truth, it was. He only spoke with that particular tone when he was about to get me naked, and it never failed to make me wet. Needy. And just a little desperate. In response to his question, I closed my eyes and nodded.

"If you open your eyes before I give you permission, I'll punish you." An involuntary shiver wracked my body. "Not that kind of punishment," he said, amusement coloring his voice. "The kind where you don't get an orgasm. Not for a long time. Maybe not at all."

That threat sent chills down my spine. He'd punished me before, but as he'd implied, I liked Adam's brand of punishment.

Just like when he'd tied me up and I'd gone off like a firecracker, the first time he'd spanked me had been explosive. At the first strike of his palm against my ass, I'd been affronted. No one hit me. Not ever.

I'd tried spanking one time with an ex-boyfriend, but it had hurt and hadn't been the least bit arousing. After that, the idea of letting some guy hit me had been repellent.

Clearly, I hadn't been spanked by the right man. Adam knew what he was doing when he punished a woman. He'd started with light smacks, enough to sting, but not truly painful. By the time he spanked me as hard as my ex had, I'd been riding high on endorphins, and the flash of pain had pushed me that much closer to orgasm.

Since then I'd welcomed any threats of punishment with a thrill of anticipation. It seemed, this time, Adam's intended punishment was something else. I didn't like the sound of being denied my orgasm.

I squeezed my eyes shut even harder. If I'd learned anything in the last month, it was that Adam wasn't kidding around when he gave an order. I didn't have to obey. But it was worth my while if I did. I felt Adam's hands on the buttons of my coat, the tug of the fabric, and the release of the garment as it fell open.

Hangers clicked as he hung the coat up. His heat was against my back, knuckles grazing the skin between my shoulder blades as he slowly lowered my zipper.

The filmy green dress had a deep V in both the front

and the back. Without the zipper to hold it together, it slipped down my shoulders and off my arms to pool around my hips.

With an expert flick of his fingers, my bra was loose. I knew better than to shimmy it off. And I didn't have to. A swipe of Adam's hand and it was gone.

Without my bra to contain them, my breasts swayed with every breath I took, my nipples tight. I expected Adam to touch me, to feel his mouth or his fingers teasing my newly bared flesh. I was disappointed.

Instead, his hands settled on my hips, pushing the light fabric of my dress to the ground where I could feel it pool around my feet. I didn't dare look, keeping my eyes tightly shut.

All that forced me to Adam's will were his words. He didn't need a blindfold. Adam's desire that I obey was the only tool he required to compel my obedience. And that only made it hotter.

"Take off your underwear," he said, his words a growl in my ear, his breath hot on my cheek. I didn't have to see the fine tremble in my hands. I could feel them flutter against my hips as I hooked my fingers in the sides of my red lace thong and pushed it off. "Leave your heels on and step away from your clothes."

His hand closed on my elbow to steady me as I carefully slid my feet free of my dress and took a step away, not wanting the narrow spike heel to catch in the fabric and trip me.

I stood there in the foyer of my apartment, naked except for my heels, my eyes closed, waiting for Adam's next command. He moved, circling me. I heard fabric rustle. Was he undressing?

I imagined I could feel his eyes skating over my skin,

touching me everywhere. It wasn't enough. I wanted more than his eyes. I wanted his hands. I wanted his touch. Needed him to take me out of myself, to drown my busy mind in pleasure.

I let out a shocked squeak when teeth closed over my earlobe and bit down, just hard enough to surprise but not hard enough to hurt. "Good girl," he said, kissing the earlobe he'd so recently bitten. "Such a good girl, Emma. Can you be good for a little longer?"

I made a sound in the back of my throat, somewhere between a squeak and a moan, nothing close to intelligible speech. Adam laughed, his lips grazing my throat as the sound vibrated against my skin. "Such a good girl," he said again.

In a whoosh, everything was upside down, Adam's strong arms around me as he lifted me, cradling me against his chest. The shock of sudden movement almost had me opening my eyes, and I squeezed them shut in self-defense.

I didn't need my eyes to tell me he was taking me to my bedroom. My apartment wasn't that big—his first few steps took us past the kitchen and the living room.

Once in my room, Adam placed me carefully back on my feet, leaving his hands on my hips an extra moment until I'd steadied myself on my narrow heels.

His hands landed on my shoulders, then slid down my arms until his fingers encircled my wrists. Those long fingers tightened, drawing my arms behind me, turning my hands palm to palm. His fingers pressed themselves over mine, weaving them together until my fingers were laced, clasped tight.

"Keep them just like that," he said. He stood behind me, and I heard fabric rustle once more, the thunk of his belt hitting the floor, a shuffle that might have been him toeing off his shoes.

Then his skin was against mine, the tight beads of his nipples brushing my shoulders, the thrust of his erection against my lower back. Hot, hard, and silky. I wanted it.

Still, he barely touched me. His voice was almost inaudible when he said, "Spread your legs."

I did, widening my stance, opening my body to his. I was almost expecting it when I felt his palm between my shoulder blades, pushing forward with a gentle but undeniable pressure. I straightened my arms behind me, palms still pressed together, using them to help my balance as I slowly lowered my chest to the bed.

I managed the feat with some grace and was glad I bothered to go to yoga every once in a while. Otherwise, I probably would've lost my balance and ended up looking like an idiot.

My cheek was hot against the cool linen of my duvet cover. Bent over like that, the air flowed between my legs, reminding me how wet I was. He was taking too long, but I knew better than to complain. Not if I wanted him to fuck me anytime soon.

My nipples slid against the fabric, the contact a delicious tease. Adam's hand, still resting between my shoulder blades, trailed down my spine, stopping at the small of my back.

He traced a figure eight with his fingertips, the light touch both too much and not nearly enough. Then both hands were at my hips, squeezing, molding my body before moving to do the same to the curves of my ass.

My palms almost fell apart when a quick, light swat landed at the exact spot where my ass met my thighs. I jumped and gasped, but my eyes remained tightly closed, hands together behind my back.

"I think," Adam said, his voice heavy with promise, "my good girl deserves her reward."

Two fingers dipped between my legs, pushing past my entrance, spreading apart to stretch me open. I couldn't help thrusting back at him, earning myself another swat on my ass.

"Not yet," he ordered, and I tried to stay still. It was hard. Almost impossible. I needed him.

My breath was coming in gasps, my heart pounding in my chest. I pressed my eyes shut, my hands together, as if my obedience could compel him to give me what I wanted.

Maybe it did, because the next thing I felt was his thick cock pushing into my pussy, stretching me open, filling me the way only Adam could.

I moaned at the pain-tinged pleasure. He was big, his cock thick and long. Sometimes he came into me gradually, with little thrusts, working his way in. And then there were times like this when I was wet enough for him to fill me in one long, slow thrust. Pressure and pleasure in one.

When he was seated to the hilt, I squeezed him, earning myself another smack. The flash of pain only gave more of a bite to the bliss of his cock in my pussy. I thrust against him, trying to take him a little deeper. Impossible when he was already in me to the hilt. But it was enough to goad Adam into action.

With a growl, he sank his fingers into my hips and began to thrust, his cock pounding into me, his balls swinging forward to smack my clit, driving me to the edge of orgasm in moments.

I gasped for breath, my closed eyes and trapped hands suddenly mixing panic with the ever-growing pleasure.

Adam had blindfolded me before, but it had never been this intense.

Somehow, blinding myself, voluntarily fixing my own hands behind my back and cutting off my sight, served to make me feel even more helpless than I'd been when Adam had done it.

Everything inside me focused on the sensations between my legs. The tease of the duvet cover against my nipples, the harsh sounds of Adam breathing, my thudding heartbeat.

When he released my hips and used my joined hands to pull me upright, I gasped a half scream, rising with him, suddenly off balance. He let go and covered my breasts with his hands, thrusting faster. I sobbed, wobbling on my heels, unsteady and skating the edge of orgasm.

"Open your eyes," he rasped. I did, disorientation flooding me as my eyes fought to adjust to the dim light in my bedroom. "Look," he demanded.

My gaze fastened on the mirror above my dresser on the opposite side of the bed, unable to take in what I saw.

Adam, the corded muscles of his chest and arms standing out, knotted with tension, his big hands overfilled with my pale, soft breasts. His eyes burned into mine as they met in the mirror.

My hair fell around us in sheets of red, my cheeks flushed a deep pink, my eyes glittering a midnight blue. Adam's hands twisted, and his fingers closed on my nipples, squeezing tightly enough to cause a heady mix of pain and fiery pleasure.

"Come," he whispered in my ear. "Come for me now."

In a rush of sharp, burning ecstasy, I did.

# CHAPTER FOUR
## AXEL

I left Emma passed out in her bed, her duvet pulled up to her chin, long hair spilling across her white sheets like a trail of flame. I'd almost fallen asleep myself. After I'd fucked her, she'd slid onto her bed, her knees weak from the force of her orgasm.

I might have been smug about it, but my own knees had been less than solid as I'd gone to the bathroom to deal with the condom. I needed her asleep to get to the next step of my plans, so I'd tucked myself into bed beside her, wrapping one arm around her waist and settling my hand against her breasts.

Emma might be a lying criminal, but she had stupendous breasts. Seriously amazing. Full. Soft, yet firm. Her whole body was like that—soft everywhere. Her hips, her ass, her stomach. Soft and round and perfect.

There were no hard edges to Emma. At least not on the outside. For the first time, I wondered if I could help her get a lawyer when it all went down, find some way to keep her safe from the worst of the trouble coming her way.

I knew better than anyone that sometimes, good people

made stupid mistakes. I'd seen it too many times to count. No way Emma was rotten to the core. I'd sense it.

I'd known people like that, empty and wrong. Soulless. That wasn't Emma. There had to be a reason she'd steal from her company and sell their secrets for profit. I just hadn't uncovered it yet.

I'd done a thorough background check on Emma when I'd taken the case. I hadn't turned up anything that explained why she would be involved in corporate espionage. Her life seemed fairly stable.

She grew up in Southern California with two brothers, older, and one sister, younger. Her parents were retired, brothers in the military, sister in grad school. No one had any outstanding debt, except for a few student loans that were almost paid off. No extravagant purchases, no expensive health problems, no gambling, no drugs. Just normal people living normal lives.

I was missing something. I had to be. No one crossed the line into criminal behavior without a reason. Some people just got off on the thrill, but if that were the case, there would've been a clue. Speeding tickets or dangerous hobbies.

Emma had plenty of interests outside of work, but they mostly involved taking classes, like the cooking class where we'd met, or hanging with her girlfriends, giggling over wine or martinis. Nothing that gave any indication why she might wake up one day and decide to start stealing from her employer.

I'd run into situations like this before. The pieces of a puzzle weren't always clear at the beginning of a job. I was used to that. But it normally didn't take this long to figure out what the hell was going on.

Laying in her bed, her soft, warm body tucked into

mine, it was hard to imagine there would be an end. Eventually, maybe tonight, I'd find what I needed, and I'd walk away. My gut tightened at the thought. Whatever my mind had planned, my body sure as hell didn't want to give up Emma.

I was drifting off beside her, the honeysuckle scent of her hair and her warm body lulling me into fantasies of luring her away from her life of crime, when my brain kicked in.

Despite the act I was putting on, I reminded myself, Emma Wright was not my girlfriend. She wasn't my lover. She was a job. Worse, a target. I had a duty to my client to get my lazy, satisfied ass out of bed and find the evidence that would prove her guilt and get her out of his company.

Repressing a sigh, I eased myself away from Emma, slipped from the bed, and grabbed my clothes off the floor, closing the door behind me.

After getting dressed, I started where I always did, with her briefcase. I checked every outside pocket, finding the same pack of tissues, lint, emergency sewing kit, and tin of mints that were always there.

The inside was the same as ever, a mostly-empty notebook, a plastic envelope filled with personal papers, and her laptop. She never hid anything in the briefcase, at least not so far, but I checked it anyway. In my line of work, it pays to be thorough.

I moved on to my real target for the night. Emma's laptop. Silently pulling it from the briefcase, I set it on the coffee table and flipped it open. I'd figured out her password the first night. Her father's birthday, not very secure.

Once I'd broken into the computer, I'd made a quick copy of the hard drive and installed a program that would tell me what had changed. It saved me searching through the whole laptop every time. So far, there wasn't much of interest.

A lot of nights she didn't even bother to bring it home, only when she thought she might have to answer emails from employees after hours.

For the first time in almost ten days, the program alerted significant changes in the file structure. My heart sped up, the thrill of the chase drowning out my conflicting feelings about Emma. This might be exactly what I was looking for.

I opened the new files and scanned them, disappointed to find that they were nothing more interesting than explanations of the company's medical and vacation benefits that had been updated the previous day.

Emma's job sounded both boring and annoying. From what she'd told me about her work, it seemed to me that she spent her days going over paperwork and listening to employees bitch about bullshit that wasn't Emma's problem.

For the most part, she chose to find it amusing, retelling some of the complaints with a laugh instead of irritation. I wouldn't have been nearly as patient.

The Las Vegas branch of Sinclair security didn't have an official human resources department. That kind of stuff was handled by our office manager, a former Marine, who'd been injured in the field.

He got the paperwork done, but nobody brought Billy whiny complaints about the coffee maker in the break room. If any one of my team ever complained about someone hurting their feelings, we'd run them out of the building.

Aside from the paperwork and the complaining employees, there were aspects of Emma's job she'd been reluctant to explain. It was those aspects that had my instincts on alert. That, and she seemed too young to head a department.

She was only twenty-eight. Harper shipping wasn't a huge conglomerate, and the company only had one location, but there were over one hundred employees, and Emma had four beneath her. Just one more thing that didn't add up.

I flipped through the files as quickly as I could, looking for anything suspicious. Finally, I hit a folder buried among insurance manuals. It was new, when nothing else in that folder had been updated in months, and it was encrypted. Nothing too hardcore.

Emma wasn't a hacker, and from what I'd seen it didn't appear that she was working with one. I'm not a hacker either. Not exactly. But I had a few on my team, and they'd taught me just enough to get by.

I had the folder open a few minutes later, but I couldn't tell if it was useful. Spreadsheets with names numbers and addresses.

I copied them to a USB drive I'd brought for that purpose, but I had a sneaking suspicion that I was looking at a list of employees and their confidential information. Not customer accounts, bids, logistical plans, or any other proprietary information that might be valuable enough to sell to a competitor. I'd check it, but so far this search, like all the others, was a bust.

At the almost silent thump down the hall, I exited out of my program and the open folders, closed the laptop, slid it back into the briefcase, and leaned over as if I was putting on my shoes.

Emma's bedroom door opened and a second later she appeared at the end of the hall, wrapped in a faded pink knit robe, her eyes squinted against the light in the living room. Her cheeks were still flushed with sleep, almost the same pink as her robe. Her eyes skimmed me, taking in my half-dressed state, and she said, "You going?"

Another woman might have said the words with an accusation or petulance. Emma offered neither, no judgment and no complaint. Oddly, that bothered me.

I shouldn't want her to want me to stay. I was here to keep tabs on what she was doing and search for evidence for my client. Fucking her was only a side benefit. I wasn't her boyfriend. So why the fuck did I care if she didn't care that I was sneaking out on her in the middle of the night? Again.

I didn't care, I told myself.

"Yeah," I said. "Got an early meeting."

"K. I'll lock up behind you," she said, her voice adorably still half asleep.

"What about you?" I asked, unable to stop myself. "Do you have an early meeting?"

Looking confused, she shook her head. Leaving my shoes on the floor, I stood and crossed the room to her. Her eyes widened in surprise when I took her face in my hands and kissed her.

Her mouth opened, her tongue stroking mine, her arms wrapping around my shoulders. I kissed her harder, crushing her full lips, pulling her flush against me, her breasts pressed to my chest, her ass filling my hand.

It was late, and I did have an early meeting. But since we were both awake, it would be foolish to waste the opportunity to get Emma naked. I was a lot of things, but I wasn't a fool.

# CHAPTER FIVE

## EMMA

I sat at my desk, my coffee cold in front of me, my stomach twisted in knots.

It was GO time.

The last few months of stress and fear had led me to this moment. If I managed not to mess up the next hour, I'd get my life back. I think I've mentioned I'm just a normal girl. I was not meant for excitement. At least not this kind.

It had all started so simply.

I took a job at Harper Shipping just out of college as a lowly assistant in the Human Resources department. My plan was to stay here for a few years, then go to grad school part-time and get my MBA.

Three months ago, I'd finished my MBA, planning to start looking for a new job eventually. I didn't love working at Harper Shipping, but I didn't hate it either.

I did like Human Resources, and my job here was good experience even if my boss, Thomas, was a misogynistic asshole who thought being female meant I was inherently less intelligent than anyone with a penis.

It might have bothered me more, but he didn't try to

hold me back so much as he was just rude and annoying on occasion.

A few weeks after I finished graduate school, Thomas' mother got sick, and he took an extended leave. To my shock, he recommended me as his interim replacement.

I was flattered, though I think he only did it because he couldn't imagine a woman angling to take his job and figured I'd be the safe choice.

I didn't care; I was excited about the opportunity. If I'd known what I was getting into, I would have run screaming.

To say Thomas was disorganized would be an understatement. I spent the first week or two on the job just trying to make sense of his system for handling the vast amounts of paperwork generated by our department.

Everything relating to employees had to go into writing. Including verbal reprimands. And Thomas had everything stacked in random piles on his desk and inside his filing cabinet.

I dragged in an intern and set to work putting things right. He probably would have been furious when he got back, but a month after he left, Thomas called William Harper, the owner of Harper Shipping, to give his resignation.

Since the Human Resources department hadn't fallen apart during Thomas' absence, Mr. Harper said that I could keep the job, at least as long as it remained apparent that I could do it.

I dove in, determined to get the department running exactly the way I wanted it. I loved everything about being in charge except reporting to Mr. Harper, who creeped me out a little bit.

He was an inch shorter than me, with narrow bones and a protruding potbelly that made him look pregnant. His shoulders slouched forward, and his watery blue eyes always seemed to be trying to look down my shirt. He'd never done anything overtly inappropriate; I just didn't like the way he looked at me.

Fortunately, we had one short meeting a week, and some weeks not even that if he was out of the office. He'd suggested once that we have our meeting over dinner, but he'd been neutral when I'd declined, as if he hadn't cared either way. He creeped me out, but as long as there weren't any problems in Human Resources, he mostly left me alone.

I should've been in heaven, heading my own depart-ment only a month after getting my MBA, especially with the increase in salary that went along with the promotion. I should have been thrilled. And I was. Until I got a phone call from the FBI.

I would've been more alarmed, but Harry Jensen, the FBI agent, reminded me of my dad. He had the same tall, bulky build that was half muscle and half fat. Similar thick brown hair that needed a cut, and his blue eyes were kind and patient. I needed that because I was seriously freaked.

I'd never even had a speeding ticket, and the only time I'd seen the FBI was on the news when they were wearing those navy blue jackets with the yellow letters on the back and escorting a prisoner or milling around a crime scene. I couldn't imagine what they might want with me. When Agent Jensen said it had to do with my job, I was floored.

Harper Shipping was not exactly a hotbed of criminal activity. The company had a huge fleet of trucks and contracted out to various distributors to drive merchandise all over the country.

I worked for the employees, not the clients, but I'd seen enough people coming in and out of the office to know that our clients were mostly corporate, from easily identifiable companies.

Agent Jensen assured me that I was right, for the most part. The bulk of our business was legitimate. Unfortunately, William Harper had gotten greedy.

According to Agent Jensen, Mr. Harper wasn't happy with the current healthy level of profit he got from shipping legitimate goods around the country. The list of 'other' things Harper Shipping transported was long and terrifying.

Weapons. Drugs. And people. Illegal immigrants to be sold as slave labor. And women, girls mostly. More immigrants, and runaways. Girls who came to Vegas for the bright lights and got lost.

They would also be sold, but for a different kind of work. I couldn't imagine it. I didn't like Mr. Harper, but I just couldn't see him masterminding a criminal enterprise like the one Agent Jensen was describing. He didn't seem smart enough, for one.

Harper Shipping was a company William Harper had inherited from his grandfather. He hadn't built it from scratch or taken what he'd been given and made it better. He barely managed to keep the company on an even keel.

When Agent Jensen explained that Mr. Harper was working with the Russian mob, everything made more sense.

And it got that much more terrifying. My first thought, after hearing about the case from Agent Jensen, was to quit my job and get the hell out of town.

I had nothing to do with any of the things he'd described. I didn't coordinate with clients, I didn't handle logistics for shipping, none of it. I occasionally did a little work with marketing, but that was the only time I ever stepped outside of Human Resources. My job was limited to benefits, company policies, and employee problems.

But the FBI needed someone on the inside, and after investigating the company for the past year, they'd determined that my new promotion made me their best bet.

Coming from below the management level, Agent Jensen was reasonably sure that I was clean, yet my new position as head of Human Resources meant I had access to the information that might prove their case against both William Harper and the Russian mob.

I'm going to be honest. I didn't want to help. I wasn't afraid of Mr. Harper, not exactly. But the Russian mob? I wasn't stupid.

I've seen plenty of movies, and the idea of getting on the wrong side of the Russian mob seemed like a great way to get myself killed.

I might not be doing anything really important with my life. Taking cooking classes and hanging out with my friends wasn't exactly curing cancer, but that didn't mean I didn't value what I had.

I wasn't crazy about putting myself in danger. I was gearing up to tell Agent Jensen he could take his job and shove it when he showed me the pictures. Girls, young women, their eyes wide and terrified. Then more pictures of other girls, dead girls.

Agent Jensen said they hadn't been able to prove it, but they believed these girls had been moved into the country and to their final destinations by Harper Shipping.

The discovery of the group of six dead young women, ages 11 to 15, had been the FBI's first tie between the Russian mob and Harper Shipping. Agent Jensen stared at me with those warm brown eyes so like my father's and begged me to help. To save the next shipment of girls, and the one after that.

I couldn't say no. Not after looking at those pictures, those girls too young, gray with death, their eyes flat and empty. So I'd begun spying on my employer for the FBI.

I was terrible at it. Really terrible. It wasn't that I got caught or even came close to getting caught. Mr. Harper seemed oblivious, and in general, the files were such a mess no one noticed what I was looking at.

On top of that, everyone had gotten used to me reorganizing my department, so it wasn't unusual to find me poring through papers in the storage rooms or poking around the company looking for something Thomas had misplaced.

But I really had no idea what the FBI needed, and Agent Jensen couldn't always be specific. So far, I'd only managed to give them a few things that were helpful.

Then Agent Jensen moved on, and Alan Tierney took over. I didn't like Agent Tierney. Agent Jensen had made me feel safe. Maybe that was just an illusion because he looked like my dad, but I'd trusted Agent Jensen to look out for me.

Agent Tierney was all about the case. I was just a means to an end for him. Disposable. It made me nervous. At this point, I just wanted to find something they could use to end all this so I could go back to my normal, relatively stress-free life.

I'd been racking my brain, trying to figure out what I could get that would provide solid enough evidence to end my involvement in the FBI's case.

It was complicated, because, like Agent Jensen, Agent Tierney didn't fill me in on the details of what he needed, and I wasn't trained in criminal investigation. If you wanted to know the limits of your health insurance policy or when you could take vacation, I was your girl.

How to determine what was useless data and what might stand up in court? I had no clue.

The day before, I'd finally caught a break. The most recent corporate cell phone bill had landed on my desk by accident and following a hunch, I'd opened it.

I went straight to Mr. Harper's call records and discovered that he'd been using his corporate cell phone to conduct criminal activity. At least, I recognized a few of the numbers he'd called as those Agent Jensen had given me.

He'd asked me to let him know if they ever came through the switchboard, saying they belonged to key players in the Russian mob. I'd memorized the numbers even though I'd been sure I'd never see them. I rarely manned the switchboard—a lot of people had to be out of the office before the head of Human Resources answered the phones.

But I'd been wrong, because here they were, those numbers I'd memorized all those months ago. I had to think that copies of these records would be helpful.

They could subpoena them from the cell phone carrier. I thought they could. But that might tip off Mr. Harper about the investigation. I had a legal right to copy these files as an employee of the company. I was pretty sure that was true.

While the bills went to the accounting department, I was listed as an admin on the account since Human Resources issued cell phones to employees.

I tried to log into the account online and download the last few months of call records, but the password Thomas left me didn't work.

When I ordered cell phones for the account I usually

did it over the phone, not online, and I'd never tried to log in. But I knew where paper copies of the bills were kept. If I could get down there, copy the records, and get them to Agent Tierney, it might be enough to end this once and for all.

I was so ready to be done with being an informant for the FBI. The week before, Agent Tierney had asked me to find a file that Harper had used to keep track of shipments for various enterprises with the Russians.

Not only had Mr. Harper kept records of all of it going back a year, but he also stored those records in his office. Agent Tierney had promised he would take care of shutting off any security that might catch me, but he said I was the one who had to steal the file.

I thought it was odd that he hadn't wanted me to copy the file, leaving it where it was so that Mr. Harper would never know I'd been there. He'd wanted me to physically remove the file from Mr. Harper's office and bring it to him, along with a scanned copy of the file. I'd done it, waiting until both Mr. Harper and his assistant were out of the office.

Agent Tierney had given me a good idea where to look, and the whole thing hadn't taken me more than a few minutes, but I'd been sick to my stomach the entire time. I really wasn't cut out for this kind of work.

My fingers were crossed that this afternoon would be my last clandestine file search. I kept myself busy at my desk until lunchtime, when I knew most of my coworkers would be headed out of the building or otherwise occupied.

I usually stayed at my desk for lunch, because employees who wanted a quiet word would often stop by then, taking advantage of the same lull in activity that I was looking for today.

I'd brought a sandwich for lunch, but I left it in my desk drawer, too nauseated from nerves to think about eating anything. At twelve forty-two, I pushed my chair back and stood, taking a deep breath to settle my nerves, and tried to force a calm, placid expression onto my face.

It was GO time. If I could find what I needed, I'd be off the hook.

# CHAPTER SIX

## EMMA

The office was quiet as I made my way to the elevators. My footsteps seemed to echo through the entire floor. In my imagination, every head turned to watch me as I passed by, making note of the time of my activity for later. I knew that was ridiculous.

No one was paying any attention to me, and even those who noticed my passage didn't care. It didn't stop me from being almost lightheaded with anxiety.

I'd hidden a tiny USB drive in my pocket. We had pretty sophisticated copiers at Harper Shipping, and the one in the file room would let me scan directly to the drive. Efficient, and far easier to be sneaky when the evidence I took with me could literally fit in the palm of my hand.

I rode the elevator alone and, conscious of the security cameras, tried not to fidget. I had every right and reason to go down to the file room. I was in there several times a week on legitimate business. No one would think this trip was any different, or so I told myself.

The doors opened, and I smoothed my jacket over my hips, using the motion to dry my sweaty palms. Nervous about getting caught, I'd dressed a little differently today than I normally did.

Most of my work clothes consisted of a variety of suits in feminine cuts that flattered my curvy figure. Nothing inappropriate, all very professional, but I've never understood why professional couldn't also be pretty.

While I knew I was unlikely to have to run for my life in the file room, I hadn't been comfortable wearing a skirt and heels today. Instead, I'd chosen one of my few pantsuits and a pair of flats. The change in wardrobe made me feel even more off-balance.

The basement of the building was deserted, the lights flickering. The energy-saving motion detection system left every room dark except those occupied by a person. I tried not to jump as the lights followed me down the hall, flicking on as they sensed me coming. They were good for the environment, and the power bill, but I'd always found them creepy, today more than ever.

I opened the door to the file room, manually flicked on the lights, and shut the door behind me. I could feel the emptiness in the room, and that, combined with the closed door, made me feel a little bit better.

The file room was huge, taking up most of the basement level. The ceiling was only nine feet, and while the room was big, the tall rows of shelves made it feel like a rabbit warren or a cave.

Not sure where the cell phone bills were kept, I searched through the room, reading the labels on the ends of each aisle, hoping to find something that looked right. I checked an aisle marked 'Billing' and found it contained invoices for clients. That might have useful information, but it would eat up my entire day to check, and I had to stay focused.

I was headed down an aisle marked 'Accounts Payable, Misc.' when my phone beeped in my pocket. I think I jumped about a foot in the air, my heart thudding in my chest from shock and fear. My hand shaking, I pulled the phone from my pocket and checked the text on the screen.

*Dinner tonight?*

It was Adam. We didn't usually go out two nights in a row. I wanted to see him. I always wanted to see Adam. Probably more than was good for me. No, definitely more than was good for me. But I didn't think I'd be free this evening. I hoped I wouldn't.

I hoped I'd be meeting Agent Tierney to hand over the evidence I was about to find, ending my involvement in the case.

*Can't,* I typed back. *I have a work thing that'll run late. Late dinner?*

I stared at my phone, torn. I did want to see Adam. And how long could it take to hand off the USB drive to Agent Tierney? Anyway, I needed something good to look forward to.

*That works. I'll TXT you when I'm done.*

*Looking forward to it.*

I shoved my phone back in my pocket and tried to concentrate on the task at hand. I was on the third section of 'Accounts Payable, Misc.' when I found it in a nondescript box marked with the name of our corporate cell phone carrier, on the fourth shelf up in a row filled with similar boxes. I pulled down the first box and lifted the lid.

It was packed with manila file folders. I groaned and flipped through them. There was no way I'd have time to scan all of these. I didn't even think my USB drive was big enough to hold that many documents. I tried to think logically.

If Agent Tierney was going to use the phone records to substantiate the files I'd given him last week, he only needed records from this year. I grabbed the box marked for the current year and headed for the copier at the far end of the room.

Scanning the cell phone bills was an enormous pain in the ass. Each bill had about fifty pages. At least, that's what it seemed like. Rather than scanning the record of every call made on a company cell phone, I scanned the first page of each bill and the section that included Mr. Harper's calls.

It still took forever. I was already nervous, but my anxiety spiked even higher as I felt the clock running down. I'd been in the basement too long. Away from my desk for too long. I was three-quarters of the way through, and I still had to get the last few months of bills to the USB drive.

"Are you almost done?" The sound of a voice behind me sent a bolt of sheer terror through my chest. I jumped, dropped the sheaf of papers in my hands, and whirled, my eyes wide with panic, one hand pressed over my thundering heart.

"Wow, Emma, are you okay? I didn't mean to scare you, sorry." It was Allison, one of the interns. She was new, sweet, and got sent on annoying errands for everyone who had the authority to tell her what to do. I rubbed my hand over my chest and took a deep breath, trying to calm down.

Gathering up the papers I'd dropped, I said, "Sorry, Allison. I'm fine. I just got used to it being so quiet in here, and I didn't hear you come in. You scared the heck out of me."

Allison started to crouch down and help me with the papers, but I threw out a hand and said, too sharply, "I've got it."

She took a step back and gave me a probing look. "Are you sure you're okay?"

I picked up the last of the papers and stood, shuffling them back together in a semblance of order. I felt my face flushing red. "Really, I'm fine. The basement always freaks me out, the way the lights come on by themselves, and how big it is. It makes me feel like a little kid afraid of the bogeyman."

"Sorry about that," Allison said again. "I get creeped out down here too. Do you need any help?"

"No, I'm almost done. Can you give me a few more minutes?" I asked, my heart rate finally back to normal. I quickly reorganized the bill I was holding and turned back to the copier.

There was no way for me to hide the distinctive logo on the corporate cell phone bills. I would just have to hope that Allison didn't ask why I was copying them. My stomach twisted in a knot, and I felt bile rise in the back of my throat. I forced it back and pasted a friendly smile on my face as I got to work.

"Sure, no problem," she said. Allison leaned against the end of the copier, too close for comfort, and began to chatter about two employees who had been secretly dating and were now in the middle of a not-so-secret ugly breakup.

I relaxed slightly. I liked Allison, but I didn't think she was bright enough to be this involved in relating gossip and also make detailed mental notes of what I was doing.

After what felt like an eternity, I scanned the last bill, put it in order, and filed it back in the box. Hefting the box, I turned and said, "It's all yours, thanks for waiting!"

I was halfway to the end of the room and almost out of sight when I heard Allison's voice behind me. "Hey, Emma, wait a sec!"

My heart jumped into my throat once more, my breath catching in my chest. I was so close to being done with this. What did she want?

I spun around to see her holding out my USB drive. Tucking the awkward file box under my arm, I took it from her gratefully, feeling like a complete idiot. How awful would it have been to go through all of that then lose the stupid USB drive? Stress had my brain scrambled.

"Thanks, Allison. I can't believe I almost left that down here," I said, trying to sound casual.

She shrugged and smiled. "Anytime, see you later."

I returned the file box without any further incidents and went straight back to my desk. As soon as I sat down, I pulled a second USB drive from my purse, this one blank, and plugged both of them into my computer. It only took a few minutes to copy the drive, but having a back-up made me feel much better.

On impulse, I copied over the scanned file Agent Tierney had asked me to get the week before so that the last few weeks of files were all in one place. Before anyone could come into my office, I pulled a prepaid priority mail envelope from my bottom desk drawer, addressed it to my best friend, and dropped the second USB drive inside.

This whole situation was making me paranoid: finding out my boss was a criminal, Agent Tierney replacing Agent Jensen, sneaking around copying files. I was uneasy handing everything over to Agent Tierney. What if he lost something?

All my work would be wasted, and I might have to do it again. I needed to have a backup, and Summer was perfect. I didn't tell her what I was sending to her, just asked her to keep it somewhere safe and not let anyone know I sent her anything. I didn't even ask her over the phone, though we talked to each other several times a week.

A few months before, I'd sent her a priority mail envelope like this one with an almost identical USB drive inside, along with a note asking her to hang onto it and not mention it to anyone, even to me, unless we were face-to-face. She'd done as I asked.

Well, I assumed she had since I hadn't seen her in person for the last few months. But Summer Winters was my best friend, and if I could trust anyone, it was her.

# CHAPTER SEVEN

## EMMA

My clandestine trip to the file room had gone according to plan, if not with seamless perfection. Almost losing the USB drive could be counted as a fail. But I'd gotten what I needed, and that was the important part. After that, the rest of my day went to hell.

My afternoon was filled with straightening out an employee's health insurance mix-up and listening to five employees, one after the other, complain about the emotional stress of having to listen to the details of two other employees' private life. The two other employees in question were the same pair Allison had been talking about in the file room.

There was a good reason you weren't supposed to sleep with your coworkers. Well, there were a lot of good reasons you shouldn't sleep with your coworkers, but in my opinion, the most important was that office affairs were a huge pain in the ass for the Human Resources Director.

I called Agent Tierney as soon as I finished putting

together the envelope for Summer. I planned to drop it in the mail before I met with him.

He knew nothing about Summer, and I wanted to keep it that way. I doubted I'd ever need those backup files, and there was no reason she had to get dragged into this. At least not any further than I'd already dragged her. But Agent Tierney couldn't meet me to take the USB drive. He said he was out of town on a case, there was no one else he trusted with my evidence, and he could meet me at lunch-time the next day.

So close... The USB drive felt like it was burning a hole in my briefcase. Now that I had what I hoped was the final piece of evidence, they'd need to put together a case against Mr. Harper and the Russian mob. I just wanted it out of my hands.

I couldn't believe I had to keep it one more day. The afternoon stretched into eternity. I texted Adam to let him know I was free for dinner, so at least I had that to look forward to.

Once I was done with Agent Tierney and the FBI, I was going to put some energy into this relationship and figure out what was going on with Adam Stewart.

By five o'clock, I was exhausted, my head pounding, and all I really wanted to do was drink a big glass of wine and go to sleep. For the first time since we'd met, I wasn't looking forward to Adam coming over.

He was there when I got home, standing at my door, carrying a bag of take-out from my favorite Chinese place. When the elevator opened, he looked up, his dark eyes warming as they met mine, then narrowing in scrutiny.

"You look beat," he said, stepping away from the door to give me room to unlock it and let us in. "Long day?"

"Day from Hell," I said. Once inside, I hung up my coat

and put down my things, eager to get out of my work clothes if I couldn't collapse on my bed and take a nap.

Before I could say anything else, Adam pulled me into his arms, taking my mouth in a sweet, slow, uncharacteristically undemanding kiss. His lips left mine and brushed across my temple as he tucked my hair behind my ear.

"Why don't you go change into something comfortable. You look like you need a glass of wine and a foot rub."

See? This is why I couldn't break up with him even if he might have a secret girlfriend. A glass of wine and a foot rub from a thoughtful super-hot guy was exactly what I needed.

Somehow, I knew he remembered that my favorite Chinese food was spicy orange chicken, just like he'd remembered to order from my favorite Chinese restaurant. Adam Stewart was crazy hot, amazing in bed, and very sweet. All of that also made him a little scary.

It didn't take me long to strip off my pantsuit, kick off my flats, and change into a comfy-but-cute pair of yoga pants with a matching camisole and hoodie.

It wasn't the most flattering outfit in my closet, but it didn't look too bad, it was ridiculously comfortable, and the deep lavender shade looked great with my eyes and hair. I was exhausted and frustrated, but I still wanted to look good in front of Adam.

My wine was poured and my food plated when I got back to the kitchen. Adam led me to the living room, carrying both of our plates, where he had a movie paused on the TV.

We got together fairly often to Netflix and chill, which meant we didn't end up watching a whole lot of Netflix. This movie was one we'd both talked about wanting to watch and never got around to.

"I thought we could eat in here," he said, handing me my plate as I sat down.

I'd never eaten my lunch, and at the smell of the spicy orange chicken, I realized I was starving. I dug in, ignoring everything but my dinner until the hole in my belly was filled. When I was done, I put my plate on the coffee table and picked up my wine, sending Adam a grateful smile.

"That was exactly what I needed. Thank you."

"Tell me what was so awful about your day," he ordered, spearing a piece of beef with broccoli on his fork and lifting it to his mouth, one eyebrow raised. I couldn't tell him all of it, obviously, but he'd probably think the employee relationship drama was funny.

"I swear," I said. "My job is fairly boring most of the time, but every once in a while... We have two employees, married employees, but not to each other. Sometime in the last few months, both of them decided life would be more exciting if they started hooking up.

"I'm not going to give you too much description because you're eating and I don't want to spoil your appetite, but let me just say that these two employees are the last two people you ever want to envision hooking up. Or doing anything that would involve taking off their clothes."

Adam laughed and said, "I don't care if I'm eating, now you have to describe them to me. Whatever's growing in my imagination has got to be worse than reality."

"It's just that she's about five feet tall and maybe weighs ninety pounds. And she looks like she's sixteen. He's past fifty, and he's a big guy. Over six feet and definitely over three hundred pounds.

"I mean, I don't even know how that works. And he's got this long greasy hair that I don't think he's washed since the 70s. She always has food stuck in her teeth and really bad breath. Her coworkers leave mints on her desk, and she just throws them away."

Adam put his plate down, still laughing, and said, "Well, everybody deserves love."

"I very strongly believe that's true," I said. "But these two already picked their soul mates. He's been married for three decades, and I bought her a wedding present last summer. Besides, it is very much against company policy to have sex at the office. I'm sorry to tell you that they were caught on camera."

"Did you have to watch?" Adam asked, laughing so hard at this point the couch was shaking. Before I could answer, he reached down, picked my feet up off the floor, and sat back, tucking them into his lap. He rolled my big toes in his strong fingers, and I let out a moan of pleasure as I answered.

"Not all of it, but enough. More than enough. I think my retinas were seared from the horror."

"So, you had to deal with them all day?"

"No, that's the worst part. They've been dealt with already. A formal reprimand, both put on action plans, kind of like being on probation. Done and done. What I had to deal with was a never-ending stream of their coworkers coming into my office to complain about the trauma of the affair when they were really just looking for dirt.

"Sometimes I think gossip is a basic human need, like shelter and food and sex. People are incapable of minding their own business, and it drives me nuts. I mean, these two already completely messed up their lives. Their jobs are in danger, not to mention their marriages. Do we really need to pick them apart during office hours, too?"

"That really sucks," Adam said, shifting his hands so he could squeeze and press my heels. It felt so good I could've lain there all day. I took a sip of wine and closed my eyes. "I'm glad I don't have to deal with that kind of thing in my office," he went on. "My team doesn't gossip."

I gave a little snort and opened my eyes again. "What? App developers don't gossip? I don't believe that. And don't tell me it's because you're all guys, though you probably are. Half the gossipers coming through my office are guys."

Adam made a funny sound in his throat, and I looked at him, surprised to see a slightly panicked expression in his eyes. "What?" I asked. He shook his head.

"Nothing," he said. "And we're not all guys."

"Yeah? How many women are on your team?" I asked. "I've read all about gender issues in tech hiring. Are you saying your company is the exception?"

"Not exactly," he admitted. "But we do have a few female programmers. And I promise we don't give them a hard time."

"I bet," I said, not convinced. But his hands were working magic on my feet, my stomach was full, I'd had half a glass of really good Riesling, and being on the edge of panic all day had exhausted me.

I didn't want to get into an argument about gender inequalities in the tech industry. That would just lead into a bigger conversation about differences in pay, the way stay-at-home moms got shafted, the way working moms also got shafted, how ridiculous it was that child care wasn't a deductible expense—a complaint I heard often—and a whole host of other topics on which we probably wouldn't agree.

I didn't want to talk anymore.

I'd never thought of my feet as an erogenous zone, but Adam's touch had reminded me that there were better parts of me he could rub than my feet. I set my wine on the coffee table and swung my feet off his lap. Before he could react, I jumped him, straddling his hips and kissing him, burying my fingers in his short, silky hair and pulling his face to mine.

I didn't get to be in control very often. I liked it that way with Adam, so I wasn't complaining, but just for a few minutes, I wanted to savor being in charge. I didn't often get the chance to make the first move.

Adam's mouth opened, his tongue stroking mine, his head tilting to deepen the kiss. It wasn't long before his palms closed over my ass and he squeezed, already taking over despite letting me be on top.

I lost myself in the kiss. This was what I needed after such a miserable day. Not the wine or the food. Adam. Just Adam. In the back of my mind, I was waiting for him to pull back, to give me an order and take charge.

Instead, he rolled to his feet, holding me in his arms. I wound my legs around his waist and kept kissing him. Adam carried me to my bedroom and lay me back on my bed, saying nothing as he broke our kiss and slowly, deliberately, stripped off my clothes.

His dark eyes raked my body, lingering on my naked breasts, then my full hips. His fingertips trailed over my skin, following the path of his eyes, his touch almost reverent.

He left me there, naked, laying at the edge of my bed, legs hanging down, knees parted. He took off his own clothes in the same slow, deliberate way he'd undressed me. I ached for his touch. I ached to touch him. His body was revealed in parts, each one beautifully male.

I loved his shoulders, broad and muscled but not bulky. Ditto for his arms. He was strong, strong enough to pick me up like I weighed nothing, but his muscle was compact and lean. Unbelievably sexy. And I could lust after his ass all day.

I wanted him inside me, my knees pulled back and my hands on that ass, my nails digging into the hard muscle as his cock filled me over and over. At the thought, I let out a low groan and my knees fell a few more inches apart.

That was all it took. The last of Adam's clothes hit the floor and his body covered mine. He pulled me with him, dragging me back until we were sprawled in the center of my queen size bed, his hips pushing my legs wider to make room for his body.

He rose up on his arms and looked down at me for a frozen moment before I felt his cock press past the gate of my pussy.

Unable to help myself, I tilted my hips more, taking him deeper, needing to feel him all the way inside me. I gasped at the stretch, and he gave me what I wanted, thrusting to the hilt.

He fell on top of me, growling into my ear, "I fucking love your body. You feel so fucking good. So tight. Your fucking pussy's so tight." He thrust harder, his breath coming in harsh pants. "Fuck, Emma, you're so soft. So perfect. I'm not fucking giving this up. I'm fucking keeping you. I don't fucking care."

His words spun through my mind and fell away. Adam rarely spoke during sex, at least not unless he was giving me orders.

He wasn't one of those guys who needed to hold a running commentary on what we were doing. Which was good because once he got me naked, I couldn't seem to pay attention to anything but the raw sensations of his body inside mine. Tonight was no different.

I pressed my knees tighter to his sides and rocked up

into him, meeting every thrust with one of my own. I always wanted Adam. But after my tense, awful day, after months of worry and stress, I just wanted this.

Adam fucking me, taking pleasure in my body and giving me the same with his own. I tried to hold off my orgasm. I wanted to stay where I was forever, to feel Adam's chest rubbing my hard nipples, his cock moving inside me for hours.

I tried to wait, but he must have been on the edge and ready to come himself because he took my mouth in a hungry kiss that drove my head into the mattress and demolished all my resistance.

Orgasm roared through me, and I arched my back, caught in a wave of hot pleasure that blanked my mind completely. Adam's hips jerked into mine, hard and fast, and he came with me, his groan of release mixing with my higher pitched scream.

He stayed where he was for longer than usual. By the time he rolled us to our sides and slipped away, I was already falling asleep. I barely felt him clean me up and pull the comforter to my chin. I had just enough time to wonder if he was leaving before I gave in to the exhaustion pulling at me and passed out.

# CHAPTER EIGHT
## AXEL

Fuck me. I was fucking the whole operation up. I'd slipped and mentioned the team to Emma. I hadn't even realized it at first. The conversation hadn't felt like part of the job. It had felt real, like I was her boyfriend and we were relaxing after a long day, telling each other stories about work while we ate takeout.

Not like I'd slipped a dose of sleeping meds in her wine and was about to fuck her until she passed out so I could search her apartment for evidence she'd committed a crime.

She'd jumped me after only drinking half the wine, which wasn't a big deal. I wasn't relying on the drugs; they were just a way to keep her out a little longer than usual. I didn't need her waking up while I was searching her place again. I could have gotten her to finish the wine if I'd needed her to.

Who the fuck was I kidding? The second her soft breasts pillowed against my chest and I had her ass in my hands, I was done for. She'd never taken the initiative like that. I knew Emma liked it when I was in charge. Taking control of her sexually was part of the way I'd hooked her so fast. It was only a side benefit that I liked it just as much as she did.

But her making the first move had knocked me sideways, and I'd lost control. Lost it all the way. Talking during sex? That kind of shit got men killed. Women too, if they were in my line of work. It was sloppy. Stupid. And for some reason, I hadn't been able to help myself.

Emma had been so fucking gorgeous lying back on her bed, her soft, round, lush body mine for the taking, her eyes heavy with desire as she'd watched me strip. She'd spread her knees, I'd caught the gleam of moisture between her legs, and my brain had taken a back seat to my cock.

I liked Emma, I liked her a lot, more than I should. My cock fucking loved her. I'd let it take control, it had buried itself inside her tight, scaldingly-hot pussy, and what was left of my brain had leaked out of my ears.

What the fuck was I thinking, telling her I was going to keep her? I couldn't keep her. Best case scenario she was about to lose her job, everything she owned, and would probably have to leave the state.

Worst case, she was going to jail for a long time. I'd thought about helping her with a lawyer, but I couldn't even do that without working against my own client. And I doubted William Harper was going to agree to let me help the woman who'd been selling out the company his grandfather had founded in nineteen twenty-three.

Once I was back to being Axel Sinclair, Emma Wright was untouchable. I would have to walk away and let her drown in the mess she'd made. I knew it in my head, I just had to convince my dick.

That was my shit to deal with. And I would. Later. While Emma was still passed out in her bed, I had to get back into her laptop and pray there was something I could use to end this charade before I managed to really fuck it up. I'd gone through the files I'd found the night before, but they'd been useless. What I'd hoped was proprietary information was actually just confidential personal data on Harper Shipping employees. Exactly the kind of thing the head of Human Resources should have had on her company laptop, and exactly what she would have stored in an encrypted file.

I took a second to listen to the quiet apartment, then got to work. For the first time since I'd sweet-talked my way into Emma's apartment, I hit pay dirt right off. A USB drive was tucked into a discreet inner pocket of her briefcase. Ignoring the fine tremble in my hands, telling myself it was anticipation and not dread, I popped open her laptop and plugged it in.

Bingo. Pages and pages of shipping contracts with job dates, client info, including bids. Schematics for the new line of refrigerated trucks Harper had told me they'd been working on. And company cell phone records. I'm not sure how they fit in, but the data on the clients, contracts, jobs, and the schematics were more than enough to hang her.

I sat back, staring blankly at the screen, rage searing through me. It wasn't until I saw the proof of her guilt that I realized I'd truly thought she was innocent. The whole time I'd been reminding myself I had to walk away, I'd been secretly certain she'd come out of this clean, and she could be mine.

Axel's woman, not Adam's. Somehow, despite all my years in this job, deep down I'd been certain I'd never find anything on Emma. That I could keep fucking her, would prove her innocent, and we'd live happily ever after. Or something like that.

The USB drive and the documents on the screen tore a

gaping hole through my half-formed plans of a happy ending. Emma was guilty as hell, and I was going to have to turn her in. If Harper decided not to call in the police, and I was sure he probably wouldn't, he'd undoubtedly end up forcing a huge payoff out of Emma.

She'd be ruined, her brand new MBA worth nothing. She might be better off if Harper called the police. At least she'd have a place to live in jail.

My gut burned. My breath was strangled in my chest. She'd started this well before we met, yet I still felt betrayed, felt as if Emma had stolen from me, sold *me* out, instead of Harper.

All my ill-conceived plans to help her went out the window in the face of my anger. I wanted her to go down for what she'd done. She was a liar and a fucking criminal. She deserved everything that was coming to her.

From behind me, I heard the sound of her bedroom door opening. Guess she didn't drink enough wine. I stayed where I was, fury coursing through my veins, waiting to see the look on her face when she realized she was caught.

I wasn't disappointed. She stood at the end of the hall, wrapped in her faded pink robe, eyes wide open and terrified. Giving her my coldest stare, I got to my feet, pulled a pair of police-issue handcuffs from my pocket and dangled them from one finger.

"Game Over," I said, and took a step forward, ready to catch her when she ran.

# CHAPTER NINE
### EMMA

I stood at the end of the hall, frozen in place, my feet glued to the floor. Adam leaned over my laptop, the screen crowded with documents. I couldn't see the details, but I saw enough to know he was looking through the package of evidence I'd put together for Tierney.

My mind spun, and I didn't know what to think. At first, I tried to convince myself that there was an innocent explanation for what he was doing.

Maybe he just wanted to check his email...

But that didn't make sense. Those documents had been well hidden and encrypted. The only way he was looking at them was if he'd been searching for them in the first place. Which meant I was in big trouble. Before I could decide what to do, Adam turned his head and saw me. At the cold rage in his dark eyes, my breath caught.

He stood, coming to his full height, his shoulders tight, eyes glacier cold. An air of menace filled my small apartment. I'd been so shocked at the sight of Adam poring over my laptop, I hadn't registered that he might be a threat.

I'd seen Adam in a lot of different moods since we'd met, but never this one. Never so cold. And never angry. Not like this. Without meaning to, I took a step back. I didn't know what he planned, but instinct told me I didn't want him coming anywhere near me when he was like this.

Adam reached into his back pocket and pulled out a pair of handcuffs, dangling them from one finger, held out as if offering a gift. Or a taunt. Handcuffs? Why did Adam have handcuffs?

There was too much I didn't understand. For months, I'd been in over my head. First with the unexpected promotion, then with the FBI. And finally, with Adam.

Whatever was happening now was just a reminder that I'd been over my head with Adam from the beginning. I'd wondered what he was keeping from me. It looked like I was about to find out.

Adam took a step closer, his eyes focused on me, merciless and unrelenting. Like a blade, they sliced through me with rage and dismissal. He held his finger out, the shiny handcuffs rocking where they hung on his fingertip, and said, "Game over, Emma."

He shifted his weight to the balls of his feet as if ready to lunge. Still frozen in place, I fought my rising panic. What did he mean, 'Game Over'? What game? As far as I could tell the only one of us playing a game was Adam.

I was doing a job. And as long as he was between me and my laptop, all the work I'd put into that job could be in jeopardy.

"Adam, I don't think you understand," I said, backing up another step. He moved closer and I tensed, somehow knowing that running from him was not a good idea.

"I understand just fine," he said, his voice hard. "I understand that you're a thief and a liar."

A thief and a liar? I wasn't the one who was lying.

"You don't know what you're talking about," I said, getting desperate as he took another step closer. "I'm not a thief and I've never lied to you."

"You're lying to me right now." Adam opened the handcuffs, ready to slap them on my wrist at the first opportunity. My stomach turned to ice.

I'm fairly tall for a woman and in decent shape, but I was no match for Adam. If he wanted to get the handcuffs on me, he would. My mind raced, searching for a solution to Adam's unexpected threat. What did I know that could help me?

I knew Adam wasn't who he said he was because the Adam I knew had no reason to go looking for encrypted files on my laptop.

I also knew that Adam thought I was someone I wasn't because he'd called me a thief and a liar. I knew I was neither.

Third, I knew that those handcuffs implied he planned to take me somewhere. I had no intention of leaving my apartment with him, but the fourth thing I knew was that he was bigger and stronger than me. The look in his eyes indicated that he didn't care what I wanted, I was going to do whatever he wanted me to do.

Every muscle tense, my eyes locked on Adam, I considered my options. The best scenario was that I could get both myself and my laptop away from Adam. Either of those things seemed unlikely to happen at this point.

The next best option was to escape long enough to put on some clothes because I had no intention of going anywhere as I was, naked beneath my thin pink robe.

I couldn't get past Adam, but maybe I could get back

into my bedroom and lock the door. That would buy me time to get dressed.

Breathing a silent prayer of thanks that I'd managed to copy and send out a backup of the data before I came home that evening, I took a deep breath, whirled on the balls of my feet, and dove down the hall and into my bedroom.

I slammed the door and turned the almost useless lock in the handle just as the wood shuddered under the impact of Adam's body.

He went straight for the handle, which refused to turn. Before I did anything else, I grabbed the wooden chair at my vanity and jammed it under the door handle at an angle.

I had no idea if that would really keep the door shut, but I'd seen it in movies, and it was the best option I had because there was no way I could drag my dresser across the room to block the door before Adam broke it down.

Tossing off my pink robe, I quickly pulled on underwear, jeans, a t-shirt, and a sweater. They were weekend clothes, more comfortable than stylish, but I wasn't worried about looking good.

I didn't bother to brush my hair, just pulled it up into a messy bun. As long as I had a ponytail holder I could do something better with it later if I had the chance. Tugging on my socks, I shoved my feet into a pair of sneakers and tried to figure out what to do next.

The door handle rattled, then gave a hard jerk before it stopped moving. He must have let go. A second later the door shuddered again in its frame. I imagined Adam throwing his shoulder into it, determined to get through.

My apartment wasn't luxurious, but the place wasn't cheap either, and it was fairly well built. Looked like the chair-under-the-door-handle trick worked. At least, it was working for now. I had no illusions that it was a viable long-term solution.

Adam wanted me out of this bedroom, and he would eventually get what he wanted. I had to come up with a plan.

Nothing was coming to mind. Randomly, I wished I'd listened to my mother and bought a fire escape ladder for my bedroom. My mother was always convinced that disaster lurked just around the corner. She had fire escape ladders in all of her second story bedrooms, just in case a fire should break out while they were sleeping.

She'd told me I should get one since my apartment was on the third floor, but I'd thought the idea was ridiculous, though I hadn't told her that.

It didn't sound so ridiculous now, did it? If I'd had the fire escape ladder, I could have hung it out of the window, climbed down, and been free. Granted, I wouldn't have had my purse or my car keys, but at least I would have been able to put some distance between me and Adam's shiny metal handcuffs.

Briefly, I thought about tying some sheets together to get out of the window, but I discarded that idea almost immediately. Not only did I have a single set of sheets in my bedroom—the linen closet was in the hallway—I did not trust my life to my knot tying skills. A girl scout I wasn't.

Just as I was beginning to face the fact that I was surrounded by dead ends, Adam's voice came through the door, low and persuasive.

"Emma, I know you're guilty. I have the evidence right there on your laptop. The best thing you can do at this point is come with me to talk with Mr. Harper. If you're lucky, he won't press charges as long as you come clean about who you've been working with. If you stay in here, this whole situation is just going to escalate, and no one wants that."

"Are you working for William Harper?" I asked. My first instinct was to confess everything. Despite all that had happened in the past few minutes, the last three weeks with Adam had given me every reason to believe he was a good man. Intense, scorchingly hot in bed, definitely bossy, but in his heart, a good man.

If he was working for William Harper, all bets were off. William Harper was not a good man. William Harper was at best involved with the mob, shipping drugs and weapons, and at worst delivering women to white slavers.

It didn't get much worse than that. If Adam was working for him, then everything I knew about Adam was a lie. And if Adam wasn't really Adam, then I shouldn't tell him anything he didn't already know.

If I couldn't figure out a way to escape, Harper would get my laptop. So far, nobody knew about the evidence I'd sent to Summer. Even she didn't know what she had, only that I'd asked her to keep the packages safe for me. So, my work wasn't lost.

I'd also told Summer that if I went missing, she should turn everything over to the FBI. Not an ideal solution, but it gave me the comfort of knowing that eventually, the evidence would end up where it belonged.

That still left me with no good escape plan on the short-term. If Adam brought me to William Harper, I didn't feel good about my chances. What were the odds Harper would call the police on me?

Considering he was up to his neck in criminal activity and had ties to the Russian mob, not very good. Whatever Harper was going to do with me, it didn't involve prosecution. I would've welcomed prosecution and the police. I could've just called Agent Tierney and this whole problem would go away.

*Agent Tierney.* That was my answer. If I could get Adam to let me make a phone call, I could call Agent Tierney for help. I don't know why it hadn't occurred to me sooner.

Oh, yeah, the handcuffs. The sight of those handcuffs had freaked me out so much it had put a hitch in my normal thought processes. Too bad my phone was on the kitchen table.

"Emma," Adam said again, this time sounding less persuasive and more irritated. "I'm only going to—"

"Adam," I interrupted, "just wait a second. I'll come out and talk to you. But I need to make a phone call before we go anywhere."

"To whom?" he asked, suspicious.

"I can explain everything if you'll just give me my phone for a minute," I evaded. I felt sick at the thought that I couldn't trust Adam, but I didn't think I should mention the FBI unless I absolutely had to.

"Fine," he said. "You can make a call. Just open the door and I'll give you your phone."

I didn't believe him. He'd agreed too easily. The part of me that still hoped we could work things out wanted to trust him. Wanted it desperately. I wanted Adam to be the good guy. If Adam was the good guy, then this was just a misunderstanding with an easy solution.

I was sure he was lying about giving me the phone, but I still had to open the door. I couldn't just sit here in my room indefinitely. Eventually, Adam would figure out a way to get to me. Sitting on my bed and hoping for rescue wasn't going to save me.

"Okay," I said. "I'm going to open the door a little bit,

and you're going to slide my phone through. Once I make a quick call, I'll come out."

A long pause.

"Fine."

I went to the door and wiggled the chair back just enough so I could crack the door open an inch. I didn't touch the handle until I heard Adam coming down the hallway towards my bedroom door.

"You have it?" I asked, wishing my voice didn't wobble with fear and hurt. Adam was so cold and in charge, and all I wanted was to climb under the covers and hide.

Maybe I should have been better prepared for something like this to happen, but betrayal by my boyfriend was the last thing I'd expected when I agreed to help the FBI. Maybe I should've known a man like Adam would have to have an ulterior motive to go out with me.

I'd always been out of my league with Adam, and here was my proof. I wasn't his girlfriend, I was a job. For a moment, the sinking sensation of loss chased away my fear.

Being with him had been like nothing I'd ever experienced before. The way he listened to me, the way he knew exactly what I wanted in bed. Now, not only was it over, it had all been no more than a lie.

With adrenaline-fired nerves vibrating through my body and a sick, leaden feeling in my stomach, I reached for the door handle and unlocked it.

"I'm going to open the door now, just a crack," I said. "Slide my phone through, and I'll get this cleared up in just a few minutes."

Adam didn't say anything. I turned the handle of the door and opened it less than an inch, looking for the gleam of my phone in the strip of light leaking in from the hallway.

The door exploded into me, and I flew back, the solid

wood slamming into my forehead and nose, sending a bolt of pain through my face. It hurt so badly I barely noticed as I landed on my rear end on the carpet and fell to the side.

I didn't have time to get my bearings before Adam was on me, rolling me over, wrenching my arms behind my back, and slapping on the handcuffs.

# CHAPTER TEN
### EMMA

I really should've seen that one coming. Now I knew—the chair under the door thing didn't work quite as well if the door was already open. Or maybe it was just the angle of the chair. It didn't matter now.

Adam hauled me to my feet and growled in my ear, "I wouldn't have believed it if I hadn't seen it for myself. You really had me fooled, Emma. I was sure Harper was wrong about you."

"Adam," I gasped, trying to talk through the pain in my face. "This isn't what you think. You need to let me make a phone call. I'm not a criminal. I haven't done anything wrong. I just need to call the FBI. I have a contact at the FBI. He can explain everything. I swear, I haven't done anything wrong."

I was babbling, pain and fear roiling inside me. Telling Adam I was working with the FBI was my last resort. If he was in deep with William Harper it would make everything a lot worse. But if he was bringing me to William Harper, things were about as bad as they could get. And if mentioning the FBI helped at all, I had to take the risk.

I tried again.

"Adam, please," I cried out as he shoved me in front of him down the hallway, my feet tangling beneath me. "Please, you need to listen to me. You have to let me make one phone call. I need to call the FBI.

"If you really think I'm a criminal, if you're not working with William Harper, and you believe that this is about me breaking the law, please listen to me and let me call the FBI. I'll even give you the name of the agent to ask for and you can call. Please, don't bring me to William Harper like this."

Adam kept dragging me to the door, relentless. "I might've fallen for the innocent act yesterday, Emma, but now I know better. I've seen everything. The video of you selling company secrets. I have the files on your laptop— everything Harper told me to look for.

"And he said you'd claim you were working with the FBI. He warned me not to fall for it. Your 'FBI' contact is really one of Harper's competitors. So, no. You can't call him."

"He's not!" I protested. He wasn't. I'd met with Agent Tierney at his office at the FBI. I'd seen his badge, checked the number with the bureau in D.C. I wasn't his biggest fan, but Agent Tierney was legit. Adam was too pissed to listen.

"I know you're fucking guilty," he went on, "and I know you're a fucking liar. I don't want to hear any more of your fucking excuses. I just want to deliver you to Harper and then never see you again."

Was it possible there was hurt beneath his angry words? Or was that more wishful thinking on my part? As he shoved my bound hands into my back and pushed me down the hall, I couldn't help but remember the last time he'd stood behind me like this.

A wave of shame chased off any hopeful thoughts that

Adam might be hurt, might have some feelings for me other than his job.

He'd used me. I'd trusted him in ways I'd never trusted another man, and he'd been using me the whole time. I'd thought Adam wasn't the usual kind of asshole guy I attracted. I'd been right. Adam was worse. He was the King of Assholes.

He propelled me through my apartment faster than I would've imagined possible, especially considering I wasn't a willing participant in the journey. He snatched up my laptop on the way, tossing it into a bag he slung over his shoulder.

The hallway was deserted when we left the apartment. I thought about screaming, had my mouth half-open, when Adam said, "Make a fucking sound and you're going to regret it. I don't want to get your neighbors involved in this, but if you don't give me a choice..."

Then I saw the gun. When did Adam get a gun? Had he always had a gun? Or was it just tonight? I didn't like guns. They freaked me out. I especially didn't like guns when one was poking into my back. That didn't just freak me out, it terrified me.

I snapped my mouth shut.

I had to accept the fact that I didn't know Adam, and I had no idea how far he was willing to go. Taking me to Harper was bad enough. I'd never be able to live with it if he hurt someone else. My nose throbbed along with my forehead, and I felt something hot and sticky on my face that could only be blood.

Stunned by the lightning shift in my circumstances, by Adam's transformation from the boyfriend of my dreams into the cold, hard King of Assholes, I fell silent and let him manhandle me into the car. I'd have to hope inspiration struck on the way to wherever we were going, because just then, I was out of ideas and out of luck.

Adam buckled me into the back seat of his black SUV, his hands rough. I gasped in pain when my face bumped the door frame, and I thought I saw him wince, but he didn't apologize.

He was angry, that much was clear. I don't know what he thought he had to be so angry about. He wasn't the one who was being manhandled, handcuffed, and treated like a criminal. *Criminal.* That was a loaded word, and he kept throwing it around like he knew something I didn't. Who was he, really?

"You work for William Harper?" I asked. I didn't think I'd be able to believe his answer, but if I didn't ask, I'd never know anything.

"William Harper is my client," Adam said, grudgingly.

Great. Well, if he worked for Harper, he wasn't going to help me. Still, it was worth a try.

"Adam, please listen to me. You keep calling me a criminal, but I'm not. I haven't done anything wrong. Harper is the one who's a criminal. He's the one breaking the law, and I've been working with the FBI to help them build their case.

"If Mr. Harper has you bringing me in, it has to be because he knows what I've been up to. You're sending me into danger. Please, please don't do this. Please let me call the FBI."

Nothing from Adam. Not a denial, not a request for more information. Nothing. The words I'd spoken echoed back in my head, and I realized the truth of what I said. William Harper had sent Adam after me, and that meant he knew what I'd been doing. If he wanted me in his custody, I was in big trouble. Seriously big trouble.

Adam had grabbed my laptop off the coffee table before he'd hustled me out of my apartment, which meant Harper wanted the evidence I'd been collecting.

He probably thought he was getting it before I'd given it to the FBI. Which was true, in a sense. Except that Summer also had a copy. Or she would when she picked up her mail in a few days. Thank God I'd never mentioned her to Adam.

He picked up his phone and made a call. His words were cryptic; *I'm bringing her to you, I've got everything.* I thought I understood who he was calling and what it meant. I was going to William Harper, along with all the evidence I'd been collecting against him.

The ramifications hit me in a rush. The handcuffs on my wrist were too tight, the metal cold and hard. Terrifyingly hard. I didn't know what William Harper had planned for me, but I'd seen the pictures of the girls they'd trafficked, I knew where those girls had ended up. I didn't want to end up like that.

I wasn't sure I had control over my own destiny any longer. Adam wasn't listening to me. Adam wasn't even Adam. Despair swept through me, and my eyes welled with tears. I'd been so stupid.

Thinking I could help the FBI make a case against somebody working with the mob, thinking it wasn't going to come back on me, thinking that out of nowhere I could suddenly have this amazing boyfriend.

The FBI part, that could have been real. But I should have known Adam was too good to be true. With my life shattered around me, I wanted to know the truth.

"Who are you?" I asked, needing to know who he was. "Is your name really Adam Stewart? Do you normally work for Harper or is this just a one-time thing, like he called you in to fix a problem?"

My voice shook with emotion and tears, and my cheeks flushed red. I hated crying, hated that he saw me falling apart. Desperation clawed in my chest, fear over what was going to happen to me when he left me with William Harper and walked away. I couldn't escape, I couldn't do anything.

"Tell me," I demanded, when Adam remained silent. "Tell me. You owe me at least that much."

"I don't owe you jack shit. You lied to me. You're a fucking liar."

His voice was ice cold, no trace of the hurt I'd thought I heard before. But if I was just a job, why was Adam so angry?

"*I'm* not the liar," I said. Then, "Your name isn't Adam, is it?"

"Shut the fuck up," Adam said, his words tight, clipped. "I can't believe I was so wrong. And to think, I'd really started to believe that you were clean. The only fucking person in all these years that was really innocent. But no, all I needed was one more day and I found everything. I was thinking about getting you a lawyer. How's that for irony?"

Yeah, sure *that* was irony. *He* was feeling betrayed. The last I checked he wasn't the one in handcuffs.

"Fine, don't tell me your name," I said. "But if it's true you wanted to believe that I was innocent, if you really were going to get a lawyer, then call the FBI. Please. Ask for Agent Tierney."

The SUV turned into a residential neighborhood with large lots and huge homes. I had no doubt this was where William Harper lived. My time was running out. The vehicle slowed, turning into a driveway. Panic overwhelmed me, and I started to beg,

"Please, please, Adam. Call Agent Tierney with the Vegas office of the FBI. Please don't leave me here and walk away. If you do I'm going to disappear. Harper's trafficking girls with the Russian mob, and you can't leave me here. Please don't leave me. Call Agent Tierney. Please."

The SUV stopped, and I shut my mouth. He came around the side of the vehicle, opened the door, unbuckled my seatbelt, and pulled me out without meeting my eyes. One glance at his face told me that his resolve was impenetrable.

He thought I was guilty. He thought I'd betrayed him. He wasn't going to listen to reason, wasn't going to give me any options.

Harper opened the front door himself, his watery blue eyes lighting with glee at the sight of me.

"You got her!" He said to Adam, with more enthusiasm than I'd ever heard him display before. "Follow me," he said, leading us through the entry hall, deeper into his house.

I barely noticed our surroundings as we walked down the long hall, more aware of Adam's steely grip on my bound hands. What I did see of the house was ornate and tacky, not a surprise knowing William Harper.

Mr. Harper was one of my least favorite parts of my job. A little shorter than me, with narrow shoulders and a protruding potbelly that made him look like he was eight months pregnant, Harper's eyes always lingered on my chest longer than they should have every time we ran into each other.

Now, standing before him in his home office, my hands secured behind my back, the slow crawl of his eyes over my body turned my blood to ice. Unconsciously, I backed up into Adam, some instinct telling me he was the safer option.

That was a lie. Everything about Adam was a lie. My new understanding of Adam was driven home when Harper said, "I was starting to doubt you, Sinclair, but now I see the rumors were true. You're worth every penny. That is, assuming you got what I needed?"

In answer, Adam dropped my laptop onto his desk. "Everything's in there."

"Excellent, good job. Took a little longer than I would've liked, but now that she's here, we're good. And you can assure me that none of the files she stole got by you?"

Adam took a step back and studied Harper. "I'm not 100% certain, no. But reasonably certain? Yes. I've been through everything multiple times and the sum total of what I found is on that laptop. There are no files in her apartment, nothing in her car, nothing in her purse. I assume you searched her office thoroughly?"

"Of course, of course," Harper said, his eyes crawling over me again. "So that's it. You can go, I'll take care of her from here."

Adam's grip on my wrist tightened a fraction before he let go. My stomach seized in fear. Right now, I hated Adam. He was the King of Assholes. But I would do anything he wanted if he just wouldn't leave me here with William Harper. Adam stepped away from me and stopped in the middle of the room.

"Do you want me to wait while you call the police?" he asked.

"No, that's not necessary," Harper said. "You know how those things are, it might take hours. I don't want to waste what's left of your evening. I'm sure I can contain one woman, especially now that you have her under control."

The look Harper gave me sent a shiver of revulsion down my spine. I couldn't stop myself from whispering, "Adam, please. Please don't leave me here."

Adam didn't meet my eyes when he said, "Sit down, shut up, and don't argue with the police. That's your safest bet."

I didn't respond. There was nothing left to say. He was leaving me, and I was totally screwed. His footsteps echoed on the hardwood as he left, calling over his shoulder, "I'll see myself out, expect my invoice."

The door shut behind him with a solid thunk. Searching for a scrap of inner strength, I looked up at William Harper to find him leering down at me.

"You're not calling the police, are you?" I asked, already knowing the answer, but needing to hear him say it.

"No, I'm not," he said. "But then, you already know I'm not calling the police. I bet you know exactly who it is I'm going to call."

I did. If my instincts were correct, and my worst nightmare was coming true, he was indeed not calling the police. He was going to call the Russian mob. And I was about to disappear into hell.

# CHAPTER ELEVEN

## AXEL

That was a fucking clusterfuck. I'd had jobs that had gone wrong before. One memorable occasion things had gone so totally sideways, we'd had to refund the client's money.

A lot of the time there were clients I didn't particularly like. If I had to like all the people I worked for, I'd have a lot of free time on my hands. But my inner radar had been pinging ever since we'd taken William Harper's case.

Emma didn't fit the profile of an embezzler. I still couldn't see her committing corporate espionage, even with all the evidence staring me in the face. And her reaction when I'd taken her to Harper had been completely over-the-top. Emma was not a drama queen.

In my gut, I didn't believe the last few weeks had been an act. At least, not on her part. Was that why I was feeling so off balance? Because I'd been lying to her? But, if I was right, she'd been lying to me.

And if I was wrong... If I was wrong, I'd just made an enormous mistake.

I got in the front seat of my SUV and put the keys in the

ignition but didn't start the vehicle. Something inside me wouldn't let me pull away from the curb without Emma.

It wouldn't hurt to double check. Clicking a button on my steering wheel, I called into the office. It only rang twice before a deep, alert voice said, "What's up, boss?" Hank Stevens, one of my best guys.

"We have ears on William Harper's phone?" I asked.

"Affirmative, boss. All's quiet."

"No calls tonight? Nothing going in or out in the last twenty minutes?"

"Only the call from you twenty-four minutes ago, lasting approximately nine seconds. Nothing else."

That wasn't good. If Harper had planned to press charges against Emma, he would've called the police by now. He should've called them right away.

If I hadn't been so blinded by emotion I would have forced him to call while I was still there. Emma had made a lot of accusations in those last few minutes. If even one of them was true, she was in danger.

"Pull the roster for the Vegas FBI office," I said to Hank. "Look for an Agent Tierney."

"Yeah, just a second." I heard the tapping of the keyboard and less than a minute later Hank was back on. "Got it right here boss. Agent Alan Tierney. Works mainly with RICO cases."

Fuck. Emma was either exceptionally devious, or Harper had played us. Played me. Normally, the thought that I'd been played would be enough to get me monumentally pissed off. This time, I wasn't angry so much as scared.

FEAR WAS NOT A FAMILIAR EMOTION FOR ME. I DIDN'T get scared. In my business fear is a luxury, one I can't afford.

I plan my jobs and mitigate risk. But I don't get scared. Not until now.

The things Emma had said on the way over: that Harper was working with the Russian mob, that they were trafficking drugs, guns, and worst of all, women. It was bad stuff. And I'd just delivered Emma to him. I'd had run-ins with the Russian mob in Vegas before, and if Harper was working with them, that meant one thing, one guy.

Sergey Tsepov.

I wanted Sergey Tsepov nowhere near Emma. I didn't want him to know she existed.

On the other end of the line, I heard, "Boss, you still there?"

"Yeah, I'm here. Do we have contact info on Agent Tierney?"

That kind of thing wasn't usually available to private citizens, but we had access most people didn't. And there had been more than one occasion when it had paid off to be able to call exactly the person we needed at the FBI. Like this one.

"Texting it to you," Hank said. I hung up and waited. My phone beeped with the number a second later, and I placed the call.

"Tierney," a gravelly, quiet voice said.

"Agent Alan Tierney of the Las Vegas FBI office?" I asked.

"Yes. Who is this?"

"This is Axel Sinclair. I need to know what you know about Emma Wright."

"I'm not at liberty to discuss anything that might impact an open investigation," Tierney said in a bored, somewhat annoyed tone.

"I understand," I said. "You know who I am?"

IVY LAYNE

"I know who you are, Mr. Sinclair."

"Good, that makes this simpler. Then you understand what I mean when I tell you I've been working for William Harper for the last month investigating a case of alleged corporate espionage in which Emma Wright was our prime target.

"Having found what appeared to be a ton of incriminating evidence on her laptop this evening, I brought her to Harper with the understanding that he'd be calling the police to have her arrested. Is this a problem in any way for you or your investigation?"

Tierney exploded into a long string of barely intelligible curses. That was bad. With every second that passed it was becoming clearer that for the first time in my career, I'd fucked up big time. Huge. And not with just anyone, I'd fucked up with the only woman I'd ever truly cared about.

I'd been enraged when I'd thought she'd lied to me. I'd felt so betrayed that I hadn't thought it through. If I'd sat down with her, or let her make that phone call, done anything other than treat her like a fucking criminal... I cringed at the things I'd said to her.

Bile rose in my throat as I remembered her face, the bleeding cut on her forehead, the blood trickling from her nose. I'd done that to her.

It had been an accident. I'd thought she was out of the way when I'd broken down the door. That didn't change the fact that I was responsible. I hadn't just handed her over to a man who might want to hurt her, I'd hurt her myself.

I'd *hurt* her. Hurt Emma.

For a second, I thought I was going to vomit. Then my brain kicked into gear. As long as she was okay, I could fix things with Emma later. First on the agenda was getting her out of harm's way without making the situation any worse.

I looked at Harper's McMansion, his attractive land-scaping lit by accent lights, the windows dark, the house quiet. She was in there somewhere. I had to hope she was still all right.

"What happened to the evidence on the laptop?" Tierney asked, interrupting my thoughts. I noticed that he didn't ask what had happened to Emma. Clearly, he was focused on his case, not his informant.

"At the moment," I said, "the laptop is with Harper."

"You really fucked this one up, didn't you?" Tierney said, not hiding how pissed off he was. "Now you have to figure out how you're going to get the laptop back, and Emma away from Harper, without blowing your cover."

"Without blowing *my* cover?" I asked. My cover? I didn't have a cover, I wasn't working for the FBI. As far as I could see, the best thing I could do was to bust into Harper's house, grab Emma, and get her out of there.

"Your cover," Tierney repeated. "If he thinks you're still working for him, we have someone on the inside," Tierney said. "Maybe that could make up for the Charlie Foxtrot you made of my case. We were days from busting him and now we have next to nothing."

"Look, I don't need to make anything up to you," I said. "I just need to get Emma the hell out of there."

"If you want to keep your business open, you need to do exactly what I say," Tierney shot back.

"You've already interfered with an FBI investigation. I'm assuming the information you gave to Harper tonight is the evidence that Emma was collecting for me. Now Harper has all of our evidence and our informant.

"You'd better fucking fix this without tipping him off that we're on to him, or I'll pull every string I can to get

Sinclair Security shut down in the entire fucking state of Nevada, do you understand me?"

"I understand you," I said, my jaw tight.

I didn't like it, but I understood. As much as I wanted to grab Emma and run, Tierney had a point. By letting my emotions blind me and not giving Emma a chance to explain, I'd thrown a wrench into the middle of Tierney's case.

Assuming Emma had been telling the truth about what Harper was up to, I didn't want to be responsible for fucking up Harper's arrest. I had to get Emma out of that house.

I couldn't do it myself. As much as I wanted to be the knight in shining armor for this one, Tierney had a point about not burning my bridges. If everything did go to plan, it would be better if I still had access to Harper.

I needed a ringer, someone who wasn't connected to my office but who I could trust to get the job done. Fortunately, I had exactly what I needed in a luxury hotel suite on the strip. I scrolled through the recent contacts on my phone and hit the name.

"I need a favor," I said, as soon as he picked up the phone. "How's your case going?"

"Dead for tonight. My targets are in their hotel room and their contact is in LA. Why?"

"I need an extraction. I have a plan. Can you head to my office? Call me when you get there, and I'll explain."

"I'm on it."

I hung up, resigned to waiting. My office was less than ten minutes from the strip and Griffen would move fast. I was lucky he was in Vegas. I ran the smaller West Coast offices of Sinclair Security, and my four brothers managed the larger East Coast division.

Griffen Sawyer was one of their best guys. A former Army Ranger, he'd spent a few years working shadow ops for the military, so far off the grid his own family had thought he was dead.

One day, three years ago, he'd abruptly quit, for reasons he'd never explained, and come back to the States. My brother Evers had served in the Rangers with Griffen. As soon as Evers got word Griffen was back, he'd recruited him.

Griffen had started his current job in Dallas and followed it to Vegas. He'd been working here for the past few weeks, getting more and more frustrated as his quarry seemed to drink, gamble, and do little else.

Like most of the men and women who worked for Sinclair Security, Griffen liked action. What I had in mind for Emma's rescue should be right up his alley.

## CHAPTER TWELVE

### EMMA

He'd tied me to the chair, as if the handcuffs weren't enough to hold me. I guess if I'd been a ninja, they might not have been. But, with my hands secured behind my back, I wasn't all that confident in my combat skills.

What was I going to do, jump up and try to kick Harper until he fell down, then stomp on him? I'm sure an MMA fighter could have handled that, no problem. The closest I'd come to MMA was a kickboxing class I took three years ago for two sessions before deciding that yoga and walking were more my speed.

Proving he was a creep, Harper had a length of rope in his desk drawer, and he used it to secure me to the chair, wrapping it all the way around my torso, over and over, until the highest strand was just at the base of my neck, making it a little hard to breathe if I struggled.

When he was done tying me, and he'd taken his time on that, letting his hands graze my breasts as often as possible, he'd taken my laptop off his desk and locked it in a safe in the bookshelves across the room.

If I'd had any idea how I was going to get out of this, having my laptop locked up would've been a real problem. But since I wasn't going anywhere anyway, losing the laptop was just one more thing in my already-huge pile of troubles.

Harper leaned against his desk, crossed his arms over his chest, and stared at me for a long moment before giving me a suggestive smile that made me want to throw up.

"Emma, Emma, Emma. I was beginning to think Sinclair would never run you to ground. Honestly, I figured a girl as clever as you would've had her evidence together by now.

"You should know, if Sinclair hadn't caught you tonight, I would've had you brought to me in the morning. Corporate espionage is a serious charge," he said shaking his head in mock disappointment.

I kept my mouth shut. I wasn't going to play his game. He wanted to banter with me? I didn't even want to be in the same room with him, much less have a conversation.

I thought about mentioning that I was working with the FBI, and Agent Tierney would be looking for me, but I wasn't sure it was a good idea. Wouldn't that just make me more of a liability to Harper? I didn't want to encourage him to get rid of me.

Until I knew what Harper had planned, I didn't think I should push him any further than I had to. I resolved to stay quiet and keep my mouth shut. My resolution didn't last long.

Harper pushed himself off the desk and uncrossed his arms, his long gangly limbs framing his bulbous pot belly making him look like a human-size orangutan.

He ambled closer, then reached out one hand and grasped my breast through my sweater. I cringed in revulsion. At my reaction, he squeezed, his grip painfully tight.

The way he'd tied me wasn't exactly artful, but it had the effect of forcing my breasts into even more prominence than usual. I was instantly grateful I'd chosen a chunky, thick, cotton sweater. I could still feel his hand touching me —so gross—but it wasn't as bad as if I'd been wearing a T-shirt.

"Get off me," I ground out, fighting back the bile rising in my throat. If he wanted to do more than grope me, he'd have to untie me. My mind instantly shied away from the thought of him doing anything else. His hand on my breast was bad enough. Squeezing hard, he reached for the other breast.

"Don't complain," he said. "I'm just trying to help you get used to it. Where you're going, a little groping is just the beginning."

I squeezed my eyes shut. I didn't want to think about that. I didn't want him to confirm my worst suspicions. As he'd already proven, Harper didn't care about what I wanted.

He moved even closer, straddling my legs and dropping both hands to my chest, squeezing and mauling my breasts while he leered down at me with a revoltingly greedy expression. My vision grayed out at the edges as I went lightheaded with fear.

"I knew your tits would feel this good," he said. "I don't have to pretend with you anymore. I know you know everything. I know you've been talking to the FBI. And I know they don't have anything, or you wouldn't be here right now. So I can tell you Tsepov has plans for you.

"Girls like you, that red hair, that white skin, all these curves? You're worth a lot of money. In a few minutes I'm gonna call him to pick you up, and in twenty-four hours you'll be out of the country. No one who knows you will ever see you again."

Harper's cheeks were flushed, and his eyes glittered as they looked down into mine. My chest rose and fell in his hands as I gasped for breath, fear so tight around my ribcage I couldn't seem to get any air. Harper touching me, leering at me, was bad enough.

The threat of being taken by Tsepov was something else. I could survive an assault. I knew I could, I had to believe that I could because I was being assaulted right then. And I had no intention of dying.

A lifetime of assaults? I couldn't do anything but survive that, if they were determined to keep me alive, yet I knew it would be the worst kind of survival.

My heart would beat, my lungs would draw air, but if Tsepov got me it wouldn't be *me* who survived. Everything that was *me* would be gone.

Harper inched closer, and I caught a glimpse of his erection pushing against the front of his khaki pants. It wasn't very big, but it was way too close to my face.

The width of the chair and its height meant the best he could do was thrust his hips somewhere in the direction of my neck, but still, it was clear what he wanted. He wasn't going to get it. If that erection got anywhere near my mouth, he'd regret it.

Maybe he sensed his danger because he turned his attention back to my breasts and started trying to pull off my sweater. He'd tied the ropes too tightly, and the sweater had a crewneck, so he couldn't do more than ineffectually yank at it. He took a step back and let go, glaring down at me.

"I know you're a hot little slut," he said. "I had a guy watching you with Sinclair, and I know you fucked him the second time you met him. If you want things to go easy with Tsepov, I suggest you play nice before he gets here."

"Fuck you," I spit out. "I'll take my chances, but if you fucking try to touch me again, I'll bite anything I can reach."

His fist flashed out and smashed into the side of my face. My head snapped back as pain exploded in my nose, my cheek, my eye, everywhere. I didn't care. I'd meant what I said, and I'd say it again. Just because he planned to hurt me didn't mean I had to go quietly.

Harper must have read something in my eyes, or he had a low tolerance for backtalk because he went to his desk and took out a roll of duct tape. Who had duct tape in their desk? But then, he'd also had the rope he'd used to tie me up. Either he'd been planning this, or he was one weird fucker.

Tearing a strip off the duct tape, Harper pressed it over my mouth, but not before I let out an ear-piercing scream. It wasn't much.

The houses in this development were too far apart to hope anyone had heard me, and it was unlikely a neighbor was out walking their dog at this hour. But as the sticky tape sealed itself over my lips, my scream gave me a moment of satisfaction.

"I was just trying to help you out," Harper said, pacing to his desk where he tossed the roll of duct tape in a drawer and picked up his phone. "I'm going to have you either way. Tsepov will see to it. It was up to you whether it went easy or hard. Since you didn't want to cooperate..."

Harper shrugged his shoulders as if to say *It's all out of my hands now*, like he was innocent and this was all my fault. Had I said Adam was the King of Assholes? I was going to have to demote him because it was clear William Harper held that title.

Harper picked up his phone and made a call. A moment later he said "I've got Emma Wright and the evidence. The FBI isn't going to be a problem any longer." He paused, then scowled. "No, I can keep her overnight if you want."

Another pause. My stomach churned. I wasn't sure what I wanted to hear him say. As creepy and awful as Harper was, I had a feeling he was a much safer option compared to Tsepov. Then he said, "Fine, fine. I'll be here."

He put the phone down on the desk and leaned back against it as he had before, his arms crossed over his chest. He studied me, this time his eyes lingering on my face as opposed to my breasts.

"Tsepov wants you untouched and unharmed," he said. "You're not exactly unharmed, but most of that was Sinclair's fault, not mine, so I'm not going to worry about it. We'll have to wait for a bit, Tsepov's men are tied up and can't come get you for an hour or so. Too bad he won't let me touch you. I'd risk it anyway if I could trust you not to talk."

I shook my head, then realized he wouldn't know if I was saying I wouldn't talk or assuring him that I would. I didn't even know which would be the better answer. I was too scared, and I felt too helpless to think things through. Worse, I had the sick sensation that, at this point, nothing I did was going to save me.

Harper pushed himself off his desk and strolled to the corner of his office where he had an antique bar cart. He poured himself a drink in a cut crystal glass, as if he were entertaining company and not holding a woman hostage while blood dripped down her face.

Making his way back to the desk, he assumed his comfortable leaning position again and continued to examine me. I was starting to feel like a bug trapped under a microscope.

"I like seeing you so scared, Emma," he said. "You were always so superior. So confident. So together. Everyone at the office likes you. Have a problem? Bring it to Emma, she'll figure it out. But you wouldn't give me the time of day, would you?

I asked you out once, and you turned me down flat. Me! William Harper! Not just your boss—I own the whole fucking company. Do you have any idea how rich I am? Richer now since I hooked up with Tsepov.

"You wouldn't believe how much money drugs bring in. Not to mention importing and exporting weapons. First, it was Central America, before my time. Now it's Africa and the old favorite, the Middle East. All these wars, all this terrorism. It's great for business. Everyone wants guns these days.

"But I have to admit, the girls are my favorite part. I couldn't believe how easy it was, especially in a city like Vegas. So many young women, running away from home with dreams and no one to care what happened to them. How does it feel to know you're going to be joining them soon?"

Tears streamed down my face as I listened, unable to respond to the ugliness spewing from Harper's mouth. He had no remorse. He didn't care about anything but the money. He got off on breaking the law. On being the upstanding businessman William Harper to the world and knowing he was in bed with the Russian mob on the side.

I was beyond trying to figure out if I had any more options to get away. I was too tightly tied. My head was pounding, my face hurt, I was bleeding, and I was so scared I could barely breathe.

Then, a loud, melodious chime cut through the house, echoing down the empty hall to the office. I didn't realize what it was until Harper's head snapped up, and he looked out of the office in the direction the front door. The doorbell?

Panic hit me, and I realized I was nowhere near the height of my fear, not yet, because at the thought that the Russian's goons were at the door to collect me, my chest tightened even further, and my lungs froze.

Harper pushed off the desk and headed for the door of the office, muttering under his breath, "He said they would be another hour."

# CHAPTER THIRTEEN

## EMMA

Harper's footsteps echoed down the hall, and I heard the front door open. An unfamiliar male voice said, "Sorry to bother you, sir, but we received a report of a disturbance. A neighbor called and said they heard a woman scream. I apologize for interrupting your evening, but I'm going to have to take a look around."

"I appreciate you coming so quickly," Harper said, his tone polite yet not inviting. "But I'm afraid I can't allow you in without a warrant." At the word *warrant*, my heart leaped. Was that the police?

"Actually, sir," the new voice went on, "while in most cases that might be true, in this one I have probable cause to search without a warrant, considering one of your neighbors specifically said they heard a woman scream. You're welcome to call your attorney while I search."

"I'll call my attorney right now," Harper blustered, and even in my own state of terror I heard the fear beneath his words. "You're not coming in my house without my attorney here and without a warrant."

"Sir, as I said, you're welcome to call your attorney. But in the meantime, I'm checking out your residence. If I have to arrest you for interfering with a police investigation, I will. But I don't see why this has to get that difficult. Unless a woman really did scream?"

My brain finally clicked into gear. My mouth was taped shut and the front door was down a long hallway from the office, but I could try to make some kind of sound to draw the officer's attention.

I started rocking the chair back and forth, screaming through my nose as loudly as I could. The noise was deafening inside my head, but I couldn't be sure how much of it was actually getting out through the tape.

I rocked harder in the chair, throwing my weight from side to side, not caring that I'd hurt myself even worse if I managed to knock it over. William Harper's office was decorated as a man's domain, and the furniture was both bulky and heavy. Rocking side to side wasn't throwing the chair off balance enough to tip it over.

I did the second-best thing and tried to throw my weight backwards. The chair was as top-heavy as it was wide. Rocking back to raise the front just a few inches was enough to send the chair careening backward to the floor, the impact driving the air from my lungs.

"Did you hear that?" the police officer's voice said. Harper remained silent. "Sir, I'm going to have to insist that you stand aside. If you don't, I'll arrest you right now, but I *will* investigate that sound."

I stayed very still on the floor, securely tied to the chair, which had tipped backward but hadn't broken. Wriggling in my bonds, I realized the chair wasn't even slightly damaged, and I was still securely tied.

I couldn't hear if Harper gave a response to the officer's

ultimatum, but a scuffle in the hallway indicated that he hadn't done as he was told. A few moments later, both sets of footsteps came back down towards the office, growing louder as they neared the door.

My heart sang at the sight of William Harper in handcuffs. Let's see how he liked it. He was escorted back into his office by a police officer, complete with a crisp navy blue uniform and a shiny badge pinned to his chest.

The officer was tall, with broad shoulders and narrow hips. His eyes met mine as he entered the room, and I got the feeling he knew exactly who I was. His sea-green gaze communicated reassurance and comfort.

The tightness in my chest relaxed a fraction. I wouldn't relax completely until I was far away from Harper's house. But I'd just about given up any hope of rescue, and this police officer was every Christmas present I'd ever wanted rolled into one.

His eyes narrowed as he took in my injuries, then he quirked a grin that softened his austerely handsome face, rounding his bladed cheekbones and making his well-formed lips even more attractive.

After the debacle with Adam, I was swearing off men for the rest of my life. But that said, I'd have to be blind not to notice that my rescuer was hot.

His lips still twisted into a half smile, he looked from Harper to me and said, "I can see why you didn't want to let me in." His eyes on mine, he went on, "If you would like to leave, nod your head."

I nodded my head, hard, despite the pain it sent through my face and skull. Knocking over my chair had drawn the officer's attention, but it hadn't done my headache any good. The officer directed his eyes back to Harper. "It looks like this young woman doesn't want to be restrained in your home. Are you responsible for her condition?"

"No! No, she was like that when she got here. It's not what you think, officer! She attacked me. I just tied her up for my own safety."

"You're going to have to try another story, sir." His *sir* dripped with irony, and Harper bristled at the lack of respect.

"Do you have any idea who I am? You can't just bust in here—" The officer gave him a shove, sending him reeling towards the couch on the other side of the room.

"If you know what's good for you, you will sit there and shut up. I do know who you are, and I don't care. You have a woman in your home who has been beaten and is tied up. She's indicated that she does not want to be here. You've got a whole lot of problems right now, and I suggest you don't make this any harder on yourself."

"I want to call my attorney," Harper shouted, but he sat on the couch. He was an asshole, but he wasn't entirely stupid. The officer knelt beside me and pulled the heavy chair upright.

As he did, he whispered in my ear, "I'm going to get you out of here. We're safe, no one is going to hurt you. But when I ask, say you don't want to press charges. Understand?"

I gave a slight nod to indicate that I understood. I didn't know who this guy was, and what he'd said gave me the impression he wasn't a police officer. Wouldn't a police officer want me to press charges? But he'd said I was safe, and that he was getting me out of here. That was enough for me.

He wasn't Harper's man, and he didn't work for Tsepov, because Tsepov didn't need any subterfuge to take me from

Harper. Maybe he was with Agent Tierney. I didn't know. But I wasn't going to second-guess someone who was trying to rescue me. Whatever he wanted me to do to help him get me out of here, I would do it.

The chair settled back into its upright position. The officer made quick work of the rope and released the handcuffs, sliding them in his pocket. I hope he didn't plan to get them out again later.

Gently, he peeled the duct tape from my mouth, careful not to bump my nose or my cheek. Helping me to my feet, he said, "Miss, would you like to press charges against this man?"

I shook my head and said, "No, I just want to go home."

"Then I guess you got lucky tonight," he said to Harper. "If the lady doesn't want to press charges, I can't take you in for this. For all I know she tripped and fell into a doorframe and then asked you to tie her up." Sarcasm dripped from his words. Harper nodded along with him but was smart enough not to verbally agree.

"Since the lady just wants to go home, I'll take her off your hands."

My rescuer steered me out of the office and into the hallway. At the sight of the front door, my heart pounded in my chest. So close to freedom. From behind me, I heard Harper cry out, "What about me? You can't just leave me here in handcuffs!"

The officer stopped beside me and said, "Can you lean against the wall for just a minute?"

I nodded. He disappeared back into the office and I heard rustling, a grunt, and Harper say, "What are you doing, you can't do this." Then more muffled shuffling and grunting. Less than a minute later, the officer was back, a wide grin stretched across his face. Gently, he wrapped his arm around my shoulders, supporting my weight as he led me toward the front door.

"What did you do with him?" I asked quietly.

He gave a chuckle and said, "I took my cuffs back and tied him to the chair he had you in with the rope he used on you. And I duct taped his mouth shut. I'm sure someone will find him and let him go. Eventually."

I didn't know who this guy was. Maybe I was just making things worse for myself by leaving with him. But after finding out he'd tied William Harper to that chair and duct taped his mouth shut? I was willing to follow him anywhere.

I didn't speak again until we were out of the house. A big black SUV, identical to the one Adam had been driving, was parked in the driveway in front of the house.

The officer led me to the vehicle, opened the passenger door, and helped me inside, saying, "Buckle up, and I'll get you out of here."

I did, fastening my seatbelt and letting my head fall back in relief. He rounded the car and was in the driver's seat a moment later, starting the vehicle with quick efficiency.

He shot a sideways glance at my face and said, "We'll get you cleaned up in a few minutes. I heard his phone call, and I want to get you out of here before Tsepov's men show up."

"Sounds good to me," I said. "Are you going to tell me who you are?" I asked, suspecting he'd refuse. He surprised me and answered immediately.

"Griffen Sawyer, ma'am," he said in an affected drawl that made me smile.

"And that's your real name?" I asked. Based on everything I'd learned that night, I'd realized there was a difference between the name a person gave you and what their name actually was, Adam case in point.

I knew Adam's real name was Sinclair and not Stewart. I still had no idea if his first name was really Adam. I wondered if I would ever find out. Beside me, Griffen Sawyer laughed.

"You're a quick learner," he said, with a smile. "Yes ma'am, my real name is Griffen Sawyer. At least according to my mama and the United States government."

Relief washed through me at the mention of the government. He must be with the FBI. Still, it seemed smart to ask.

I'd trusted him enough to get me out of Harper's house, but that didn't mean I could trust everything he said. And it wasn't smart to make assumptions. I'd made enough of those; they had gotten me into this mess in the first place.

"Are you with the FBI?" I asked, afraid of what his answer would be. Giving credence to my fear, he slanted me another sideways look and gave a short shake of his head.

"No, I'm not," he said dropping the drawl and the amusement. "I didn't get all the details, but I know enough about what happened to you tonight. I understand that you'd be smart not to trust anyone you don't know. And probably half the people you do know."

"Are you going to tell me who you are? And why you helped me back there?"

"It's not my job to give you explanations," he said. "I'm sorry about that, since I know an explanation, the truth, would make you feel a lot better right now. My job is to get you someplace safe."

"And if you're not willing to tell me who you are, or what's going on, then why should I go with you?" I asked, annoyed that I was being asked to trust someone I didn't know. Yes, he'd helped me. And yes, he seemed trustworthy. But my judgment hadn't proved spectacular of late. Just because he was funny, and seemed friendly, didn't mean a god-damned thing.

"I'm not cleared to tell you anything," he repeated. "My job was to get you out in one piece. It was also to get the laptop, but I didn't see that anywhere, and I didn't want to blow my cover by asking." He raised an eyebrow at me, inviting an explanation. I didn't think there was any point in not telling him.

"Harper locked it in his safe," I said. He shrugged.

"It's the FBI that wants the laptop. My orders were only to get it if it was easy and available. My mission was you."

"And why was I your mission?" I tried again. A second head shake and he smiled, giving me another look, this one clearly amused.

"He said you were sharp. But I can see you've taken a few shots to the head. I'd like to make this easier for you, but frankly, I've stepped right into the middle of this mess, and I think the less said, the better, until we get where we're going, and we can straighten all this out.

"But here's the thing," he went on. "You don't know me. I can tell you I'm not working with Harper or the mob. I can tell you I just want to get you somewhere safe, somewhere you can get your bearings, and can figure out where to go from here. I can tell you all of that, and you have no reason to believe me.

"But what are your other options? If you're as smart as he says you are, you'll know jumping out of my car and running away is only going to leave you vulnerable to the bad guys. If you're loose out there without protection, Harper or Tsepov will pick you up. If they get you a second time, they won't make a mistake.

"Harper's an entitled ass, but I'm not from Vegas and even I know about Tsepov. You don't want to get mixed up with him. If he takes you, it's going to be a hell of a lot harder for us to get you back.

"I know you're not much of a gambler, but take one more risk and give me some time. I'm going to take you somewhere safe. Somewhere you'll get explanations for everything that's been going on. If you don't like those explanations, if you can't live with them, I'll bring you somewhere else and help you."

He took his eyes off the road, fixed them on me, and said, "I promise."

My judgment hadn't been great lately, but I believed him.

"So, when we get where we're going, if I say I don't want to be there, you'll take me somewhere else? Somewhere safe?" I asked.

"I will," he said. "But you have to give it a few hours. You have to give him a chance to explain. This whole case has been a disaster, and you got the worst of it, no question. But I have to tell you, he doesn't make mistakes, and this one is killing him."

I didn't like the way that sounded. Who was *he*? I had a sinking feeling that I knew exactly who Griffen was talking about. If I did, I wanted nothing to do with him. Nothing. No that wasn't true, I wanted to fly him to the top of a volcano and drop him in just before it erupted. That wasn't nothing.

I did *not* want to talk to him or hear his explanations. But I was getting ahead of myself. Maybe he wasn't talking about Adam Stewart, a.k.a. Somebody Sinclair.

Maybe there was another player in this whole disaster of an investigation, one I hadn't heard of yet. It was possible since it seemed I had no idea what had been going on this whole time.

I closed my eyes and tipped my head back. I didn't want to think about it. Just for a little bit, I wanted to be quiet and appreciate that I was safe, at least temporarily. Whatever came next, I would deal with it later.

"When will we be there?" I asked in a whisper.

"Not too much longer," Griffen answered. "Close your eyes and take a nap, we'll be there before you know it."

My eyelids were as heavy as cement blocks. Exhaustion overwhelmed me. I took Griffen's suggestion and fell asleep.

# CHAPTER FOURTEEN
## EMMA

I didn't wake up until the car stopped. My eyes opened slowly, and I looked around. We were in a driveway, in front of a house that, in the dim light, appeared both low and long. I couldn't see much more than that.

"Where are we?" I asked.

Griffen turned off the engine and opened his door, the overhead light illuminating his face as he said, "Near Lake Mead. Let's go inside and get this over with, then you can get some rest."

I didn't like the way that sounded. Get *what* over with? I thought I knew, and I wasn't sure if I wanted my suspicions to be correct just so I wouldn't have to face one more surprise.

Obediently, I got out of the car and followed Griffen up the walkway. He didn't bother to knock, just turned the handle and opened the tall rustic wood and black iron door as if he belonged there.

"Is this your house?" I asked.

A familiar voice said, "No, it's mine."

With a sinking feeling, I looked up to see Adam standing in front of me.

"I knew it," I shouted, suddenly furious at the sight of him. "I didn't want to believe it, but I knew you were behind this." I whirled to face Griffen and said, "Take me somewhere else. You promised you'd take me somewhere else if I didn't want to be here."

He shook his head, an apology in his kind green eyes.

"I said you had to hear him out. Then, if you still wanted to leave, I'd take you somewhere else. You've only been here a minute."

I punched him in the shoulder. I thought it was a good punch. It carried enough frustration that it should have knocked him out. Griffen didn't react at all.

I knew it wasn't fair to strike out at him; this whole mess wasn't Griffen's fault. I was just so pissed and hurt, and I didn't trust myself to get close enough to Adam to hit him.

Still focused on Griffen, trying my best to ignore the lying bastard who had been my boyfriend, I said, "Please, Griffen. I don't want to stay here with him. He lied to me. He used me. He slammed the door in my face."

I knew my face looked like a mess. I also knew Adam hadn't hit me with the door on purpose. I didn't really care.

My nose wasn't broken—I was sure I'd know if it had been broken—but it still hurt like hell. I could feel the bruise on my cheek, hot and tight. I didn't need a mirror to guess that I looked awful.

Griffen's eyes narrowed on my face, then flashed at Adam. "*You* did this to her?"

Adam ignored Griffen and looked at me.

His eyes soft and heavy with regret, he said, "Emma. Emma, I fucked up. I fucked up huge. I don't even know where to start apologizing."

Turning his attention to Griffen, he went on, "I *am* responsible for hurting her, but it was an accident. I would never, ever, hurt Emma like that on purpose."

"No, you'd just lie to me for weeks, use me, and then turn me over to someone who was going to sell me into slavery. That's so much better than accidentally slamming a door into my face."

All the stress and fear I'd been holding back exploded inside me, set loose by my close call that evening. I couldn't keep it together anymore.

I'd known something was off with Adam. My gut had told me he was too good to be true. But I'd been falling for him. Falling hard. And now I'd hit bottom.

The man I'd thought I might be in love with had lied to me and used me. The sick thing was a part of me wanted to forgive him.

A tiny, wounded voice in my heart whispered that I could trust him. That he'd apologized. Maybe he meant it. Maybe he really cared.

The memory of Harper's greedy eyes, the hungry tone in his voice when he said he was going to fuck me, reminded me that I couldn't trust a thing Adam said.

I wouldn't have been there for Harper to touch if it hadn't been for Adam. I wanted him to shut up, but he kept talking.

"Emma, if I'd had any idea what Harper was into, I never would've left you with him."

"That's not the point," I said, my voice rising. "You should have trusted me. You should have believed me when I told you I was innocent. Instead, you handcuffed me. You brought me to him, even after I begged you to help me, and then you just left me there."

"I didn't leave you there. Not exactly. I was outside in

my car the whole time. I knew something was wrong, and I checked on your story. I'm sorry, Emma. I'm so sorry."

"You were there the whole time?" That just made me angrier. "While he had me tied to a chair? While he was groping me? You were just sitting outside, safe in your car, making phone calls?"

Adam's eyes went dark and cold. He turned them on Griffen and said, "He touched her?"

"Not that I saw, and she was so shaken up when I got her out I didn't think it was the right time for an inquisition," Griffen answered, his voice tight.

"I'll fucking kill him," Adam said.

I had to stop thinking of him as Adam. At least assuming that wasn't his real name. Annoyed by everything I didn't know, I snapped out, "Is your name even Adam?"

"No," he said, looking sheepish. "It's Axel. Axel Sinclair."

"Adam Stewart. Axel Sinclair. Close. I guess close enough that you wouldn't get confused, right?"

Adam/Axel didn't answer, just shrugged his shoulders. Probably smart. I couldn't think of any response that wouldn't have pissed me off further.

I didn't want to be here. I didn't want to be facing this new person, Axel instead of Adam.

I wanted my boyfriend back. Adam, who rubbed my feet and knew exactly how to boss me around in bed. Adam who texted me at work and laughed at my stories. Not this intimidating stranger with the cold eyes and new name.

He stood there, his handsome face filled with regret and determination, and he scared me almost as much as William Harper.

I knew Harper was the enemy. But Axel was Adam and I was still so unsettled by everything that had happened.

I wanted someone to trust. It would be so easy to forget his lies, so easy to believe that Axel really wanted to make everything all right. Easy, and dangerous.

"Is there somewhere I can go to wash my face?" I asked, needing to get myself together before we took this confrontation any further.

"Down the hall," Axel said gesturing to his left. Without thanking him, I followed where he pointed and found a spacious powder room. An oversized wood framed mirror hung over the sink, and the room was lit by a black iron chandelier. It was not the average powder room. It looked like Adam—interesting and elegant.

Absently, I wondered how an app developer could afford a house like this. Then I reminded myself that Adam wasn't an app developer. He wasn't even Adam. He was Axel Sinclair, and I had no idea what he did for a living, except that it involved working for criminals and lying.

My stomach clenched when I caught a glimpse of myself in the mirror. I'd guessed I looked pretty bad, but this was way worse than I'd expected. My hair probably didn't help. It had worked its way free of the loose bun and stuck out in bright red tangles around my face.

My skin, where it wasn't covered with dried blood, was sheet white. My nose was a little swollen, but definitely not broken. Blood trailed from both nostrils and my right cheek-bone was puffy, already bruising. Not a surprise that it throbbed and ached like a bitch. I could see the beginnings of a black eye above the bruise.

I was going to look so very charming for the next few days. Lovely.

I took one of the hunter green hand towels folded neatly by the sink, wet it, and went to work cleaning up my face. When I was done, I pulled out the bun, used my fingers to roughly comb my hair, and pulled it back into the best French braid I could manage. I didn't look great, but I looked less like a disaster. It would have to be enough.

I left the powder room and went back down the hall to face down Axel. I needed answers. It seemed he wanted me to stay at his house, and it was possible that was the safest location, considering I now had both my former boss—I was sure as hell quitting my job—and the Russian mob looking for me.

Before I made any decisions, I wanted to hear Axel's explanation for everything that had happened since we'd met.

Walking back into the room, I took in the sight of Griffen and Axel, standing close together, murmuring in low voices, and said, "I'd like a cup of tea. Do you have any tea?"

"I do," Axel said, looking relieved that I hadn't renewed my demands to leave. "If you'll go sit in the living room, I'll make you some." To Griffen, he said, "You can go, we're good here."

"No," I said, also to Griffen. "We're not good here. You made me a promise."

Griffen gave Axel an apologetic look and said, "I did make her a promise. And whatever your explanation for why you cuffed her and delivered her to that asshole, it had a better be good."

Axel had already started toward the kitchen. At Griffen's words, he stopped, turned, and fastened his dark eyes on Griffen. "What, exactly, did you promise her?"

"I told Emma that she had to let you have your say. If she didn't want to stay after that, I'd take her somewhere else and keep her safe until she's out of danger."

Axel's eyes narrowed, and for a moment, he looked like

he was going to explode. This gave me a perverse sense of amusement.

He didn't like being thwarted? Did he feel helpless? Betrayed by someone he trusted? It was a small thing, but the frustrated anger on his face made me feel better.

"You work for me," he said. Griffen laughed and sent me a flirtatious wink. I smiled back. Axel scowled at the both of us.

"Not really. I mostly work for your brothers," Griffen said, shoving his hands in his back pockets, looking like he was enjoying baiting Axel. "But I don't do what they tell me either. I'm an operative, not a trained puppy. Emma's been through enough. She's held up surprisingly well, considering the circumstances. And if you can't satisfy her..." — this said with an intentionally comical leer in my direction —"then I'll take over her case."

"She's not a case. Not anymore," Axel ground out through clenched teeth.

"If she hires me to keep her safe, then she is. She's my case and my client."

If Axel ground his teeth together any harder, I thought they might shatter. He was riding the edge of his temper, and after the way he'd lost it in my apartment, I didn't want to see his temper set free again.

It had been ugly, and the memory hurt. I could tell he was holding himself in check. For me or because he didn't want to lose it in front of Griffen?

I didn't know. I also didn't know why Griffen was poking at him, but I wouldn't pretend I wasn't enjoying it. Appreciating Griffen for both needling Axel and for giving me something to smile about, I said, "I'm not sure I can afford you, Griffen."

He shot me a melting grin that had a bit too much

smolder in it to be genuine, and said, "Darlin', for you, I work cheap."

I couldn't quite think of what to say to that. I was pretty sure Griffen was flirting to piss Axel off, which was fine with me. But for once, I couldn't think of what to say to flirt back.

Axel was practically vibrating with rage at Griffen, and I didn't want to set him off. Griffen, on the other hand, looked highly entertained and completely at ease.

Eyeballing Axel's glare and tight shoulders he said, "Your brothers are going to love Emma. She'll fit right in."

I wasn't sure I liked the sound of that. If Axel's brothers were anything like him, I'd be in big trouble.

## CHAPTER FIFTEEN

### EMMA

**A**xel must have decided that he was done trying to reason with Griffen. Turning to me, he said, "I'll go make your tea. The living room is just through there, why don't you make yourself comfortable? I'll be back in a minute. We can sit down, and I'll explain everything."

I nodded and followed his direction to the living room, an open space with huge plate glass windows that, so late at night, looked out into darkness. The room was furnished with comfortable sofas and chairs in dark leathers and fabrics.

I sank down into one of the large armchairs, ensuring that no one could sit beside me. Griffen and Axel's sparring had been funny, but I was done with it.

I was going to face Axel, and I wanted to do it on my own. Griffen sat on the couch, facing the big glass window, leaving Axel the other armchair, opposite me.

Griffen reached for a remote on the coffee table in front of him and clicked the button. In the corner of the room, a fireplace flared to life. It wasn't cold outside, but I was chilly, despite my sweater.

In a low voice that wouldn't carry back to the kitchen, Griffen said, "From what I know about what went down with Axel, you have a right to be angry. But give him a chance.

"He didn't do the right thing tonight, but it's the first time since I've known him that he hasn't. Worst case scenario, even if you can't forgive him, you're safest with Axel protecting you."

"What about you?" I asked. Griffen shook his head with a wry smile.

"If you really can't work things out with Axel, I'll take you wherever you want to go, but I'm just a single operative.

"I'm good. I'm damn good. But Axel runs the whole Western division of Sinclair Security, and he's got his brothers running the Eastern division at his back. He has resources at his fingertips that I have to work for.

"It gets more complicated if I'm working outside the company, which I might be if Axel gets pissed enough about me taking you away. I know you're mad at him, but he's crazy about you."

"I doubt that," I said. If he was crazy about me, how had he lied to me for weeks? If he cared that much, he would have believed me when I told him I was innocent. It burned that he hadn't.

I could understand him seeing what was on my computer and assuming I was guilty. But the way he'd denied me the chance to defend myself and had thrown me to the wolves wasn't forgivable.

Griffen shook his head at the stubborn look on my face. "Even if you can't forgive him, you're a hell of a lot safer with him protecting you than you are anywhere else. Keep that in mind when he pisses you off again."

At that moment, Axel came back into the room carrying

two steaming mugs. He sat down in the armchair opposite me, as I'd suspected he would, after placing my mug on a coaster on the coffee table in front of me.

He didn't try to hand it to me directly, seeming to understand that I needed some distance. Maybe he was worried I'd toss the hot liquid in his face. It was an option, but I wasn't that mean. Griffen looked at our two cups and asked, "What about me?"

"Get your own fucking tea," Axel growled at him. "And don't interrupt us unless you have something constructive to say."

"How long have you been working for Harper?" I asked, suddenly tired of putting this off. I was exhausted, and I needed answers.

Axel put down his mug and met my eyes. "For almost a month. He asked me for an appointment five weeks ago. He told me he had reason to believe that an employee was stealing proprietary company information and selling it to competitors.

"He showed me photographs and video of you going through company files, then delivering the files to an individual he claimed was a competitor. He also showed me photographs of the competitor in question that matched up with the video.

"I had the video tested and it was genuine. I had no reason to believe that the suspect, you, was anything but guilty."

"And you thought the best way to deal with this was to ask me out?"

That was the part that hurt the worst. Not that Harper had lied to him about me being a criminal. Not even that he'd believed it. But that of all the ways he had to prove his case, he'd pretended to care about me.

I'd worried that I was falling in love with him, and he'd just been thinking about the job.

"You want me to say I'm sorry, don't you?" he asked. "To say I'm sorry I pursued you, sorry I seduced you."

"*Yes*," I said, incredulous. Wasn't that obvious? "Yes, I want you to apologize for being a lying bastard."

"I can't do that, Emma. I won't apologize for that. I was doing my job. And I seduced you because I wanted to. Because you're beautiful, and smart, and funny, and sexy. There was no way I was going to watch you for weeks and not touch you.

"Once we started spending time together, I only wanted you more. I'm sorry for everything that happened tonight. I should have known better. I should have known that you could never be guilty of the things Harper said you did. I should have known there was another explanation for what I found on your laptop."

"Then why? Why wouldn't you listen to me?" I asked, appalled to hear tears choking my voice. I clamped my mouth shut and cradled my tea in front of my face like a shield.

Axel looked at Griffen, then down at his tea. Griffen, possibly understanding some silent guy-speak that was over my head, murmured an excuse, stood, and left the room. Axel looked up from his mug and met my eyes, his dark gaze locked on mine.

"Emma," he said in a soft voice. "I fucked up big time tonight. My judgment was off. So far off. I fucked up because you're not just a job. You haven't been just a job since the night we met. My gut was telling me you were innocent, and I couldn't trust it because I was completely upside down about you."

"I don't even know what that means," I said, my voice

shaking. I didn't trust him, and I didn't trust myself. I wanted to believe he was telling the truth, but I hadn't thought he was lying before. He said his judgment was off—that was something we had in common.

He went on, "I started falling for you the first night, in that cooking class. Every night since it's only gotten worse. I think about you all the time.

"Something happens at work, and I want to tell you about it. I'm tired at the end of the day, and I want to be with you. I've never felt this way about a woman. I guess I just didn't know what the fuck I was doing."

He let out a huff of air and sat back, looking helpless for the first time since we'd met. I wanted to reassure him, which was stupid. He'd lied to me. If the case hadn't ended, he would have gone on lying.

"I just don't think I can trust you," I said, my eyes blurring with tears. Axel was telling me everything I wanted to hear, and I wanted to believe he meant it. I wanted to believe it so badly. But I couldn't. Not yet. Words were too easy, and I was so very tired.

I did, however, trust Griffen. Not much, but more than I trusted Axel. If he was right, I was safer with Axel than out there on my own. Griffen hadn't said he'd be putting his job in danger by helping me, but I didn't have to be a genius to figure out that math.

He worked for Axel's company. Maybe in a different division, but if Axel and his brothers owned Sinclair Security, then I didn't want to put Griffen in a position where he'd be endangering his job. I owed him for getting me out of Harper's house. I wasn't going to pay him back by asking him to get himself fired.

I looked at Axel, my head spinning, unable to make a decision. Instead, I said, "Did you talk to Agent Tierney?"

"While you were with Harper," he said, his eyes narrowing at the reminder that I'd been alone with his client. "I also called him to let him know you were safe. He wanted to come pick you up and put you in protective custody."

"When will he be here?" I asked, relieved at the easy answer to my problems with Axel. My relief faded when Axel shook his head.

"No," he said. "No protective custody. The FBI is good, don't get me wrong, but Tsepov will find you if you're with the FBI. Tierney can't keep you as safe as I can."

I didn't know if that was true, but my gut, which had never warmed to Tierney, thought it might be.

"Fine, I'll stay with you. But that doesn't mean I forgive you, or that we're going to pick up where we left off. Got it?"

"I know it's going to take some time for you to trust me again." Axel stood and said, "Let me show you to your room, and you can get some sleep. We'll figure out the rest of it in the morning."

Almost numb with exhaustion, I followed Axel down another hall to a guest bedroom. A man's T-shirt had already been laid out across the bed. Without another word, he left me in the room and shut the door behind him. I peeled off my clothes, pulled on the T-shirt, fell into the bed, and promptly passed out.

# CHAPTER SIXTEEN
## AXEL

I gave Emma enough time to fall into a deep sleep before I slipped into bed beside her. Griffen was gone, back to his hotel on the Strip and out of my hair. I knew he was a good guy, but if he'd kept flirting with Emma, I would've knocked him out. It didn't help that she was responding, even if it was only to piss me off.

Emma wouldn't be happy when she woke up and found me in bed with her. I should have cared about that. I should have been overwhelmed with remorse over what I'd done. I should have given her space and let her make up her own mind. That would be the gentlemanly thing to do.

I wasn't a gentleman. Everything that had happened to Emma tonight had been my fault. I knew that. And I would make it up to her. But I wasn't going to let her pull away from me. I'd given her plenty of reasons to hate me, and while Emma was easy-going, I suspected she could hold a mean grudge. I had no intention of letting her get away from me.

I'd let her think I was giving her space so she would

relax enough to fall asleep. She was exhausted, and likely in some pain if the look on her face was any indication. Just the thought that I was responsible for that bruising, the blood, and the black eye she'd have in the morning made me sick.

I wanted to beat the hell out of William Harper for daring to touch her, but the worst of the damage was on my shoulders. Like everything else, I would make it up to her.

She knew it had been an accident. I'd been sure she was out of the way before I busted open the door. I still couldn't believe I'd made such a mistake. It was a reminder of what could happen when I let emotion make my decisions.

I was going to have to be careful. Emma stirred me up, made it hard for me to think clearly, and we had a tricky situation with Harper and Tsepov.

She was in danger, and I couldn't afford to get distracted by the way she made me feel. If I was smart, I'd send her away. That wasn't going to happen. I needed her with me.

She'd be angry to find me in her bed, but I still wasn't leaving. Moving closer, I wrapped my arm around her and pulled her back against my chest, burying my face in her hair, letting the sweet honeysuckle scent of her wash over me.

I hadn't taken very good care of her so far. I'd been too wrapped up in fear, too used to walking away to understand that this time, I didn't want to go. I was done with that now. Emma was mine.

I was going to do anything I had to: bust my ass, bleed myself dry, call in every marker, anything I could to fix this with her. I knew in my gut that I meant something to her. She'd been falling for me before I fucked it all up.

I just had to remind her of what we'd had. I would have time, because no matter what happened, I was never letting Emma go again.

# CHAPTER SEVENTEEN
## AXEL

The sun rose, and I stayed in bed, my arm wrapped around Emma's sleeping body. I was usually up before the sun hit the sky, but Emma needed her sleep, and I wasn't letting her wake alone. It probably would have been safer for me if I had. She wouldn't be happy to open her eyes and find me beside her.

I knew Emma. If I let her build a wall to keep me out, she could hold me off forever. I didn't want to wait. I wanted my Emma back. I knew I deserved to suffer.

Every time I caught a glimpse of her swollen cheek and saw the bruising that had turned into a black eye, I felt sick. How could I have made a mistake like that?

I'd never forget the impact of the door into Emma's body and the terrible realization that I'd hit her with it. I'd been furious, my mind overwhelmed with rage, but I never would have hurt her on purpose. I'd never hurt a woman before unless it was in the linc of duty, and then only very rarely.

It didn't help in the slightest to remind myself that I'd

thought Emma was a guilty target. I should have known she was innocent. I should have trusted my gut, not my head.

Emma would forgive me. I had to believe that. Until she did, I was keeping her close. It wasn't fair. I knew that.

I could let Griffen take her back to Atlanta with him, and my brothers could take care of her. They could keep her safe and give her time away from me. I was sure she would have jumped all over that option if I'd given it to her.

I'd send her away if it was the only way. I'd do anything to keep her alive. But for now, she was safe enough at my side. And if I were with her, I could win her back. I had to. The idea of losing Emma for good was intolerable.

Before Emma, I'd never been into cuddling. I took care of the women I fucked, in bed and out, but I wasn't affectionate. With Emma, I couldn't resist the excuse to touch her soft body, to pull her against me as close as I could get her and keep her there.

Leaving her during the night for the last three weeks had sucked. Now that the truth was out, I didn't have to go. She was with me now, and I was keeping her.

Emma slept like a rock until well past seven o'clock. The moment I realized she was waking up, I started my campaign to win her back. Not fully alert and warm from my body wrapped around hers, I knew she wouldn't be on her guard.

I started slowly, nuzzling the back of her neck and sliding my hand beneath her shirt to rest on the silky skin of her stomach, just above her panties. I loved how soft she was there, her body so giving.

Still half-asleep, Emma didn't remember that she hated me. Her body recognized me, and it loved me.

Her hips wiggled back into mine, her round ass cradling

my cock. We'd never woken together. It was one more thing I'd denied myself when she was a target. Now she was mine, and we'd be waking together every day. Sleepy Emma was delicious.

I had to move quickly before her brain kicked into gear and reminded her that she wanted nothing to do with me. Carefully, I slid my hand down over her hip to her thigh, winding my fingers around her knee. I lifted her leg, pulling it back over mine, opening her to my touch.

My plan was simple. Get her so hot that by the time she woke up, she couldn't resist me.

My fingers went straight to the heat between her legs, stroking her through her panties, swirling circles around her clit with a light touch. Emma stood no chance against me. I knew her body. I knew when she wanted it hard and when she wanted it gentle. It didn't take long before she was squirming.

Time for step two. My fingertips nudged the elastic of her panties aside and slipped between her hot, slick folds. If I'd had more time, I could have teased her for hours. I would have touched her and stroked her until she was begging for more. I'd done that before and it had been amazing. Teasing was for another day. I had to go straight for the orgasm.

I slipped one finger inside her, my cock twitching with jealousy at the way her tight pussy clamped down on my finger. She was getting wetter by the second, making almost inaudible little moans in the back of her throat. I pressed the heel of my hand against her clit and a second finger joined my first, stretching her, getting her ready for me while I pushed her to the edge of orgasm.

Her eyes flickered open as she moaned again, her legs spreading wider. She thrust her pussy into my hand, her body chasing its pleasure as her mind slowly came back online. I knew she was awake when she moaned, "What are you doing in my bed, you bastard?"

"Do you want me to leave?" I asked, grinding my palm down until she shuddered, just on the edge of coming. "Or do you want me to fuck you?"

"Fuck me," she whispered. "Fuck me and then get the hell out."

"I'll fuck you," I said, pulling my hand from between her legs so I could strip off her t-shirt and underwear. "But I'm not leaving you, Emma. Not again."

"Stop talking," she said, panting for breath. "I hate you. Stop talking and make me come."

"Anything you want," I said, happy to oblige. I loved the way she glared at me with lust-darkened blue eyes. She was still too tight to take in one thrust. I had to work my way in, rocking my hips in little jerks that dragged halting moans from her throat.

Emma kept her eyes squeezed shut, trying to block me out, but it wouldn't work. She couldn't pretend I was someone else. Not when it was *me* her body wanted.

It took forever until I was in her to the hilt. I'd fucked a lot of women—probably too many—but not one had felt like this. Her silky wet heat sucked on my cock every time I withdrew, squeezing me tight as I thrust back in.

It was a good thing she was on the edge of orgasm. So was I. I'd have to hold off. I wasn't just going to make this good for her, I was going to make it spectacular.

Ready to let her come for the first time, I set a hard pace, fucking her fast and deep. Release hit, and her knees rose to grip my hips, her fingers digging into my ass as she screamed my name. Axel. My real name. She was pissed at me, but she knew who was inside her.

I fucked her through the orgasm, fighting off the need to join her. It was close to impossible. If Emma's pussy was normally hot, it was something else entirely when she was coming. Like a fist, it squeezed my cock in fierce pulses that begged me to spill inside her.

I'd never fucked her without a condom. I almost lost it, overwhelmed by the feel of her coming on my cock for the first time without anything between us. But I'd promised myself this was for her, not for me.

I moved back, sliding out of her as she came down, just enough that I could reach her breasts with my mouth. I loved how tall she was. In the right position, I could get my mouth on her breasts while we fucked. Heaven.

Filling one hand with her breast, I set to work on the other, teasing her nipple with slow passes of my tongue, making sure she only came down so far from her orgasm before she started back up again.

Emma loved it when I played with her nipples. They were sensitive, but she liked it a little rough. I'd tried clamps on them the week before and she'd gone wild. We'd have to do that again. For now, I had my teeth.

I went gently, wary of being too aggressive with her after the night before. I blocked out the knowledge that William Harper had touched these breasts. It didn't matter that he'd touched her through her clothes; it was still an assault. If Emma had flinched from my touch because of him, because I'd brought her there, it would have killed me.

Listening to her breathing quicken, I bit down on her nipple, worrying it between my teeth, tugging as it tightened in my grip. She cried out in pleasure and wrapped her leg around my back. That was all I needed to know.

Emma was turned on enough to want a little pain. I nibbled and nipped, teasing her, not going as hard as I could. I'd push her boundaries another time. This was about bringing her pleasure and reminding her why she wanted to keep me around.

I played with her breasts until she was writhing beneath me. By then, I was so close to the end I thought I was going to come on her leg like a teenager.

Just to be safe, I slid down her body to take her pussy with my mouth, partly to make sure she came before I did, but mostly because I wanted the taste of her on my tongue.

I wanted to have her everywhere, to mark myself with her. I needed to claim Emma with every part of me—my hands, my cock, and my mouth.

Emma always tasted so fucking good. I slowed down a little once I got between her legs, happy to linger over her swollen, slick pussy. Salty, warm, and sweet. That was my Emma.

I traced her pussy with my tongue, holding her hips down when she squirmed, trying to get more pressure on her clit. She needed to come, and so did I.

Closing my lips over her clit, I drew it into my mouth with hard, rhythmic sucks that sent her flying. Her orgasm hit her like a sledgehammer, preceded by a high-pitched, wailing cry.

Desperate for her, I rose over her body and slammed into her, fighting the tight grip of her pussy as it pulsed around me. I was spilling inside her a second later, helpless against the pull of Emma's body.

I'd set out to use sex to bind her to me, but it had worked out the other way around. Every time she shared her body with me, I wanted her more.

I'd said Emma was mine, and she was. But with the lies swept away from our relationship, I was learning all the ways that I was Emma's, whether she wanted me or not. I belonged to her, and she to me. I just had to keep her safe long enough to prove it.

# CHAPTER EIGHTEEN
### EMMA

I was still reeling from two intense orgasms in a row when Axel kissed me on the temple and slipped from the bed, saying, "I'll go get breakfast started. You can put that T-shirt back on, and there's a pair of sweatpants in the dresser if you don't want to put on your jeans from last night."

Before I could respond, he was gone. Sneaky jerk. I was still buzzing from the way he'd made me come so hard. Twice. The night before, I would have sworn a blood oath I would never, ever let him touch me again. Not in a million years.

I'd love to say I didn't know who he was this morning, that I'd been half-asleep and it hadn't really been consensual. But that would be a big, fat lie. I knew his touch. Adam, Axel, whatever name he was using—I knew him.

I knew the feel of his hands on my skin. I knew his scent, woodsy, masculine, and only him. I knew exactly whose hands were touching me when I woke up, and they'd felt so good I couldn't bring myself to argue.

I wasn't sorry. I'd be nuts to be sorry about what had

happened in that bed. If Axel had proven anything, it was that he knew my body as well as I knew his.

Good sex was the best antidote to stress, and I'd needed the release. Two in a row had been even better. Instead of strung tight, anxious, and angry, I was relaxed with a dopey, happy smile on my lips.

Should I give him points for that? For making me come so hard my brain felt like it had exploded and every muscle in my body was jelly?

It wasn't enough for me to forgive him. Not nearly enough. But maybe I was willing to give him just a little bit of credit for taking care of me. Even if I hadn't asked him to.

I dragged myself out of bed and headed for the bathroom. The mirror told me I looked like a creature from a horror movie, with rat's nest hair, bruises on my face, and nose still swollen. Not my best look. Resigned, I turned on the shower.

I didn't have a change of clothes or any makeup—not that my stash of makeup included anything that would cover my bruises. A little concealer and powder wouldn't come close.

My chest was tight at the idea of facing the world with messy hair and a bruised face in yesterday's bloody clothes.

Usually, I'm not too vain. I like to look good, but I don't spend hours on my hair and makeup. Like any woman, I had lines I wouldn't cross. I didn't always fix my hair. Sometimes I left it loose, and it got a little out of hand.

At times, I was happy to hang out in old leggings and a t-shirt, though I usually tried to coordinate my clothes so they showed some style. But I never, ever left the house without makeup.

I didn't wear a ton—a little concealer if I needed it,

blush, some eyebrow grooming, eyeliner, and shadow. If I were going out, maybe I'd do more with my eyes.

There were times I used a little powder if my skin was having a bad day. At the idea of going out with a naked face, especially with these bruises, I wanted to climb back into bed and hide.

Sadly, that wasn't an option.

I would just have to brazen it out and try to forget that I'd be facing the day without my usual armor. No hair tools, no makeup, and dirty clothes. I wasn't sure I had it in me to deal with what was coming when I was such a mess, but I guessed I'd find out.

At least the shower was nice, with plenty of hot water, dual shower heads and a shelf stocked with shampoo, conditioner and bath gel. I could tell from the lack of clutter on the counters and in the cabinet that this was a guest bath, not one regularly used, but it was set up to make guests comfortable.

By the time I was done, I felt much steadier. Being clean worked wonders. It wasn't clothes and makeup, but it was a start.

I pulled on the T-shirt and sweatpants after salvaging my somewhat-clean underwear off the floor. A fresh pair would've been ideal, but I wasn't going commando in front of Axel. Not anytime soon.

I wasn't sure who it was I didn't trust—him or me. Maybe neither of us. The scent of fresh coffee and cinnamon hit my nose as I entered the hallway to the rest of the house.

We'd never been together for breakfast, but I knew Axel could cook. My stomach growled, not caring that he was a betraying asshole, more interested in what he might be up to in the kitchen. I wanted some of that coffee. I decided to play nice, at least until he fed me.

My stomach flipped over at the sight of him in the kitchen wearing gray dress pants, a black belt, and a dark eggplant button-down that brought out the warmth in his brown eyes.

*No*, I told my traitorous body. *We don't trust him. I'm not sure that we even like him. Just because he's super-hot while holding a spatula and making us french toast, it doesn't mean that we're going to go soft.*

My brain cheered at my resolve, but my stomach and other base impulses disagreed. All they saw was a super-hot guy cooking breakfast. My libido and my stomach were easy. I clamped my mouth shut in case I said anything nice when I wasn't sure how I wanted to handle him yet, and I headed straight for the coffee.

Correctly sensing my mood, Axel didn't try to force me into a conversation. His eyes stroked me from head to toe, slowly, as if he liked what he saw.

I told myself he could have half a point for that, but it still wasn't enough for me to forgive him. Besides, I knew better than anyone that Axel was an excellent liar. Just because he was being nice and acting like he didn't mind that I was wearing baggy sweatpants and had no makeup, it didn't mean I could trust him.

The memory of him leaving me with William Harper was too fresh. Just the thought of him walking away brought back the hollow, desolate feeling at the realization I'd been betrayed. French toast was nice, and so were the orgasms, but they didn't erase what he'd done.

"You can sit at the bar," he said. "This will be ready in a minute."

Coffee in hand, I took a look around and saw the bar.

The kitchen was a large rectangle, with the stove on one side, an island in the middle, and on the other side, open to the living room, was a raised bar with three stools. I sat on one and spun it around to check out the rest of the house.

It was an open plan, the kitchen flowing into the living room, then to a dining area on the other side of the house. A long floor-to-ceiling plate-glass window connected all three rooms.

The night before it had been too dark to see anything, but in the light of morning, the windows gave a breathtaking panoramic view of Lake Mead. The lot had to be huge. I saw other homes in the distance, but Axel didn't appear to have any close neighbors.

The Adam I had known was successful, with a luxury car and expensive clothes, not to mention the restaurants he took me to. But this house was another level entirely. A successful, well-off man did not own a house like this.

I could tell that the furnishings in the home were all custom and high-end. The stove was professional grade, and the rustic-style woodwork in the main area of the house was handcrafted.

Not to mention what the lot itself must have cost. I wasn't into real estate, but I knew the view of the lake didn't come cheap.

If this was his place, he wasn't just doing well—he was very wealthy. I wanted to ask if he owned the house, but that would have violated my policy of not talking to him. I kept my mouth shut and continued to study my surroundings.

The design was interesting, with lots of wood and black iron and a feel that was both rustic and modern. It was masculine, but not so much so that a woman would feel uncomfortable. I liked that. It was elegant and still comfortable. It suited him.

Axel laid a plate in front of me filled with generous triangles of french toast, sprinkled liberally with powdered sugar, each with its own pat of butter and a drizzle of maple syrup, plus three strips of bacon.

I didn't care how mad I was at Axel—it looked amazing. Continuing to ignore him, I picked up the knife and fork he'd placed on the bar and dug in.

Considering Axel's talents, I wouldn't go so far as to say the french toast was better than sex, but it was pretty freaking good: crispy on the edges, tender but not raw in the middle, with just the right amount of cinnamon and sugar. Yum. If he was trying to soften me up with good food, it might work.

He took his own plate and walked around to my side of the bar, sitting on the stool next to me. He didn't attempt to talk, just focused on his food. Good. If he'd interrupted me while I was eating that breakfast, he would've lost all the points he'd gained by making it. Well, not all of them, but a good chunk.

When I was finished, he looked over and asked, "More?"

I shook my head. I was stuffed and feeling much better than I had been earlier. I still could've used a visit to my own closet, or maybe a do-over of the last few months of my life, but some sleep, a shower, and a delicious breakfast were a good start.

"How do you want to do this?" Axel asked, his dark eyes gentle on my face.

"Do what?"

"We have two issues here. First, we need to deal with the fact that I've spent most, almost all, of our relationship lying to you about who I am, and you're justifiably angry about that.

"You also have good cause to be angry about what happened last night. I should've listened to you, and I know we have to talk about that."

"I'm not sure what there is to talk about," I said, aggravated that while he recognized we needed to talk, he also assumed that the talk was going to fix everything he'd mentioned.

My fear, the bruises on my face, and what had almost happened to me last night with Harper were all too fresh to consider that a simple conversation about what he'd done wrong and another apology were going to erase it all.

I wasn't ready to go there yet. I also wasn't ready to start the conversation, and I sensed any protest about it would just get it rolling. Instead, I said, "What's the other thing we have to talk about?"

"Your cover is blown at Harper Shipping," he said, letting me switch gears without a protest.

"You can't go back. And not only does Harper want you, it's likely that Tsepov does as well. You aren't safe on your own. I can protect you, but you're going to have to trust me, which I understand isn't going to be easy."

"I'll just go with Agent Tierney, then," I said. Axel shook his head.

"Not a viable option. Agent Tierney wants you in protective custody. FBI protective custody is good for the average person.

"The average person doesn't have access to Sinclair Security. I can guarantee that I have no leaks. No one in my office is working for Tsepov or Harper. Tierney can't promise you that.

"There are too many ways Tsepov could find out where

the FBI has you stashed. We know he's got moles inside already; we just don't know who they are. Are you willing to take that risk with your life? Because I'm not."

"How do I know you can keep me safe?" I asked. I wasn't going to argue with him about the FBI's security. I didn't know what I was talking about, and it sounded like he did.

It would be stupid for me to insist that the FBI was safe when he seemed so sure they wouldn't be. Even if he was wrong, my protests weren't going to change his mind.

"I can keep you safe," Axel promised. "Finish breakfast, and I'll take you downtown to my office. You can see where I work, and I'll tell you more about what I do. Then you can make up your mind. Does that sound fair?"

I nodded. Part of me was still so angry. I wanted nothing more than to run away and hole up in my bedroom with weepy chick-flicks and a tub of ice cream. I couldn't forget how easily he'd pinned and cuffed me the night before. If I trusted him and he turned on me, I'd be helpless.

On the other hand, if Axel was planning to turn on me, he'd never let me leave, so I might as well play along for now and let him have his say. If he really was going to betray me again, I couldn't think of a reason he'd put all this effort into winning me back. Why not just handcuff me again and get it over with?

Comparing Axel to Agent Tierney, there was no question who could keep me alive. Agent Tierney's goal was the case. Axel claimed his goal was to keep me safe. I had to face reality.

Axel had been an asshole. He'd been the King of Assholes. He'd also apologized. I could choose not to trust him and take off on my own, or I could take my chances with the FBI.

Axel wasn't perfect, but he claimed to want to help me. I was in trouble, and it was the kind of trouble I couldn't fix on my own. No matter how angry I was with Axel, if he could keep me alive and away from Harper and Tsepov, I wasn't going to fight him, even if I wanted to.

# CHAPTER NINETEEN

## EMMA

I changed back into my jeans before we left, unable to bear the idea of going into Axel's offices wearing a pair of sweatpants. I would've put my sweater back on, but it had blood on it. I was pretty sure I never wanted to touch it again. I did salvage my T-shirt, so at least I was wearing my own clothes, even if they weren't clothes I would've chosen.

I still wasn't exactly sure what Axel did for a living. Both Griffen and Axel had mentioned Sinclair Security. I knew Axel's last name—his *real* last name—was Sinclair, so I was assuming that he was in charge.

Griffen had said he worked for Axel's brothers, but Axel had implied that meant he also worked for Axel, which further implied that Axel didn't work for anyone.

I was a little intimidated. I had a feeling, based on Harper's comment about Axel's fees and the big house overlooking Lake Mead, that Axel's business was pretty high-profile.

On top of all my other misgivings about any relationship

with Axel, I felt a niggle of insecurity. I wasn't the kind of girl who dated fabulously wealthy men with lake houses.

The ride back into town was quiet. I didn't remember how long it had taken to get there the night before, but I knew it would take about an hour to get back to Las Vegas, assuming that's where Axel's office was.

We rode in silence the entire way, and I grew more curious as we entered the city. When we headed downtown and Axel abruptly pulled the SUV into an underground parking garage, I was surprised.

I don't know what I had expected, but the building above looked just like any other. Had I thought it would look like James Bond worked there?

The SUV wound its way deeper underground in the parking garage until we turned into a brightly lit alcove beside an elevator. As Axel opened the driver's side door to the SUV, the elevator doors slid open.

At this point in our relationship, I knew better than to get out of the car by myself. If Axel hadn't liked me to do that before my life was in danger, I figured he probably wouldn't want me to do it now.

He was at my door a moment later, taking my arm to help me out and lead me to the elevator, the door still open, as if it were waiting for us. Maybe it was.

"What's up with the elevator?" I asked.

"When my SUV entered the garage, it signaled the control room upstairs. Whoever is on duty would've seen me, known where I was going to park, and sent the elevator."

"Nice," I said, impressed. That was pretty cool. The elevator itself was slick, a generously-sized box of brushed steel, the buttons flush with the panel and nearly invisible, with no numbers.

"How do people know which button to push?" I asked. There were more than twenty buttons on the panel. It must be annoying to have to find the right one every time you used the elevator.

Axel grinned and said, "Mostly we don't have to bother. This elevator is for company use only.

"You can reach all of the floors on it if you need the buttons, but if you're going to our offices and you have your ID on you—which you need to get in through the door anyway—the elevator reads it and knows where you're going."

I realized I hadn't seen him push any of the buttons when we got in. Very slick. The elevator carried us smoothly upward, and with every flight, my curiosity grew. Finally, the doors slid open.

If I'd been looking for James Bond, here he was. The foyer of Sinclair Security was elegant and expensive, every surface black, gray, or brushed steel.

The room was small. Surprisingly small. Then I realized it wasn't so much a foyer as it was a containment room.

We left the elevator and entered from the side. Two solid brushed steel doors were to my right, and opposite them, a second set of elevator doors. Beside the steel doors, an oversized flat screen monitor was built in flush to the wall with a keypad underneath.

On the other side of the doors was a smaller flat screen, also set flush to the wall. It didn't look big enough to be a monitor.

There was nothing else in the small room aside from a sign on the wall with the words *Sinclair Security* in a bold script, with a double S logo beneath it. I expected the doors to click open at Axel's approach as the elevator had.

They remained solidly shut. He reached over and

placed his palm on the smaller of the monitors. Not a monitor then, but a hand scanner. The screen briefly glowed an alien green and went dark. A second later, I heard a lock click.

"What if you don't have the right handprint?" I asked. Axel tipped his head toward the large monitor on the other side of the door.

"You can dial the front desk from there."

He led me through the first set of doors, and I found myself in a reception area, not unlike one you might find in any upscale office, with black leather couches, light gray walls, darker gray carpet, and brushed steel accents everywhere. The office screamed power.

Adding further to this impression, the man sitting behind the shiny black and steel desk did not look like any receptionist I'd ever seen before.

Bald, with graying stubble and keen brown eyes, he wore a button-down shirt that did little to disguise his bulky shoulders and muscled arms. A scar bisected his nose, and another ran down his cheek.

With his eyes on his computer, his face was hard-angled and forbidding. At our entry, he looked up and grinned at Axel.

"Got your orders this morning. Everything's in your office. Lola works fast," he said.

Axel nodded. "She does. Would you bring in some coffee?"

The man nodded and looked at me, raising his eyebrows. Axel, remembering his manners, said, "Billy, this is Emma Wright. Emma, this is Billy. He manages the office. He's my equivalent of you."

Billy let out a surprisingly jolly laugh. In explanation, Axel said, "Emma's in human resources."

Billy kept laughing and said, "I bet you'd handle the crew around here a little differently than I do. But then, if we had someone as gorgeous as you trying to wrangle these guys, no one would ever get anything done."

"That's for damn sure," Axel said. He wound his arm around my waist and led me past Billy's desk to another brushed steel door. He didn't do anything to unlock this one —maybe Billy did it—but I heard the click of the lock as we approached.

I guess I shouldn't have been surprised that a security company had so many locked doors.

It looked like they could withstand a siege.

I wondered how easy it would be to get up here from the lobby if you didn't have an appointment. I suspected it would be nearly impossible.

We went down the hall, then turned down another hall, both of which were lined with closed doors. We didn't pass a single person on our way.

"Does anyone else work here?" I asked. "It's so quiet." Maybe security specialists didn't work on weekends. It *was* Saturday.

Axel opened the door at the end of the hall and ushered me into a spacious office.

Keeping true to theme, it had a long, wide black desk, black bookshelves, and a black leather couch on the opposite side of the room. The couch was covered with what looked like Neiman Marcus shopping bags. They were the only thing in the room that wasn't black, gray, or brushed steel.

Two black leather chairs sat opposite the desk. Axel led me to one and took the other for himself.

"I've got a good-sized team," he said, "but most of them are in the field. Or they were in the field last night and they haven't made it into the office today. I don't micro-manage. They have their assignments, and I know they're getting them done."

"But doesn't anyone work in the office? Or is it so quiet because it's the weekend?" I asked.

"Weekends are a little slower, but there are always two people in the control room. And I have some IT people—" the way he said *IT* made me think they were less network administrators and more like hackers, "but they have their own space on the floor above us. I try not to bother them unless I have to. They don't like their focus interrupted."

Billy entered carrying two steaming mugs of coffee on a tray, along with a small stainless steel pitcher of cream and a matching bowl of sugar. He placed the tray on the desk and said, "Anything else?"

"No, we're good. Thanks, Billy."

Billy gave a half-mocking salute and left, closing the door firmly behind him.

I couldn't contain my curiosity any longer and gestured to the mess on the couch. "What's all that?"

"That's yours. You had to leave your clothes behind last night. Since it's not safe to take you back to your apartment, I didn't want you to be stuck in the same jeans and T-shirt until we get this worked out. I had my personal shopper set you up."

My jaw dropped. The couch was *covered* with Neiman Marcus bags. I loved Neiman's. I could spend many deliriously happy hours in Neiman Marcus, usually at the sale racks.

I made a great salary, but when you love to shop, even a great salary doesn't go that far if you buy everything you like, especially in a store like Neiman Marcus. There were *a lot* of bags on the couch.

"How much did you think I'd need?" I asked.

Axel shrugged. "I told her your sizes and that you wouldn't have any clothes or any other personal items for a few weeks. She figured it out from there."

"But how did you know my sizes? And what do you mean she figured it out?"

Axel gave me a level stare. "There is very little about you, Emma, that I haven't noticed. I know what size clothes you wear. I know what size shoes you wear. I know that you have bigger than average feet, and they're on the narrow side.

"I know you like boot cut jeans, you don't like them to ride too low on your hips, and you prefer Lucky's. I know you like comfortable fabrics, but you still like to look tailored and never messy.

"I know a lot about you. I don't know a lot about makeup, but I had Billy send a picture from your file so Lola would have an idea of your coloring. She's very good at what she does, but if anything doesn't work, we'll send it back."

I couldn't stop staring at the pile of bags and boxes on the couch, especially not now that I knew what they were. I wanted to forget all my troubles and dig in.

It would be lovely to get out of this T-shirt and jeans and even better to be able to put on a little makeup, maybe even do something with my hair.

After all the confusion, pain, and fear of the last twenty-four hours, I would feel so much better if I knew I looked presentable. Then reality hit me.

"Axel, I can't afford any of this. I have some money saved up, but not so much that I can blow it all on a wardrobe I don't really need. I already have a full closet."

Axel shook his head. "You are not paying for any of this. It's my fault you had to leave everything behind. It's my fault I can't take you back to your apartment. It's only fair that I cover the costs of solving that problem."

"Explain to me why I can't go back to my apartment," I said.

Unable to resist the siren call of new clothes, I got up from my chair and went to look through the bags. I could listen to Axel's explanation and check out my new stuff at the same time.

"Agent Tierney asked me not to blow my cover with Harper. Now that you can't go back to the office, they don't have anyone on the inside. Technically, my job with Harper is done. But as far as he knows, we parted on good terms.

"Tierney asked me not to compromise that unless I have to. It's likely they have someone watching your place. If I, or any of my people, take you there, he'll know I'm helping you. Even if they don't make us, they'll know where you are. It's not worth the risk."

That made sense. I pulled out a lightweight red and navy striped sweater with cute button detailing on the three-quarter length sleeves and a pair of Lucky jeans in my favorite style. Lola *was* good.

Fortunately, she'd included underwear. Most of it was high-end-yet-basic bras and panties. Everything was gorgeous, but it was for every day.

Sorting through the bags, I found a few pieces that were definitely not functional lingerie. I spotted a red lace bra and panty set that wouldn't do much to support my generous breasts, but I'd bet would look spectacular. A silk and lace negligée as light and thin as a whisper. A nearly transparent camisole with matching thong.

I'd never worn La Perla, and as pissed as I was at Axel, I wasn't starting today, but I knew I'd put it on eventually. I didn't think I had it in me to be angry enough at *anyone* to resist La Perla for long. I took what I needed, plus the bag of makeup, and asked, "Bathroom?"

Axel indicated the back corner of his office, where the wall became a panel. It could've been a door, but it was missing a handle. I raised an eyebrow and looked at Axel for further direction. "Just walk closer and push on it. It'll open if it's empty. If you're in there, it'll stay locked until you come out."

Good enough for me. I picked up my coffee from the desk and disappeared into Axel's bathroom. Sitting around in those bloodstained jeans and yesterday's underwear, with messy hair and no makeup, I couldn't seem to settle down. Maybe it was irrational, but I wanted to pull myself together before the day went any further.

I was too annoyed at Axel to mind leaving him alone, so I took my time. Besides, it was his office, and this was a workday. I was sure he had plenty to keep him busy. I tried not to think about my empty desk at Harper Shipping. I'd worked hard for that job. I didn't want to face that it was over.

Instead, I got dressed. The jeans and shirt fit perfectly. The jeans were a touch tight, not a surprise since they were brand new, but they looked good. And the sweater had a scoop neck and nipped-in waist that made me look like I had an hourglass figure. I loved it. I pulled on clean socks and the sneakers I'd brought with me, and I tried to fix my hair and face.

The makeup Lola had chosen fit my coloring, but it wasn't heavy-duty enough to cover the bruises. My black eye still looked pretty bad, even with some powder and blush to tone it down.

I finished my makeup and dealt with my hair. Lola had included a travel hairdryer, flat iron, curling iron, and a selection of pins and barrettes. I could do a lot with all of that.

It didn't take me long to finish drying my hair and put it up in a casual braided side bun. I couldn't do anything more about the bruising on my face, but I felt a million times better now that I didn't look like I'd just rolled out of bed after losing a bar fight.

Outside the door of the bathroom, I heard Axel's voice, raised in aggravated annoyance. Packing up my things, I pressed open the door and went to see what was going on.

# CHAPTER TWENTY

## EMMA

"What are you doing here?" Axel was asking as I walked into the room and did a double take.

An Axel clone was standing on the other side of his desk, dressed almost identically—if you exchanged the gray pants and eggplant shirt for black pants and steel gray shirt, and the dark brown eyes for ice blue.

Otherwise, they had the same short, dark hair, the same lean but powerful build, were the exact same height, and had identical chiseled cheekbones. They were like carbon copies.

This must be another Sinclair. The Axel clone turned in my direction and gave me a slow, thorough perusal from the top of my head to my sneakered feet, wincing as he took in my black eye. I squared my shoulders and crossed the room, my hand out.

"I'm Emma Wright," I said. "And you are?"

He grinned at me, a dizzying replica of Axel's grin, and took my hand in his, giving it a firm yet lingering shake. I returned his grin when Axel glared down at our clasped hands. The Axel clone said, "Evers Sinclair. It is very, very nice to meet you, Emma Wright. Griffen has all sorts of complimentary things to say about you. What he says about my brother is less approving."

"Why are you here?" Axel asked again. Why *was* he here? I thought Griffen had said Axel's brothers worked out of Atlanta.

Evers released my hand and said to his brother, "Aren't you going to offer me coffee?"

"No." Axel set his jaw, a mulish expression on his face.

This was a new side of Axel. If I didn't know better, I would have thought he was a ten-year-old boy for all the sullen irritation in his tone. I put the bags I was still holding down on the couch and went back to retrieve my half-empty coffee cup from the bathroom.

As I came back into the room, I saw that the brothers seemed to be locked in a staring contest. Shaking my head, I said, "I'd love some more coffee. Mine is cold."

Axel scowled at me. Then he hit a button on the phone and asked Billy to send in more coffee and maybe some food. I sat back down in the armchair I'd used before. Evers took the one beside me, forcing Axel to choose the chair behind his desk. For the first time since I'd met him, he seemed to be at a loss for words.

Evers had a twinkle in his eye that assured me he knew exactly how much he was annoying his brother, and nothing could have made him happier. Except maybe to annoy Axel even more.

Turning to me, Evers said, "Griffen called last night after he got back from your adventure. He filled me in on what he knew, and I thought I should fuel up the plane and come see what my big brother was up to."

"I've got this under control, Evers. Emma and I were just

going to go over the specifics of her case and figure out what we need to do to keep her safe. We don't need your help."

"Oh, I'm not here because I think you need help with the case, Axel. You should know better than that." Turning to me he said, "I love to bug the shit out of Axel—out of all my brothers—but you're safe in his hands. I can promise you that."

"That's what Griffen told me," I said.

Evers nodded in agreement, deliberately ignoring Axel's growing irritation.

"Griffen is a good man," he said. "We were in the Rangers together." I nodded, sensing that Evers was telling me this only so he could continue to push Axel out of the conversation. I hated to say it, but I was almost starting to feel sorry for Axel.

I had two older brothers and a younger sister. I knew precisely how maddening siblings could be. I risked a glance at Axel and saw that his jaw muscles were clenched so tightly they'd turned his cheeks white.

"If you're not here to help with the case, what are you doing here?" Axel asked for the third time.

"Because," Evers said with a grin, "Griffen said he'd never seen you so tied up in knots over a woman. Since I've never seen you in knots over *any* woman, *ever*, I had to come out to catch the show."

Axel had no response. He sat frozen behind his desk, his teeth gritted as if deciding whether to explode. I wondered if I'd have to break up a fight or if it was smarter to run for the door and wait until the mayhem was over.

Then, surprising me, Axel tipped his head back and let out a bark of laughter.

"Fine," he said, grim amusement in his dark eyes. "You want to give me a hard time over Emma? Have at it. She's found herself in the middle of a shit storm, and since she's mine, it's all hands on deck until we get her out of it. If you're between jobs, then you can jump on board."

The door opened, and Billy entered with a brushed steel carafe in one hand and a tray of pastries, muffins, and what looked like blueberry scones in the other. Without a word, he set them both on Axel's desk and left, closing the door behind him.

While I poured myself a new cup of coffee, refilled Axel's, and got Evers a cup, Axel explained my situation to his brother. I didn't enjoy listening to a replay of everything that had happened, and I was glad Axel kept it short.

When he got to the part about handing me over to Harper, I saw Evers' jaw tighten, though he didn't say a word. He just looked at the bruises on my face, then glared at Axel. Axel finished the story, and I waited to hear what Evers would say. His response surprised me.

"This doesn't make any sense," Evers said, shaking his head. "I can see why you took the job. From that perspective, Harper's story holds up. But now that we know what's really going on, I don't get it."

"I know," Axel said. "Once I realized Emma was innocent, the whole thing started to fall apart."

"I don't understand," I said, putting my coffee down on Axel's desk. "What do you mean it falls apart?"

"I mean," Axel said, "if you're guilty and Harper needed the evidence to fire you, then his hiring me makes complete sense. But if you're informing for the FBI, and Harper wants to stop you, then why hire me to gather evidence? Why bring me into this at all?

"He would've been better off just having Tsepov take you out. If he thought you knew too much, a random carjacking or a mugging would've solved the problem. It happens to FBI informants all the time."

The casual way Axel spoke of them killing me to solve their problem was chilling. And he was right. The easiest way for them to deal with me, once they knew I was giving evidence to the FBI, would have been to kill me. Then why had they hired Axel?

"You say William Harper is working with the Russian mob? With Sergey Tsepov?" Evers asked. Axel nodded. "It doesn't sound like Harper is smart enough to handle that."

"He's not," Axel agreed. "My guess is that he wanted me to get the data back from Emma before she could pass it to the FBI. He could have had Tsepov take care of her, but then he would have had to admit to Tsepov that he'd fucked up by letting her inform on him in the first place."

"Sergey Tsepov does not have a forgiving reputation," Evers said.

"Tsepov already knows about me," I said, interrupting. "Harper called him to come pick me up last night." Axel's eyes darkened at the reminder.

"This is just a guess," Axel said. "But I have a feeling that's a very recent development. If Tsepov had known about you this whole time, there's no way he would have let you go around collecting evidence against them. There's something else that we're missing."

He picked up his telephone and hit a few buttons. "Send me the audio from last night; everything happened while Emma was in Harper's house."

I didn't want to listen to a replay of the night before. I tried to think of an excuse to leave the room, then told myself to stop being such a wimp and woman up.

Yes, the situation was scary. And yes, the night before with Harper had been awful. But I was safe, and Axel wasn't going to let anything happen to me. Listening to the conversation I'd had with Harper couldn't hurt me.

A minute later, Axel clicked on his laptop and William Harper's voice filled the room. I nibbled on a blueberry scone while we listened, reminding myself that I was safe and out of William Harper's hands.

Axel's jaw was tight as he heard Harper threaten me. Evers narrowed his blue eyes and focused completely on the conversation, seeming to absorb every nuance of Harper's words.

When the recording ended, he sat back and said, "He really is a fucking moron. Granted, he had no reason to think he was being taped, but he just admitted to all of it. And now that Emma got away, she's more of a liability than she was when she was just gathering evidence."

"I know," Axel agreed. "I'm surprised Tsepov went into business with this guy. He's usually sharper than that. If we had that laptop, we could bring it to the FBI and put an end to all of this. Emma's evidence combined with the confession should be enough."

"You didn't have a warrant for the recording," Evers said, "or we could use that. But the FBI might be able to scare him with it, even if it wouldn't hold up in court. Too bad we lost the laptop." Evers gave Axel a pointed look, clearly blaming him for the loss of the evidence.

My mind raced. So far, I'd kept Summer out of this. But Axel and Evers had to know the evidence wasn't lost. I wasn't doing myself or the case any favors by keeping my mouth shut at this point.

Desperately hoping I was doing the right thing, I said, "William Harper has my laptop, but he doesn't have all of the evidence."

Axel's eyes snapped to me. "What do you mean?" he asked.

"I've been sending copies of everything I found to a friend of mine. She doesn't know what it is, only knows that I asked her to hold it for me." Two sets of eyes pinned me to my chair.

I tried to explain. "It just felt weird gathering all this information and then handing it over. What if Agent Tierney had lost it? Now I'm glad I was so paranoid."

"Who is this friend?" Axel asked, leaning forward. "Where is she? How soon can we get the evidence from her?"

"Summer lives in Marietta, but she travels a lot for work," I said. "I have to call her and see if she's in town. I mailed her a package yesterday, so it won't be there for a few days."

Axel slid his phone across his desk toward me. Summer's was one of the few phone numbers I knew by heart, and I dialed. She picked up on the third ring.

"This is Summer," she said, her standard greeting when she didn't recognize the incoming phone number.

"It's me," I said, knowing Summer would recognize my voice after years of friendship.

"Hey, babe, what's up?"

"Nothing," I lied. We hadn't talked about any of this over the phone yet, and I had no plans to start now. "Just taking a few days off work, and I thought I might fly out there and visit. Are you around?"

"Not until the end of the week. Can you wait? How much time do you have off work? I'd love to see you! I'm in Houston for a conference and I won't be back until late Friday night. Can you come for a long weekend? I can take Monday off."

"I've got a few days coming," I said. I hated lying to Summer. I wanted to tell her everything, listen to her sympathize over Axel's betrayal, and get her sage advice on what I should do with him. But I couldn't put her in any more danger than I already had.

It was beyond paranoid to think anyone was listening to her phone, but nothing about this situation was normal. Being paranoid felt smart, not crazy. "I'll be there this weekend," I said. I'd have to wait until then for Summer to help me figure out my life. "Have fun at the conference. I'll call you Friday."

"Sweet! I'll see you in a couple of days. Love you, babe."

"Love you too, Summer." I hung up the phone, suddenly missing my best friend so badly tears sprang into my eyes. Just hearing her cheerful voice had felt like getting one of her trademark tight hugs. I had no idea how all this was going to work out, but if I could see Summer anytime soon, I knew I'd feel a million times better.

"So, we're in a holding pattern until your friend gets home," Evers said, sitting back and propping his ankle on his knee.

"Looks like it," Axel said. "I have some guys doing some digging into Harper and Tsepov, but our number one priority, for now, is to keep Emma safe."

"Agreed," Evers said.

"Then we're just going to wait around until Summer gets home?" I asked, not sure I liked the sound of that. "If I can't go home, how does this work?"

Axel stood up from behind his desk. "That's easy. You'll stay with me." Looking at Evers, he said, "Billy can hook you up with one of the apartments upstairs. I'm going to take Emma to my place."

I *really* didn't like the sound of that. Axel and me, alone in his place, was the opposite of what I wanted. I thought again about calling Agent Tierney. Then I thought about FBI informants getting killed. Staying alive was more important than avoiding Axel. All I had to do was say *no*, right? How hard could that be?

# CHAPTER TWENTY-ONE

## EMMA

After gathering my shopping bags from the couch and saying a quick goodbye to Evers, Axel led me back to the elevator and ushered me inside. The elevator was pretty big, but between the two of us and all my Neiman Marcus bags, we filled it easily.

I expected him to press the button at the bottom of the panel for the garage, but instead, he pressed the one at the top. The elevator car slid smoothly upward. I asked, "Where are we going?"

"My place," Axel said.

"You live here?" I asked. "I thought this was an office building."

"It is. It's my building. Sinclair Security owns all of it, and we use it all. It's not a requirement that staff live on-site, but a lot of them choose to. It's extremely secure. I think you'll like my place."

If it was anything like his lake house, I knew I would. A moment later, the door slid open, and I saw that Axel's place was nothing like his lake house, except maybe in size. If I had to guess, I'd say the penthouse covered the entire floor of the building.

Stepping out of the elevator, I faced a long, sleek table beneath an enormous painting that looked like a Jackson Pollack. Maybe it was.

The wall was open on either side to the room beyond, giving me glimpses of a modern space with sharp angles, clean surfaces, and white everywhere, except where it was broken up by splashes of bright color, much like the painting in front of us.

Axel tossed his car keys on the table and led me out of the entry into the main living space of the penthouse. The huge room spread out before me, everything immaculate and beautifully designed.

It was so different from the lake house that I had to ask, "Did you decorate here, or did you tell someone what you wanted and she put it together?"

Axel laughed. "No, I had nothing to do with the way this place turned out. I learned my lesson, and for the lake house, I actually had a conversation with the decorator. But here I used the same person who designed the offices.

"She must have thought, based on what I wanted for the business, that I liked the modern look, because this is what I ended up with. I'm usually so busy with work that I haven't gotten around to warming the place up."

"It is a little cold," I said, trying to be diplomatic. "It's beautiful, though." It was. The penthouse wasn't my style. I was far more drawn to the warmth of the house at Lake Mead, but there was no denying that the austere, modern lines of the penthouse were both dramatic and gorgeous.

"Follow me. I'll show you where you can put your things."

Axel led me past the kitchen—more brushed steel here,

with gray marble and black lacquered cabinets—and through the living room with its low-slung, angular couches and a lot of steel with glass, and down a long, white hallway that ended in what could only be Axel's bedroom.

"I'm not staying in here," I said. Axel ignored me, and I followed him, prepared to argue further. His bedroom looked much like the rest of the penthouse: high ceilings, open space, and modern art.

The bed, however, did not fit the rest of the penthouse. It wasn't modern at all. It was huge, made of black leather and dark wood, the design a better fit for the rustic look of the lake house.

The enormous king-sized frame was dominated by a plush, tall, black leather headboard, accented by leather straps and buckles that would have looked at home on a saddle. A matching wood and leather trunk sat at the foot of the bed.

I wondered what Axel would keep in a trunk at the foot of his bed. If he were anyone else, I would have assumed spare blankets and maybe an extra pillow. I didn't think that's what Axel kept in his trunk. I told myself I didn't want to find out. I was lying.

I was so distracted by the sight of the bedroom that I didn't realize that Axel had disappeared. I called his name, and he stepped out through a doorway on the opposite side of the room.

"You can keep your things in here," he said. I remembered my earlier objections.

"I'm not staying in your bedroom. And I'm not putting my things in your closet."

Axel crossed his arms over his chest. "Emma, I know you're angry with me. We need to talk about that."

I dropped the Neiman's bags on the floor and crossed

my arms over my chest, mimicking his posture. "You can't just apologize, expect me to forgive you, and then move me into your bedroom. It's not that easy."

"I know that, Emma," he said, his tone giving me the impression his patience was wearing thin. Tough luck. "You don't have to sleep in here with me if you don't want to. But your clothes are going in my closet."

"Are you telling me you don't have a guest room in this entire place?" He had to have a guest room. The penthouse looked like it was huge.

"I do," he admitted, "but the closet isn't very big. Mine is much better."

Arguing with Axel was pointless. I didn't have that many clothes, and there was no good reason a guest room closet wouldn't work. He was just being stubborn. I decided to take a different tack and bring up something else that had been bugging me all day.

"You didn't use any protection this morning. After everything that's happened, and the fact that you knew I didn't want you in my bed in the first place, I can't believe you didn't use protection."

Axel narrowed his eyes at me and said, "You're on birth control." I was, but that wasn't the point. Reading my mind, Axel went on, "And I know you're clean. So am I."

"How do *I* know you're clean?" I asked, suddenly very tired of Axel making decisions for me. "You should have asked me first."

Axel shook his head and dropped his eyes to the floor for a long moment before meeting mine again. "You're right," he said. "I should have. I didn't think. I have a bad habit of not thinking where you're concerned, Emma. I'm sorry."

"Fine." I didn't know what else to say. He'd apologized,

and it wouldn't happen again, because I was never going to sleep with him again. Ready to be done with the whole discussion, I said, "I'm going to take a nap." I needed one. I'd only gotten up a few hours before, but I hadn't had much sleep and I was exhausted. Axel shook his head.

"We still need to talk about the situation with Harper and Tsepov," he said. "Let me send one of my guys to get the evidence from your friend. I don't want you traveling until I know you're safe."

"No way," I said. "I don't want one of your people to scare Summer. She isn't involved in any of this except for holding some mail for me. I don't want to worry her."

"It's too dangerous. You're safe in here. Out there, anything can happen to you. That's an unacceptable risk."

Did that mean what it sounded like? "So, I'm just going to stay here until what? Harper and Tsepov are in jail? Do you have any idea how long that could take?"

"You're going to stay here until I'm sure you're safe," Axel said.

"You're not my keeper," I said.

Axel unfolded his arms and stalked across the room toward me, a familiar glint in his eyes. I knew that look. Intimately.

As always, when he looked at me like that, it sent a dizzying combination of nerves and heat twisting through my belly. Hadn't I just promised myself I wasn't going to sleep with him again? Why was it that he could give me one look and I melted for him?

I was so weak. Or he was that good. He *was* that good. The best I'd ever had, not that I had a ton of experience. Why should I deny myself the best sex of my life just because Axel was a jerk? I shouldn't.

I could keep my body and my heart separate. Men did it

IVY LAYNE

all the time. I could shove aside all my worries about trusting him, all my questions about what he felt for me and take what I wanted from him. I was tired of being a victim of circumstances. This time, I was taking control.

Straightening my spine, I lifted my arm and held my hand up, palm out, ordering him to stop where he was. Axel came to a halt a few feet away and quirked his lips like he was trying not to smile. He'd been the King of Assholes, but he was seriously hot, especially now, his eyes dark with desire and focused on me.

I said, "I told myself I wasn't going to sleep with you again. This morning doesn't count. I still don't trust you, even if I believe you want to keep me safe. But then I realized that I'd be punishing myself. I don't have to trust you to have sex with you."

Now Axel was grinning at me, looking both amused and triumphant. "So, you're saying that you don't *like* me, but you're going to let me protect you and give you orgasms."

"Basically, yes." The way he put it, I sounded like a bitch. I reminded myself that the night before, he'd turned me over to a man who wanted to sell me into slavery.

It was less than twenty-four hours later, and I was willing to live in Axel's home and let him tell me what to do. Just because I hadn't forgiven him—might never forgive him —it didn't make me a bitch. I wasn't willing to explain all of that, so I said, "You get to have orgasms, too."

A quick laugh escaped, and then he was on me.

I don't know how I thought I could resist Axel. The second his hands touched my skin, my body came alive, heat gathering between my legs, nipples hardening, my breath speeding up.

I wasn't sure I liked Axel. I couldn't decide if I trusted him, but I knew I wanted him. His mouth came down on mine, and he kissed me with utter possession, pulling me to him, one arm around my back and a strong hand gripping the back of my neck.

My proud declaration that I was using him for sex was just words. Here was the truth. My body wanted him. So did my mind. Only my heart shied away, diving for cover as the rest of me gave in.

# CHAPTER TWENTY-TWO

## EMMA

A bruptly, Axel broke the kiss and stepped back, spreading his arms as if offering himself. "You want me?" he asked. "Take off my clothes."

I hated being told what to do—unless it was Axel and we were getting naked. Then, all it took was his deep voice giving me an order and my panties were immediately soaked.

Despite my anger and distrust, this time was no different. My hands trembling with the surge of lust, I went to work on the buttons of his shirt, avoiding his eyes.

Seconds later, I was peeling it off, baring his lean, muscled chest and his chiseled abs. His body didn't just look good. I knew from experience that he was strong and fast. He had a few scars marring his sleek skin, but they did nothing to detract from his sheer male beauty.

Axel half-naked was mouth-wateringly gorgeous. Fully naked would be even better. I had his pants open with my next breath, pushing them down his hips, trailing my fingers over his tight, perfect ass. At the thought of sinking my nails into that ass as he fucked me, a pulse of heat throbbed between my legs.

Axel hadn't said a word since I'd begun stripping him. That meant I was to keep going until he gave me a new order. Dropping to my knees to finish removing his pants, I wondered if I could push him into letting me take the lead.

I sat back on my heels and went to work, tugging his pants down his legs, deliberately ignoring his hard cock as it brushed my forehead.

He lifted one foot, then the other, allowing me to pull off the remainder of his clothes. When he was naked, I shifted to my knees and looked up, allowing my cheek to graze the silky, hot skin of his cock.

Turning my face an inch to the right, my lips slid over his erection. I looked up and met his eyes, waiting to see what he would say.

His eyes burned into mine, so dark they were almost black. There was something unbearably erotic about being on my knees, fully clothed while he was naked and towering above me.

His cock was so close to my mouth, I wasn't sure who was teasing whom. I wanted to taste it, wanted the control, the power of taking him between my lips and giving him pleasure. He kept me needing him, all the time, his mastery over my body a form of control over me. I wanted that power back. I could tell he knew exactly what I was thinking.

"Stay there, and strip," he ordered. I was more than happy to comply. I'd loved the outfit when I'd put it on, but now I was desperate to be as naked as Axel.

I had to roll onto my back to squirm out of my jeans, pulling them off—along with my underwear, socks, and sneakers—in one quick shove.

The sweater, t-shirt, and bra were gone a second later. Then I was back in position, kneeling at his feet, my breath ghosting over his straining cock, teasing him.

"What do you want?" Axel asked, his voice so low it caught in his throat.

"I want to suck your cock," I said. "I want to make you come in my mouth."

Axel groaned and shook his head. "Not this time. I have other plans."

I barely had time to register my disappointment when he leaned down and scooped me up, striding to his bed with my body firmly tucked into his arms. I loved his strength, the way he could pick me up like I weighed nothing. He dropped me on the mattress and said, "Don't move."

I didn't. He vanished to the end of the bed, and I heard a creak and a thump. Curiosity bloomed. Was that the trunk? What was he getting? I didn't have to wait long to find out. Axel came back into sight holding two straps.

I should have known he'd have sex toys in the trunk. Climbing on the bed behind me, he guided me to my knees, leaning me forward until my hands rested on the headboard of the massive bed.

Loops at the end of the straps slid around my wrists. The straps fastened to the buckles on the headboard, holding me in place. The position made me feel trapped and vulnerable, but it wasn't uncomfortable. I waited for Axel to move behind me.

I wasn't expecting him to roll to his back and slide between my legs. He adjusted my hips over him, propping himself up on a pillow so he was half reclined, my bare breasts dangling just above his mouth, my pussy spread inches from his straining cock.

"I know you want to run from me, Emma," he said,

trailing his fingertips down my sides, tracing my body, his touch feather-light, setting every nerve on fire. He looked up at me, his gaze capturing mine.

I wanted to look away, to shut him out and lose myself in his body. It seemed he wasn't going to allow that. His fingers explored, gliding over my breasts, pinching my nipples, skating over my belly, all the while his eyes never leaving mine.

"You want to shut me out. I get it. But I'm not going to let you. You're mine. All of you. You can try to lock away your soul, but you won't keep me from your body."

He cupped my breasts in his hands, squeezing and molding them, his hands big and hard, the calluses on his palms scraping my nipples with a delicious friction. Ducking his head, he took one nipple into his mouth and sucked, sending a blast of white-hot pleasure between my legs.

Axel's mouth on my breasts never failed to drive me crazy. One night he'd played with my nipples for over an hour, making me come that way, teasing me until I'd begged for him to fuck me. I'd come three times that night, the last time so hard I'd almost blacked out.

Dropping his head back to the pillow, he cupped my breasts again, letting them fill his hands. "I love your body, Emma. It was made for me. You're lush. Gorgeous. I could spend all day on your breasts. They're perfect."

Releasing my breasts, he slid his palms down my back and gripped my ass. "And this... fuck, Emma, your ass is phenomenal."

His fingers dug into my skin, holding me tight, pulling me down so that the head of his cock grazed the slick folds between my legs. I couldn't help it—I let out a whimper. He was so close.

"You want my cock, Emma?"

"Yes," I whispered. *Want* didn't begin to describe how I felt about his cock. "Please."

"Not yet," he said. "Open your eyes and look at me."

I did, gasping when he tugged my hips down just a little further. The head of his cock settled into the gate of my pussy, a breath away from being inside. I squirmed, trying to take more of him, then I let out a wail as he hauled me up a few inches, taking his cock away.

"Axel," I cried out, the game too much.

"No," he said. "You only want me for sex? Fine. But the rules stay the same. I'm in charge when we fuck. If you don't like it, go fuck someone else."

The thought of touching another man scored through me. Never. I couldn't imagine letting another man put his hands on me after being with Axel. He didn't mean it. I knew he didn't.

"Okay," I said, giving in. I wanted him. In here, he was mine. He might have betrayed me out there in the real world, but in bed, he'd never let me down. All I had to do was follow his direction, and I'd get what I needed. "I promise I'll do whatever you want."

"That's my good girl," he said, sliding his hands to my lower back and leading me down until the head of his cock was once more barely pressing into me. The urge to move was unbearable, but I stayed still.

This time, I wanted everything; his cock inside me, his mouth on my breasts, and my orgasm blinding me with pleasure, driving the rest of the world away. When his fingers dropped to stroke my clit, I almost screamed from the sharp, sweet sensation, from the need to move, to do something.

I forced myself to remain as I was, motionless, afraid

that if I did anything, he'd stop. Again, he stroked my clit, his touch light, teasing. Another tug on my hips and the head of his cock was inside, stretching me, giving me just a hint of how good it would be when he was all the way inside me.

In this position, so open to him, I was frozen in the moment of invasion, the slice of time when my body and his became one. It was unbearably intimate, not just about sex, about his cock and my pussy. This was more than sexual desire. It was our bodies bringing us together, making us one.

I would have cursed him for doing this to me, but I could barely breathe from the effort of holding still beneath his caresses. I fisted my hands, my body trembling from the strain.

Circling a wet finger around my clit, he lifted his head and locked his lips around one hard nipple, sucking me, stroking with his tongue as he played with me. I teetered on the edge of orgasm, body shaking, tears filling my eyes.

"Please, Axel. I'm going to come. Please. Let me come, let me have you inside me."

"Not yet." His finger fell away as he pulled me down another inch. It wasn't enough, but it was better.

"Please," I begged, unable to form thought into words. With his mouth back on my nipple, he settled a finger on either side of my clit and squeezed, gently the first time, then harder. I gasped, the pressure exploding in a white-hot flare of ecstasy, shooting me straight into an orgasm.

I forgot everything about holding still and letting Axel take control. He thrust up into me as I came, filling me with his cock, digging his fingers into my ass as he fucked me, drawing out the release until all I knew was Axel—his hands on me, my hips grinding down on his and taking all of him, over and over.

I came back to myself later, tears wet on my cheeks, my body draped over Axel's, still trembling, my hands unbound. He left me for a moment to deal with the condom, then he slid into the bed and pulled me over to him, holding me close, stroking his hands over my bare back.

"Shh, it's okay Emma. Everything's okay." A callused thumb came up to wipe a fresh tear from my cheek, and I realized I was crying. My emotions careened inside me, nothing making sense.

I'd had a plan for my life, and I'd been following it. Good job, great friends, shiny future. Then the FBI had burst in to turn it all upside down, and Axel had broken my heart.

So why, in this whole crazy mess, was he the only thing that seemed to make any sense?

I had no idea what I was doing anymore. I'd thought that if I tried to shut Axel out I could stay in control. But he'd proven me wrong.

I didn't want to shut him out. I wanted him, all of him. Lost and uncertain, I lay there and cried into Axel's warm skin, letting the tension of the past twenty-four hours drain away in my tears.

# CHAPTER TWENTY-THREE
## EMMA

That began the two most surreal days of my life. After my crying fit in bed, I'd fallen asleep. Axel had woken me a few hours later and fed me homemade pizza with a fabulous red wine, then curled up on the couch with me to watch old episodes of my favorite geeky cooking show.

He'd cleared our dishes and led me to bed early, then made love to me, slow and sweet, his touch reverent, until I was close to tears once more. Before I could lose it again, I'd fallen asleep, tucked safely into Axel's arms.

The next morning he'd cooked me breakfast, eggs Benedict with smoked salmon, and we'd settled in to binge watch a show the rest of the world had been obsessed with the year before but both of us had missed.

We didn't talk about the case or the FBI, not even when Evers called with an update. We did have sex three times: once on the couch—we'd had to restart that episode—once in the shower, and the last time was at the foot of the bed, with me on my back and strapped to the trunk like a virgin sacrifice.

The day after was the same. Good food—this time I cooked for Axel—more television, and a lot of sex. I stopped trying to push Axel away. It was a useless effort anyway. I didn't have the emotional resources to keep a true distance from Axel. It wasn't me.

I'd tried to tell myself I could use him for his body, but that had been a lie, me fooling myself so I could justify letting him back inside my defenses. Once I'd let him back in, I couldn't muster the desire to push him out.

He'd hurt me. And I was on my guard. I couldn't help it. His phone beeped with text messages every few minutes, and I wondered if any of them were from William Harper.

A tiny part of me worried that I was a fool, and this was all part of a bigger plan that would make his earlier betrayal look like a little white lie. But that was my fear talking.

I didn't really believe he was lying to me. Every kiss, every shared laugh convinced me he was telling me the truth, that this thing between us was real and it meant as much to him as it did to me.

On the evening of the second full day we'd spent secluded in Axel's penthouse, he surprised me. We were curled up on the couch, mostly naked, kind of watching television.

I was dozing, my head pillowed on Axel's chest as he stroked my hair. It was heaven if I forgot about everything waiting for us outside of the penthouse. Axel proved that not all of the world outside was a threat.

"Do you want to get out of here for a few hours?" he asked, his lips tracing the shell of my ear, sending a shiver down my spine. It was a little scary how easily this man could turn me on, especially considering how much sex we'd had in the past two days.

"Is it safe? I thought you said I couldn't leave," I said. As much as I loved this interlude with Axel, I knew I'd start going stir crazy soon. His penthouse was big, but when you can't leave, even a big place is too small.

"I have a plan," he said, nipping my earlobe with sharp teeth. I squirmed. I loved it when he used his teeth. "Do you want to meet my friends?"

"How?" I asked, suddenly intrigued. Axel's friends had been a sore spot as our relationship developed. I'd never said anything, but I'd always been aware that not only had I never seen his home, but I'd also never met a single one of his friends.

"Dylan has excellent security that I can augment with my own and a private entrance to a private dining room. It's not the same as taking you on a normal date, but it's the best I can do under the circumstances."

I rolled over on the couch and stared at Axel. He'd proven he could be an asshole. I'd been over that ground repeatedly. Now it seemed he was devoting himself to proving he could be sweet as well. The asshole part hadn't been a big surprise, less so now that I knew what he did for a living.

A man had to have some very sharp edges to thrive as a high-profile security specialist. But the sweet—*that* was a surprise. He'd spent the last forty-eight hours showing me all the ways he could make me happy. Now, in the midst of hiding me away, he wanted to take me on a date with his friends. I only had one answer for him.

"I'd love to."

He was off the couch and lifting me into his arms a second later, carrying me back to the bedroom. He set me on my feet in the master bath and herded me into the shower, turning on the water until it steamed.

"Shower sex first," he said, positioning me under the

spray and drizzling apple scented soap over my breasts. His hands slipped over my skin, working the soap into a thick foam, teasing me with his touch. Two could play at this game.

Before he got me so turned on that I forgot what I was doing, I grabbed the bottle and squirted some of the fragrant gel on his chest. I couldn't get enough of touching his body. Hard where I was soft, the planes and ridges of muscles, so strong under his silky skin, were irresistible.

You'd think we hadn't had sex in months with the way we shot right past the foreplay. Only a few minutes after we hit the shower, Axel was lifting me, bracing me against the tile wall, my legs wrapped around his hips.

We'd decided to forget about condoms the day before. It meant a lot that Axel hadn't argued about using them when we didn't need to, but as we'd started having sex all over the penthouse, the condoms had just gotten in the way.

He filled me easily, aided by the slippery soap and my arousal. I didn't know what it was—maybe pheromones—but my body was always ready when Axel was around. Even when my heart and mind weren't sure, my body knew what it wanted: Axel. Only Axel.

Another explosive orgasm later, we got out of the shower and I followed Axel into his closet, looking for something to wear.

Axel's personal shopper, Lola, had set me up with plenty of clothes for a few weeks, all carefully chosen to both fit my style and flatter my abundantly curvy figure. Whatever happened in the future, I had to meet this Lola. I loved to shop on my own, but she was a genius at finding outfits that were both comfortable and stylish while making me look like I had a perfect hourglass figure.

"How dressy is dinner?" I asked, flipping through hangers. Two more deliveries had arrived since we'd come to the penthouse, one each day. These had included more shoes and cocktail dresses as well as lingerie. A lot of lingerie. Not that I'd had a chance to wear much of it. Axel might like buying me lingerie, but he liked taking it off even more.

"I'm wearing a suit," he said, shuffling through his own hangers, then pulling out a crisp blue shirt and a steel gray suit. "The girls will probably be in cocktail dresses."

"The girls?" I asked, nervous all of a sudden.

"Leigha and Chloe, Dylan and Sam's girlfriends. Fiancées, actually."

"They're both engaged?" I asked, pulling a dress from the hanger to study it more closely.

A Carolina Herrera Doupioni silk shirtdress, it was a play on the classic little black dress—formal enough to be a cocktail dress, but with puffed sleeves and a wide belt, it had a vintage flair. The A-line cut and button-up bodice would show off my curves, and the deep black of the silk would look fantastic with my red hair and pale skin.

I avoided looking at the price tag as I carefully removed it. I'd window shopped for Carolina Herrera before, and I had an idea that the simple dress probably cost more than my mortgage. I wasn't even going to look at the tag on the box that held the shoes I'd selected.

The patent leather t-strap spike heels were crazy hot, but the distinctive red sole told me that the shoes cost about as much the dress. I wasn't going to worry about it. It wasn't every day a girl got her dream wardrobe from Neiman Marcus. I had enough to fret about; the clothes didn't even make the list.

"Both of them," Axel said as I wiggled into a matching bra and panties and stepped into the dress, his dark eyes intent on the sight of my breasts swaying in the sheer red lace bra. At the heat in his eyes, I forgot what we'd been talking about. Oh, his friends' engagement.

"When are they getting married?" I asked, half listening and half thinking about what to do with my hair. It would take forever to dry it. I was better off putting it up.

"I have a feeling Sam and Chloe are going to elope," Axel said. "Dylan and Leigha are planning a huge wedding and it has them spooked. I'm sure you'll hear about it at dinner. I think Leigha would have been fine with something small, but Dylan owns the Delecta. He doesn't do anything small."

The conversation finally penetrated my preoccupation with getting dressed. "Your friend Dylan is Dylan Kane?" I asked, shocked. Dylan Kane was practically a celebrity: ridiculously wealthy, powerful, and gorgeous, he was photographed all the time with supermodels, usually at some exclusive event.

Taking in the sight of Axel in his perfectly cut suit, his sculpted cheekbones, and dark eyes, I shouldn't have been surprised he was friends with someone like Dylan Kane. I wondered what kind of woman Dylan would be marrying.

Was she going to sit there through dinner pretending to eat and giving me sideways looks for being with a man like Axel when I wasn't model material? I hated to admit that I cared, but I wanted his friends to like me, and that meant fitting in with their future wives.

I pushed my worries away and finished getting ready. My bruising had faded somewhat—not enough for the light makeup Lola had provided to cover the damage, but I was able to hide the worst of it.

I emerged from the bedroom to find Axel on his phone again, typing out a message. It made me nervous when he did that. I didn't really think he was going to sell me out, but his open line to Harper was unsettling. Needing to know, I asked, "Work?"

The guilt in Axel's eyes when he looked up made my heart sink. "Harper wants a meeting. He doesn't come straight out and say it, but it sounds like he wants to send me after you again."

"Well, that should be easy, since you already have me," I said in a falsely bright tone. I was trying to hide my doubt. From the look in Axel's eyes, I don't think I did a very good job. He came forward and wound his arm through mine.

"Don't even joke about that," he growled. "Harper is never getting his hands on you again. I'll have to take the meeting—go in with a wire and see what we can get him to admit—but he's not getting anywhere near you, Emma. Never."

"Okay," I whispered, the conviction in his voice soothing most of my fears. I had to stop doubting him. I would. I just needed a little more time.

"You look gorgeous," Axel said as he led me to the elevator and pressed the button for the garage. "I almost wish I didn't know what you were wearing under that dress. I'll be hard all through dinner."

He turned to face me and tugged the sides of the bodice together, trying to fasten one more button. I had the top three undone, showing a fair amount of cleavage. Not too much, but more than I might have revealed during the day or at work.

If I'd been built differently, Axel might have succeeded, but my breasts didn't want to be contained by buttons up to my chin. With a sigh, he gave up and ran his finger along the line of the fabric, tracing over the skin of my breast.

"I've never been possessive about a woman before," he admitted, sliding his finger to the first fastened button, then

183

up the other side. "But I don't want anyone else seeing how sexy you are."

"I think you're exaggerating my appeal," I said. I knew I looked good in the dress, but not so good that every man in sight would be plotting to steal me away from Axel.

"I'm not. You're luscious and beautiful. Thinking about some guy staring at you makes me want to cover you up. Or keep you home."

"Such a caveman," I said as the elevator doors opened.

"I *am* a caveman," he said, "but only with you, Emma."

Axel opened the car door and helped me into the rear seat. I didn't have to ask why. The front window had a tint, but the back windows were so dark no one would be able to see me.

I'd rather be sitting next to Axel, but the back seat was better than riding in the trunk. I couldn't help but notice the two matching black SUV's that followed us out of the parking garage. Axel wasn't taking any chances.

# CHAPTER TWENTY-FOUR

## EMMA

"**W**ait there until I come to get you," Axel said, parking the SUV in a small area of the underground lot.

He'd had to show an ID to get into this section, and after a quick word with Delecta security, he helped me from the SUV and escorted me to the elevator, followed by two men in Delecta uniforms and three others who I assumed worked for him.

I was torn between being impressed and being nervous about Axel's level of paranoia. Five armed guards was a lot just to take me to dinner. If things were this dangerous, should we be going out at all?

As we progressed up the elevator and down several hallways, we lost two of the guards and picked up a new set. We weren't exposed to the general casino population at any point between the secure parking area in the garage and the plush private dining room that was our destination.

The room wasn't huge, but it was clearly intended for a much larger party than our six. Two men and two women waited in the dining room, all standing around a flickering gas fireplace, holding glasses of wine and watching our entrance with unabashed curiosity.

I recognized Dylan Kane immediately. I wasn't a gossip hound, but I read the paper often enough to know what he looked like. He had his arm wrapped tightly around the waist of a woman about my age with shining dark hair, a friendly smile, and a figure a lot like mine.

Dylan might have been photographed with a lot of stick-thin models, but he was marrying a woman with a lot of curves.

She wore a glittering black cocktail dress with a plunging V neckline. It was classy but definitely sexy. Her shoes were red spike heels that matched her lips. She was beautiful, but not at all what I'd expected. Taking the lead, she broke away from Dylan and came toward us, her hand outstretched.

"Hi, I'm Leigha," she said. "I'm so glad to meet you! Chloe and I have been badgering the guys to invite you over since we found out Axel had a real girlfriend and not some piece of fluff. Sorry you're having such a bad time. Come meet Chloe."

I didn't have a chance to respond—not that I knew what to say—before she was leading me to another woman, this one as curvy as Leigha and myself, but a few inches shorter, with honey gold skin, loose chestnut curls, and warm brown eyes.

"You must be Chloe," I said, holding out my hand as soon as Leigha let go. "I'm Emma."

Between Leigha's enthusiastic welcome and Chloe's sweet smile, I didn't have a chance to get nervous. Leigha spilled that she and Chloe had been tempted to fix Axel up, but Dylan and Sam had warned them off. I couldn't help laughing at the idea of anyone setting Axel up on a date.

He brought me a glass of wine, introduced me to Dylan and Sam, and then left me to get to know Leigha and Chloe a little better, whispering in my ear that I didn't have to hide anything, but he wouldn't mind if I didn't tell them exactly what a jerk he'd been.

At their open and kind curiosity, I shared a little of what I'd been going through, though I went out of my way to downplay Axel's mistakes. It was one thing for me to be pissed at him, but I didn't want to throw him under the bus in front of his friends.

Chloe took my hand when I mentioned the Russian mob, admitting that her brother was tied up with them and she'd met Sergey Tsepov in person. With a shiver, she said, "He's terrifying, Emma. Seriously. Elegant, urbane, very intelligent, and he'd kill you in a second if he thought it would benefit him. I don't like that he's after you."

"Axel won't let him get to me," I said. I wasn't entirely sure of our relationship, but I knew Axel would do everything he could to keep me safe.

"Axel's the best," Chloe agreed. I wasn't going to argue with that. Looking across the room, watching him as he had a quiet conversation with Dylan and Sam—probably filling them in on the past few days—I felt like I'd stepped out of the turmoil of my life and into a dream world.

The elegant dining room, with its dark red walls and walnut wainscoting, the beautiful and friendly women, and the three examples of male perfection all belonged in a story, not real life.

Dylan Kane's thick, dark hair and vibrant green eyes were even more arresting in person than in the paper. Sam was the perfect match for Chloe with his messy blond hair and piercing blue gaze.

And Axel. He was all mine.

While Dylan and Sam were undeniably handsome, Axel was in a class all his own. He wasn't just gorgeous. He had an air of danger, of control that was irresistible.

Catching my eye, he ended his conversation with the guys and came to get me. "Sorry, ladies. You can have Emma all to yourselves another time. Right now, I don't like letting her out of arm's reach."

We settled into chairs around the fire, and I discovered that the guys were hot, but also genuinely welcoming. We talked about everything and nothing, avoiding any discussion of my problems, sipping wine and nibbling on hors d'oeuvres until tuxedoed waiters brought in our dinner.

I loved seeing Axel kick back with his friends. They joked and gave each other shit, but the underlying affection was clear. And the women were wonderful: smart, kind, and fun, not unlike my own friends.

"What do you think, Emma?" Leigha asked, her gray eyes glittering with laughter.

"Hmm?" I said, not sure what we were talking about. Dylan had been explaining something about their upcoming wedding, and my attention had drifted. I liked a good party, but their wedding sounded like a three-ring circus. Or a military campaign. Way too much work to be fun.

"Are you in favor of a big wedding or eloping?"

I glanced around the room, catching Dylan and Sam's amused looks as well as Leigha and Chloe's curious ones. My gaze snagged on Axel, who didn't look either amused or annoyed at the topic of conversation. I flushed, not sure what to say.

Axel and I were barely on the good side of an almost-breakup, nowhere close to talking about marriage. It had been a while since I'd thought about the perfect wedding, and for a moment, I considered dodging the question.

Then Axel asked, "What do you think, Emma? Big or small?" The way he asked made the question personal, as if he wasn't asking if I liked big weddings but asking if I wanted *our* wedding to be big.

I swallowed, blurting out what was on my mind. "Small. I wouldn't want to elope, but I'd only want close friends and family."

"With big families, that could still get out of control," Axel commented. My heart lurched in my chest and my cheeks felt hot. What was he saying? We hadn't known each other nearly long enough to be talking about marriage.

Nervous, I deflected. "Size isn't really what's important. I want to hear about the dress. You have to have a picture on your phone that I can see."

Leigha jumped up, a brilliant smile on her face as she took the bait. The conversation went on a side trip to honeymoon destinations, and I stayed quiet by admiring pictures of Leigha's beautiful gown. I looked up once to see Axel watching me, his dark eyes serious. I looked away, my cheeks still pink.

The rest of dinner was fun, without any more embarrassing moments. I was hiding a yawn by the time we called it a night, trading numbers with Leigha and Chloe with promises to get together once my troubles were cleared up.

Axel led me out of the dining room and we left as we'd come in, surrounded by guards, except this time I was tucked tight into Axel's side, my head on his shoulder, eyelids drooping. I almost drifted off in the elevator.

We really needed to sleep more at night and save the sex for daytime. On second thought, never mind. Sleep was overrated.

At first, I thought the two sharp, loud bangs were a car engine backfiring. A blaze of agony cut across my arm and another down my cheek, and my sleepy brain scrambled to understand what was happening.

Axel knocked me to the ground, covering me with his body while shouts echoed through the parking garage and tires squealed.

"Are you okay?" Axel said urgently in my ear. Was I? I was crushed beneath him, struggling for air, but aside from the pain in my cheek and arm, I thought I was all right.

"I'm fine. Just a cut or something," I said, feeling sticky blood drip down my arm. "What happened?" I couldn't see much over Axel's shoulder, just feet running and the concrete ceiling.

"Someone took a shot at you," he said.

Looking past me, he nodded at someone and moved off me, picking me up and carrying me to the back of his SUV. Another man got in the front and said, "Where to, boss?"

"One second," Axel replied, examining my injuries. "Fuck, Emma. That first bullet hit a glass panel. This cut on your arm needs to be stitched."

"Hospital?" the driver asked.

"Not secure enough. Take us to the office and call in the doc. I want this taken care of right away."

"How could anyone shoot at me?" I asked, thoroughly confused. No one should know where I was. I'd been out of sight for most of the trip to the Delecta. "This is crazy," I said.

"Not crazy," Axel responded, stroking my cheek with his thumb, his eyes dark and furious. "Not if we have a mole."

# CHAPTER TWENTY-FIVE

## AXEL

We had a fucking mole. How the fuck could we have a mole? It wasn't one of my guys. I knew everything about my people. Everything. I couldn't believe one of them had betrayed us to Harper or Tsepov.

It was possible that someone at the Delecta was compromised, but Dylan hadn't told any of his security team who we were, just that a high-profile guest was coming in. And I'd vetted his security staff when he'd hired them.

Yet the shooting proved that there was a leak somewhere. Emma had almost been killed. I wasn't letting her out of my fucking sight until Harper and Tsepov were neutralized.

In his arrogance, Harper had told her too much, making her more of a target than when she'd simply been working for the FBI. If Tsepov had any idea how indiscreet Harper had been, he'd come after Emma with everything he had.

I cradled her closer to me, wiping away the blood on her cheek with the cuff of my sleeve. Her face was pale, her skin cool to the touch. Shock. She'd been under too much stress lately. Nearly getting shot didn't help.

My phone rang in my pocket as we neared the Sinclair Security building. Tierney. What the fuck did Tierney want?

"What?" I answered.

"Tell me the report of shots fired in the Delecta garage didn't have anything to do with you," he said.

"They had nothing to do with me," I answered, semi-truthfully. They hadn't been about me. The shooter had been after Emma.

"Bullshit. Do you think I'm not watching you? Is Emma all right?"

"She's fine," I said, his interference one more thing I didn't need.

"I'm coming to your office. We need to talk."

"We don't. Make an appointment, and I'll see you tomorrow," I said. I knew the FBI and respected them most of the time. But Tierney didn't give a shit about Emma. He'd already made that clear. I wanted to get Emma taken care of and inside the walls of the Sinclair building. I didn't have time for Tierney's demands.

"Not tomorrow," Tierney insisted. "Now. I'll be at your office in ten minutes. If you can't reassure me that you can keep Emma alive, I'll arrest you and take her into protective custody. Got it?"

I hung up the phone without answering. Five minutes ago, I would have said getting shot at was the worst part of our day. But if the FBI was going to try to take Emma from me, things had just gone from bad to worse.

# CHAPTER TWENTY-SIX

## EMMA

**A**xel held me against his chest, his arms locked tight around me, with one hand clamped on my injured arm and a wadded up piece of fabric—I think his tie—soaking up the blood. Too much had happened too quickly, and I was still trying to get my bearings. Someone had shot at us in the parking garage of the Delecta.

No one should have known we were there. Axel claimed it was proof that somewhere, there was a mole. I assumed he wasn't referring to a small woodland creature, but rather some kind of leak in our security, but I wasn't really up to date on spy lingo.

A leak was the only explanation that made any sense. I'd been well hidden in the back of the SUV, and access to that section of the Delecta parking garage was restricted. The only way for the shooter to know I was there was if he'd had inside information.

I looked up at Axel's face, illuminated by the streetlights as the SUV sped back to his office. I was more worried about the rage I saw in his eyes than I was about my own safety.

Axel had put himself between me and the bullets. The second he'd sensed danger, his only priority had been to protect me. I'd been cut by flying glass, but all things considered, that wasn't much of an injury.

Axel had proven he'd do anything to keep me safe, but his temper was volatile. I had a feeling it could be our biggest weakness.

We were on our way to meet with Agent Tierney, and, based on comments Axel had made in the past about the FBI, I was afraid he was going to blame Agent Tierney for the attack in the garage. I didn't think that was going to go over very well.

I was right.

The Sinclair Security building wasn't far from the Strip, and we pulled into the secure garage not long after we fled the Delecta. Axel carried me to the elevator, unwilling to put me down.

"I can walk, Axel," I said. His grip on me tightened, his arms steel bands around me. He dropped his lips to my ear and whispered, "Stay still. I don't want you on your feet yet. Not until the doctor takes a look at you."

"I'm fine," I said and settled my head on his shoulder. He seemed to need the reassurance of control, and if carrying me to the office made him feel better, I wasn't going to argue. We'd have plenty to argue about later, especially if he started a fight with Agent Tierney.

A man I didn't recognize met us at the door and followed us back to Axel's office, giving him an update as we went.

"Doc is on his way. ETA less than five minutes."

"Expect Agent Tierney of the FBI," Axel said, his tone brisk.

"Am I letting him in?" the man asked.

I got the impression that if Axel told him to keep the FBI from the building, he would do it, no questions asked. My stomach rolled as I contemplated the ramifications of going against the FBI. I didn't like Agent Tierney as much as I'd liked Agent Jensen, but he was still the FBI, and I was still his informant.

I understood all the reasons Axel claimed to lack confidence in their security, but I didn't agree. The FBI wasn't our enemy. Harper and Tsepov were the ones we had to worry about. The FBI were the good guys.

"Let him up," Axel said. "Check him for wires and weapons before you bring him in."

"Got it," the man said. Then he was gone, back to the front of the office without another word.

Axel set me down on his couch and peeled his blood-soaked tie off the wound on my arm. My skin and dress were stained red and sticky with the mess, but the cut looked worse than it was. It couldn't be too bad, because while it hurt like a bitch, it had mostly stopped bleeding on our short car ride.

"I'm fine, Axel," I said. "I don't even think I need stitches."

Axel crouched before me and examined the cut on my arm, then the smaller slice on my face, gently stroking his fingertip over my cheekbone as he traced the red line the glass had left on my skin.

"When my guys catch the shooter, I'm going to kill him," Axel said in a level voice that sent a chill down my spine.

"Axel, you can't kill anybody," I protested, knowing very well that anything I said was unlikely to change his mind. I knew him well enough by now to understand that when Axel was angry, he got stubborn.

"What did you mean *when your guys catch the shooter?*"

"Don't mention this to Tierney, but I had more men watching us than the three you saw. The second they got eyes on the shooter, they went after him. When they catch him, they'll bring him here. Then I'll deal with him."

Alarmed, I jerked into a sitting position and grabbed Axel's arm. "What are you going to do with him? If you catch him, you should take him to the police or the FBI."

Axel shook his head. "We can't afford for this guy to be out in the general population, even in jail. We don't want anyone to know you and I are together, especially not whoever sent him after you."

"Whoever sent him after me? Isn't it obvious?"

"Odds are it's either Harper or Tsepov," Axel said. "But I don't want to make any assumptions that could end up getting you killed."

I heard footsteps in the hallway. Axel leaned in and whispered in my ear, "That's either the doctor or Tierney. Say as little as possible. Don't under any circumstances mention Summer or the backup evidence to Agent Tierney, understand?"

I nodded. The door to the office opened, and the man who'd greeted us earlier ushered in another man, this one younger and carrying a black bag that looked so much like the stereotypical old-fashioned doctor's bag, I couldn't help but smile. He returned my smile, earning a glare from Axel, and said, "What happened?"

Axel laid out the cause of my injuries, my blood loss, and how much pain he thought I was in. In my opinion, he underestimated the amount of blood and overestimated my pain level. The doctor was efficient, checking the cuts with a bright light, and cleaning them thoroughly with something that stung like hell.

When he was done, he applied bandages to both

injuries, assured Axel I didn't need stitches and left. Moments later, Agent Tierney was escorted into the office. When his eyes hit the bandage on my face, he turned to Axel and said, "This is how you keep her safe? What the fuck happened?"

Axel stared at Agent Tierney, arms crossed over his chest, his eyes narrowed in fury. If we'd been in a comic book, I would have expected a laser to flash out of his eyes and incinerate the FBI agent on the spot. Taking the offensive, Axel said, "This is not my fuck up. You have a mole."

"How do you know the leak is on my end?" Tierney asked.

Axel gave a derisive laugh. "You think it's on my end? I would bet my life none of my people would sell me out. Would you do the same? Can you guarantee no one in the Las Vegas FBI office is working for Tsepov? Don't even answer, because he's got his fingers all over law enforcement in Vegas."

Tierney didn't respond verbally, but his cheeks flushed in frustrated anger. I took that to mean he wasn't going to argue the accusation that Tsepov had sources in the FBI. Which made his next comment all the more terrifying.

"I'm taking Emma into protective custody," he said.

"The hell you are," Axel roared. "She almost got shot tonight because of you. You're not taking her anywhere."

"We haven't determined who leaked Emma's location," Tierney said, refusing to back down. I didn't think that was a good sign. He was too calm, absolutely assured that he was going to get his way.

I didn't understand a lot of what was going on, but I knew, despite almost being shot, that I'd rather stick with Axel. I definitely did not want to go into FBI protective custody, and I said so.

"I don't want to go into protective custody."

Agent Tierney didn't even look at me. He kept his eyes on Axel. "What you want, Miss Wright, is irrelevant at this point. I'm taking you. I will arrest you to do it if I have to. And if you try to stop me, Sinclair, I'll arrest you, too."

"You can't do that," Axel said.

"Do you want to try me? You're impeding an FBI investigation. If she won't come with me, so is Emma. I will do whatever I have to do to secure the evidence, which, at the moment, is Emma, and get you out of the way before you completely fuck up my case.

"I will not hesitate to take you both into custody. Separately. In fact, *separately* would be my preference."

Fear clutched at my stomach at the thought of being separated from Axel. If Axel was in jail, who knew what he would have to do to get out? Agent Tierney didn't seem to like him very much. If he wanted to, I had a feeling he could make things very difficult for Axel.

I had no doubt that Axel and Sinclair Security had excellent lawyers on retainer, ready to jump whenever they needed anything. But I watched a lot of TV. I knew it wasn't always that simple.

What if Agent Tierney brought him in but didn't book him properly? He could disappear into the system much in the same way that Axel was apparently planning to make my attacker disappear. If they didn't press formal charges, his attorney might not be able to get him back out.

Axel was the only person I trusted, and he'd put himself in danger to help me. I couldn't let Agent Tierney take him away.

"I'll go with you," I said, "but only if you promise not to press charges against Axel."

Agent Tierney shook his head. "I'm not making any

promises. If he doesn't stay out of my way, I'll do more than take him into custody, I'll have this fucking company shut down."

Axel cocked an insolent eyebrow at Tierney. "Your threats just crossed the line. You can try to take me into custody. Maybe you can make some charges stick. But I would think very carefully before you go up against the Sinclairs," he said.

"You're one agent in a regional office. Do you know who our contacts are in D.C.? I think you do. I'll play along—for now—but don't forget who I am and who you're dealing with."

Agent Tierney's bluster faded at the mention of D.C. With a quick intake of breath, he rallied and said, "If you do as I tell you, I'll let you come into custody with Emma. That's the best I can do."

"I choose the location," Axel shot back. "We can continue to stay here. We won't leave. This is the safest building in Las Vegas."

"I don't doubt that," Agent Tierney said. "But after tonight, your enemies know you two are together, and this is the first place they're going to look. Nowhere associated with the Sinclairs is safe."

"I've got other options," Axel said.

Agent Tierney shook his head again. "No. You come in my custody to an FBI safe house, with my agents. No compromises."

"That's unacceptable," Axel said through a tight jaw.

"Ever since you got involved in this mess," Tierney said, "you've been fucking things up for me. This time, we're playing it my way, or I *will* have you arrested, and I'll deal with the consequences later. It's your choice.

"Stay with Emma and both of you come with me, or I'll

have my agents arrest you, and I'll take Emma. We're running out of time. Make a choice before you don't have any left."

"Fine," Axel ground out. "We'll come with you."

Everything moved quickly after that. Axel, his arm protectively wrapped around my shoulders, followed Agent Tierney and several other FBI agents down to the parking garage, where we got into a somewhat shabby beige sedan.

I looked at Axel in the dim light in the car with questions in my eyes. He gave a shake of his head in response. I wanted an explanation for his change of heart, but it looked like I was going to have to wait.

A little lost at the quick shift in our circumstances, I resigned myself to wait until later to find out why Axel had agreed to go into custody. I settled myself against him in the back of the car and let my head rest on his shoulder.

In the confusion of almost being shot, getting back to Axel's office, the doctor, and Agent Tierney, I'd forgotten how tired I was. In the quiet of the car, my exhaustion came rushing back, and with my head on Axel's shoulder and his strong arm around me, I drifted to sleep.

# CHAPTER TWENTY-SEVEN

## AXEL

Emma fell asleep in the car, exhausted from the night's events. She'd been ready to pass out before she'd almost been shot, so I wasn't surprised she dropped off. Careful not to disturb her, I eased my phone from my pocket and tapped out a quick text to Evers.

He was working with Griffen or he would have joined us for dinner, but I knew, even if he had his phone turned off for the moment, he'd get my message eventually.

*Assassin at the Delecta. 3 men on him. Bringing him back to office. E & I in FBI custody.*

My phone illuminated with a message less than a minute later.

*At office w/G. Shooter in safe room. Information?*

I typed back, *Get what you can. Need to be sure who $$ him. Hold him.*

There was no answer, but I didn't expect one. I didn't trust a lot of people—it was a drawback of being in the security business.

Divided loyalties were so common that at any moment,

a former ally could be your enemy. And it seemed like people always had a second, or even third, agenda. But I trusted my team, and deeper than that, I trusted my family.

My brothers and I loved to give each other shit. It was a sibling curse and a privilege, depending on which side of the shit-giving you were on. But no one in this clusterfuck would have my back like Evers.

When I'd first seen him in my office, I'd been pissed. Things had been bad enough with Emma without my brother showing up to complicate them even more. Now I was relieved he was here. I knew he had everything at the office under control, so I could focus on Emma.

Agent Tierney was determined to be a pain in the ass. He and I both knew we were safer outside of FBI protective custody. Why had he forced us into it? I could think of a few reasons, none of them good.

The first was ego and the need to control his own investigation. It might be as simple as that. So far, I hadn't been overwhelmed by his intelligence, and it was possible he was just that stupid. Even so, I wasn't buying it.

The other explanation was that he knew we were less secure in FBI custody and he wanted it that way to give someone else a chance to get to us. I'll admit, part of my emphasis on the vulnerability of FBI informants was to encourage Emma to stick with me. It wasn't a lie.

History would show that a private security company like Sinclair could keep an individual safer than the FBI in circumstances like this. That was a fact. But I wasn't above using that fact in my favor, especially when Emma had been ready to run from me.

I was armed with more weapons than anyone seeing me in my suit and tie would guess. I was trained for this, and I had full confidence that I could keep Emma alive even in an uncertain situation. That didn't mean I liked it.

The best that could come out of this was confirmation on the source of the leak. My people didn't know where we were going. If we were attacked from this point on, we'd know the FBI was the problem. It was cold comfort.

I would rather have locked Emma in my penthouse until the case was resolved. Whatever happened, we wouldn't be staying with the FBI for long. Emma's friend would be back from her business trip on Friday, and the package with the evidence would have arrived by then as well.

I planned to have Emma out of FBI custody and on a plane Thursday night without Tierney's knowledge. I had seventy-two hours to figure out how I was going to pull that off. Plenty of time.

The car finally slowed as we pulled into a generic tract home neighborhood in Henderson. *Perfect.* The setting was straight out of a cheesy movie where they grab the witness and stick her in protective custody.

The sedan turned into a driveway, and I got my first look at the safe house. The FBI hadn't killed its budget on this one.

For one thing, the place was all kinds of exposed. It was on the end of a cul-de-sac, and if it had had open desert behind it, with some nice bright lights in the backyard, that would have been a plus. But, as we pulled into the drive-way, I caught a view of the backyard.

It had been attractively landscaped with various plant-ings and a gazebo that looked like it was falling apart, but it would provide cover for anyone approaching from the rear. There were houses on either side, both close enough that they, too, would provide cover.

On top of that, the general quality of the neighborhood told me that our accommodations were not going to be top of the line.

For myself, I didn't really care. I preferred the best when it was available. I could afford it, so why not? But I'd spent years in the military, and a lot of my assignments had involved sleeping on the ground, often in miserable weather. Then there were the things I'd had to do since I'd been working at Sinclair.

High-profile security sounded glamorous, but a lot of it was waiting and watching, rarely in comfortable locations.

We pulled into the garage and I lifted Emma into my arms, carrying her into the house, escorted by two agents and Tierney. I'd been right—the accommodations were crap.

Tierney only turned on one light, trying to keep a low profile, though the two vehicles pulling in at this hour would have been noticed, regardless of how many lights we turned on.

The kitchen was a time warp of avocado appliances and almond countertops. The family room boasted a worn and stained rust-colored shag carpet. Deep shag carpet. *Hello, 1970s.*

I thought wistfully of my so-very-secure, almost-impenetrable-without-a-rocket-launcher penthouse. Then of the three other safehouses we had secreted around the city, also almost impenetrable. I had agreed to bring Emma here?

I had a gut feeling that sticking with the FBI was the best way to flush out the mole. On top of that, there were Tierney's threats of arrest.

He couldn't hold me, and I wasn't worried about disappearing into the system once the FBI had me. I was way too high-profile, and there were too many people that knew of Tierney's connections to me and my work on his case.

I hadn't been bluffing when I'd brought up the Sinclair connections in D.C. Tierney could have arrested me, but he wouldn't have been able to hold me longer than twelve hours, and it likely would have ended up costing him his job.

It was the time I'd spend in custody that had me worried. Time away from Emma was time she'd be completely vulnerable. My brothers and my team could have gone after Emma for me, but that would have caused a shit storm that would've been a lot more complicated than me staying by her side.

So here we were, in this dilapidated safe house with an unsecured perimeter and two FBI agents for protection, both of whom looked like they'd only been shaving for a few years. I barely listened as Tierney gave me a quick lecture about behaving myself. I declined to respond.

I set Emma on her feet and she leaned into me, still sleepy. Stifling a yawn, she looked around, then said in a low voice, "Is this it?" Her eyebrows were raised in doubt. I laughed. Like me, she was clearly unimpressed with the FBI's safe house.

Rubbing my hand up her spine, I said, "This is it. It looks a lot more secure than my penthouse, don't you think?"

She wrinkled her nose and said nothing. Smart girl. Tierney scowled at both of us.

"I need your cellphones," he said. "They can be tracked, and they're not secure."

"Emma doesn't have hers," I said. "And I'm not giving you mine. It's untraceable and unhackable. You're going to have to take my word for that."

Tierney tried to stare me down, clearly weighing the

cost of demanding the phone against my unwillingness to turn it over. Proving he wasn't as stupid as I thought, he backed down and let me keep the phone. Good thing for him.

I could handle Tierney stashing me in this unsafe safe house with our inexperienced guards and only a handful of weapons, but I wasn't letting Tierney take away my access to my team and my brother.

I worked out of the office so often that I had everything set up so that if I had my phone, it was the next best thing to being there myself.

"You have two agents in the house," Tierney said, "and an agent outside watching for an approach. You're completely covered, and you're safe. I'll check in tomorrow."

"You're leaving?" Emma asked. "You're dumping us here and leaving?"

Tierney gave her an oily smile and said, "You're safe here, Emma, I promise. I have leads to follow. The sooner I get this case wrapped up, the sooner this will all be over.

"If lover-boy there," this he said with a sneer, "hadn't lost the evidence, I wouldn't have to work twice as hard to get this wrapped up. We have you as a witness to Harper's confession, but it's not enough. Stay out of trouble, do what the agents tell you to, and this will all be over before you know it."

Tierney let himself out through the garage and was gone. Emma turned to me with wide eyes and opened her mouth to speak. I shook my head and said to the two agents in the room, "I'm taking Emma up to bed. She's exhausted. You two will have the first floor covered?"

"Yes, sir," the taller of the agents said. I led Emma upstairs, tucking her behind me on the narrow staircase, and checked every room before choosing what was supposed to be the master suite, though *master suite* was a stretch of the imagination.

It had a king size bed, so that was something. When we were in the room with the door shut, I turned on the taps in the bathroom sink to create some background noise.

Pulling Emma close, I dropped my head and whispered in her ear, "It's a safe bet that they're listening. Don't say anything you don't want to be caught on tape." She nodded and whispered back, "Did you tell Agent Tierney about the tape? That Harper confessed to me?"

My girl was smart. I'd wondered if she'd caught that. "No, I didn't. Either the FBI has ears at William Harper's house, or Tierney is working with someone who does."

Emma pulled back and looked up at me, her blue eyes wide with horror. She hadn't entirely believed me when I'd said the leak had to be in Tierney's office. His slip indicated I was right. Protective custody just got that much more dangerous.

# CHAPTER TWENTY-EIGHT

## EMMA

**A**xel couldn't stop pacing the bedroom. I sat on the bed, watching him walk back and forth, every so often ducking to the side to peer through a tiny crack in the blinds.

I knew he didn't want to be in FBI custody, but I hadn't realized how strongly he felt until we were here. His shoulders were tight, his eyes too sharp, and I was beginning to hate the way he looked when he clenched his jaw.

I knew it wasn't my fault this was happening, but all the same, I felt guilty. Axel's life was upside down. He didn't need to be here, locked in this run-down house with me, waiting for the other shoe to drop.

"You should go to sleep," he said without looking at me.

There was no way I could sleep, even though I was exhausted. I wasn't pacing the room, but I was as wound up as Axel. The second Agent Tierney had mentioned Harper's confession, my adrenaline had surged, and my brain had begun to spin.

How had he known Harper had confessed his crimes to

me? Could he be working with Harper? Or worse, Tsepov? I couldn't believe it. I wouldn't.

It was more likely that the FBI had bugged Harper's office, just as Axel had. After all, Axel had been Harper's client, and he'd still bugged his office. Why wouldn't the FBI, who were investigating Harper, do the same?

It made sense. But if there were such an innocent explanation, then why was Axel so tense? I was intelligent and had reasonably good judgment most of the time, but there was no denying that Axel had far better instincts when it came to stuff like this. If he was too tense to sleep, then so was I.

"I can't sleep," I said. "I'm too wired."

"You were exhausted when we left the Delecta," he said, still pacing from one side of the small room to the other. "You need to rest."

"Are we safe here?" I asked. "I mean, for now. Do you think we're safe?"

Axel stopped his pacing and gave me a long look. "Safe enough. Why?"

"Come sit next to me," I said, patting the worn comforter on the bed. I was trying not to wonder when the house had last been cleaned.

Reluctantly, Axel came to sit beside me. He vibrated with contained energy and the need to move.

I couldn't help him with the case. I'd done everything I was able to where that was concerned. But I couldn't stand seeing him so wound up and knowing it was my fault. If I couldn't do much to help him with the FBI or Harper, at least I could help him relax.

As soon as he was seated, I stood and faced him, my hands going straight to the top button of his shirt. He looked up at me, eyes tense, the dark brown lighting with heat as his mind shifted gears and he realized what I was up to.

I rarely initiated sex since we'd gotten together. Axel's need for control and my desire to give it to him put him in charge of our encounters—most of the time. Not tonight. Axel needed me. His instincts had him too on edge to unwind on his own. I'd had a plan the day before, one Axel had thwarted. This time, I was determined to get my way.

I didn't need him naked, but I liked him that way. I finished unbuttoning his shirt—carefully, methodically, appreciating every inch of skin that I bared. For once, Axel was content to let me take charge, and I reveled in his compliance.

I wouldn't go so far as to call it submission. I don't think Axel had it in him to submit. But compliance was close enough.

Once his shirt was stripped off and laid out on the bed beside him, I dropped to my knees and went to work on his belt. His erection pressed against the fabric of his pants. My hands brushed his length as I worked the leather belt free of the metal buckle and pulled down his zipper.

"Up," I commanded. Axel's lips worked in a half smile, but he did as I ordered, lifting up just enough for me to slide his pants and boxers over his ass and down his legs. I placed a hand on each knee and urged his legs apart, scooting forward so I knelt between them.

It was exactly where I wanted to be. His cock rose before me, thick and hard, a pearly drop of pre-come beading on the tip. I opened my mouth and my tongue dipped out to taste him. Salty, a little bitter, and all mine. Before I could taste more of him, his guttural voice said, "Take off your clothes."

I thought about objecting, just to remind him that this

was my show. Then I remembered that I didn't want the barrier of clothing between Axel and me. I wanted to be naked, on my knees, his hard cock filling my mouth. Maybe this time we could both be compliant.

I had my clothes off in seconds and was back where I had started, tucked between his legs, my mouth open, ready for him.

Oral sex hadn't always been my favorite thing. With Axel, it was different. I loved the feel of him on my tongue, the heat of him, his scent—earthy and all man—the way his silky skin slid over the steely muscle as I stroked him from base to tip.

I couldn't take all of him in my mouth, but I was getting closer. To make up for the lack, I circled my fingers at the base of his cock and squeezed, sliding them up and down in time to the rhythm of my mouth. My other hand was busy between his legs, cradling and stroking his balls.

Above me, Axel's breath was ragged, coming in short gasps.

His hands buried themselves in my hair, his strong fingers cradling the back of my skull, not guiding me so much as holding me, feeling the play of muscles in my neck and my jaw as I worked him with my mouth, sucking and licking at him, reveling in the knowledge that I was bringing him the kind of pleasure he so often gave to me.

His thumb stroked down my cheek just before he said, "I'm getting close, Emma. Do you want me to come in your mouth or your pussy?"

Every cell in my body wanted him to fuck me. Sucking Axel's cock always made me hot. I wanted to be filled with him, needed it. But this was for Axel. I knew he'd take care of me. Not once had Axel ever left me hanging.

Now, though, I wanted to feel him come in my mouth. I

wanted to swallow everything he had to give, to drink him down as he shuddered under my mouth and my hands. In answer, I sucked harder, wrapping my tongue around the head of his cock in a slow, thorough lick.

He groaned, the sound low and guttural, more animal than man, sending another rush of heat between my legs. I loved that I could do this to him, make him as mindless with passion as he made me.

His fingers clenched tightly in my hair, his grip just on the edge of painful, as he thrust his hips up and pulled my face down, his control slipping as pleasure tore through his body. I swallowed quickly, trying to catch every drop.

I kept my mouth on him until he grew too sensitive and nudged me back. I sat on my heels and looked up at him, loving the sated, lazy look in his dark eyes.

He slid his calloused thumb along my lower lip, collecting a drop of his come and stroking it across my tongue. I sucked it off, my body flushing with another wave of desire.

Leaning forward, Axel hooked his hands under my arms and pulled me up, drawing me on top of him and rolling us both to the center of the bed. Dropping his head beside mine, he whispered, "Your turn."

Axel took his time, laying gentle, almost chaste kisses on my jaw, my collarbone, the slope of my breast, my ribs, and my hip bones, avoiding all of the obvious erogenous zones. He worshiped my body slowly and with great care, never missing a square inch of bare skin.

I've never felt as good about my body as I did with Axel. Though I was mostly confident about my curvy shape, it was hard to really love my body in a world dominated by models and movie stars who were little more than skin and bones.

With Axel, the thought that I could stand to lose a few pounds never crossed my mind. His obvious adoration of every curve was too clear for me to misunderstand. While I'd had plenty of occasions to wonder about his devotion to me, I never questioned how much he loved my body.

His hands stroked and caressed, his mouth following their lead, until he got all the way to my toes, laying a kiss on each one before moving back up. By the time he used his palms to spread my legs wide and swiped his hot tongue over my pussy, I was shaking with the need for more.

His mouth closed over my slick folds, his tongue stroking and swirling around my clit. At my moan, he lifted his head and said, "Shh. Not a sound, Emma. Unless you want those two agents downstairs to hear everything."

He was teasing, but also reminding me we had an audience. I'd been so wrapped up in sucking his cock that I hadn't noticed how quiet he'd been. His hands in my hair and his low, almost silent moans had communicated his response clearly enough, but I realized he'd barely made a sound.

I was not usually quiet in bed. When something felt good I had a hard time lowering the volume on my response. If he'd reminded me that someone was listening earlier, I would have been too tense to relax. Now I was too far gone, needed him too much, to let our eavesdroppers dampen my desire.

Instead, the knowledge that someone was listening only made me hotter. Biting my lip to lock in any sounds, I squirmed beneath Axel, suddenly desperate for more. He didn't make me wait. His mouth moved over me, licking and sucking my clit until I teetered on the edge of orgasm.

Just when I thought I would tip over, he rose above me,

pulled my knees up to his hips and thrust deep, filling me in one long stroke.

A gasp escaped my lips before I clamped them shut again, and I wrapped my arms around his shoulders, pulling him down, as if his weight on my body would stifle my need to moan aloud.

He started slowly, moving inside me in a deliberate, drawn out rhythm that pushed me to the edge of orgasm before easing me back again, building me higher and higher until the need to cry out was too much, and I sank my teeth into his shoulder.

Axel got the message. His lazy thrusts sped up and he fucked me hard, stretching me open as he pounded inside me, shoving me over the edge so abruptly that the explosion of bliss caught me off guard.

Silent sobs of passion caught in my throat as the wave of pleasure waned, and I loosened my bite on Axel's shoulder and dropped my head back to the mattress.

Axel was braced on his elbows above me, a smug smile on his handsome face. He didn't say a word—he just kissed me, a lazy, indulgent kiss filled with affection and sated passion.

Maneuvering us beneath the covers, he wrapped his body around mine, nuzzling his lips to the back of my neck. He whispered, "Go to sleep, sweet Emma. Everything will seem better in the morning."

I wasn't sure about that, but with his strong arm around my chest and his leg twined over mine as if he could protect me with his body even in sleep, I knew that whatever faced us the following day, we would handle together.

# CHAPTER TWENTY-NINE
## EMMA

I woke the next morning to faint light leaking in through the drawn curtains. Awareness hit me all at once. It was earlier than I usually woke. I lay there staring at the ceiling for a moment when Axel's phone buzzed, and I realized an incoming text had pulled me from sleep.

I shifted under the covers, and Axel's arm tightened around my waist. He squeezed me close before releasing me to roll over and grab his phone off the nightstand. Settling back beside me, he held up the phone and checked the screen. Curious, I sneaked a quick glance. My breath froze in my lungs when I saw the message.

*Been calling your office. They say you're on a case, but we need to talk. I have a job for you.*

It was from William Harper. I didn't have to guess what the job would be. *Me.* Harper hadn't had any luck finding me on his own because Axel was protecting me. The irony of him trying to hire Axel to find me would have been amusing if the whole situation didn't scare the shit out of me.

"What are you going to say?" I whispered, my words so quiet that I barely heard them myself. Axel raised his eyebrows, then he said in a louder tone than my own, "Take the meeting."

"What?" I asked, no longer worried about whispering. If Axel needed me to be quiet again, I was sure he'd let me know. "What do you mean, take the meeting?"

I didn't want to doubt Axel. I'd spent enough time doubting him, and he'd more than proven that I could trust him. Hadn't he? But this meeting with William Harper—I didn't like it. I knew what Harper wanted, and until he was in jail, I'd never feel truly safe.

Axel's sharp eyes studied my face before he answered me. "It's the best way to find out what he wants," he said. "As soon as we're up and dressed, I'll call Tierney and see what he thinks. I'm sure he's going to want me to take the meeting. Maybe this time, we can get a taped confession we can use."

"And if he tries to hire you to find me and bring me in?"

"Then I'll take the job," Axel said, sounding surprised that I would ask.

"What?" I screeched, the part of my brain capable of higher reasoning drowned out by my instinctive denial of Axel's words. I sat up and started to get out of the bed. Axel grabbed me and pulled me back down, rolling until he was on top of me, holding me still with his weight.

"Relax, Emma. This will be the first time in the history of my career that I'll take a job I have no intention of doing. I'm trying to keep you safe.

"Harper is still after you, and he thinks I'm on his side or at least willing to work for him. If I can find out where he stands and what's really going on, it's worth taking the meeting."

"What if it's a trap?" I asked, fear for Axel's safety overcoming fear for myself. "What if he knows we're together, and he's calling you to flush you out?"

"It's a possibility," he said. "We don't know who the mole is or who they're reporting to. My gut tells me it's not William Harper. I don't see him having the brains to infiltrate the FBI."

"Or your office," I said, reminding him of the other possibility. As I expected he would, he gave a sharp shake of his head.

"The leak is not in my office."

"We don't know that," I reminded him. "Until we find the mole, we won't know for sure if it's on your side or Agent Tierney's."

Axel didn't respond. He knew his team better than I did, but everything was too uncertain for me to trust a bunch of people I didn't know. Until we figured out who the mole was, I was willing to suspect everyone.

"If it is a trap, how are you going to protect yourself?" I asked.

"Emma, you have to trust me. I know what I'm doing. William Harper is not going to put one over on me, I promise you."

It rankled that I didn't have a choice *but* to trust him. I wanted to believe in him. I did, mostly. I believed Axel wouldn't do anything he knew would put me in danger.

I still didn't like the idea of him leaving me here with the two FBI agents while he went off to meet with William Harper to talk about finding me so that William Harper could sell me into slavery. Or maybe he and Tsepov were done with that plan and they just wanted to find me so they could kill me.

As Axel had pointed out, killing me was the most efficient way to deal with me.

In a lower tone than he'd used before, Axel said, "I also need to see if I can get my hands on your laptop."

I thought it was weird that everyone was so focused on my laptop. We didn't need it since Summer had all the evidence I'd stored on the hard drive, plus what I'd gathered earlier in the investigation.

"Get up, sweetheart. I'm going to call Tierney and Evers while you get ready."

"Why Evers?" I asked.

"You think I'm going to leave you here with only the FBI for protection?" Axel asked, shaking his head. "There is a very short list of people I trust with your life, Emma Wright. My brother is one of them. I wouldn't meet with Harper if I didn't think it was the right move, but I'm not leaving you open while I do it."

"Agent Tierney isn't going to like that," I said.

"I don't give a fuck what Agent Tierney likes," Axel said. "Go ahead and take the bathroom first while I get things rolling."

I did as he said, wondering if he really wanted me to get dressed first or if he just wanted me out of the room while he made his phone calls.

Trying not to be so suspicious, I went to the small, ugly bathroom to do what I could to get ready to face the day, wishing we'd been able to bring all the lovely things Lola had chosen for me. Instead, I'd be getting ready—again—in the clothes I'd worn the day before, with no makeup, not even a hairbrush.

When I got out of the bathroom, Axel was sitting on the edge of the bed, his phone to his ear, murmuring into it in a low voice. I couldn't catch what he was saying, just that he sccmcd to be agreeing with whoever was on the other end. He looked up and smiled when he saw me.

"Tierney will be here any minute," he said. Standing up, he crossed the room to me and pulled me into his arms, kissing me slowly, his hands reaching down to squeeze my ass. The contrast between the sweet kiss and the grope made me giggle, shaking me out of my worry for just a second.

"Wait for me before you go downstairs," he said and disappeared into the bathroom. I heard the water turn on, then off again, in what had to be the fastest shower in creation.

Axel emerged from the bathroom a minute later, his short dark hair still dripping, a towel tied around his waist. For just a second, I imagined forgetting everything we had to deal with and tearing off the towel. There wasn't time. Even if we could be quick enough, getting my hands all over that lean, muscled body would have to wait.

When this was over, we needed to go on a vacation, just the two of us, somewhere we could be mostly naked all the time. I stared, completely unashamed, as Axel dropped the towel and pulled on his clothes.

His suit from dinner the night before was a little rumpled, but it still looked great. My black shirt-dress? Not so much. Again, I wished for my new wardrobe, which was hanging in Axel's closet at his penthouse.

Taking my hand, Axel led me to the door of the bedroom and down the stairs, where the scent of stale coffee lingered in the air.

Two agents greeted us—not the same as those I'd met the night before. There must have been a shift change while we'd been asleep. Axel stopped in front of them, held out his hand, and said, "I.D."

I got the impression that they knew whom they were dealing with, because they didn't argue. They just produced their FBI identification and gave it to Axel, who opened his phone and dialed.

He double checked their information, and, when he was satisfied the agents were who they claimed to be, he returned their identification and said, "We're going to be having a visitor shortly—my brother, Evers Sinclair."

Identical expressions of alarm bloomed on the agents' faces. Like the agents from the night before, these two looked fresh out of the Academy and uncomfortable with their assignment. The older of the two protested, "You can't invite people to a safe house, Mr. Sinclair. Agent Tierney—"

"I spoke with Agent Tierney already," Axel said, unruffled by the agent's protest. "He's on his way. He'll be here in the next ten minutes, probably before Evers. You can speak to him about it then, or feel free to call him now."

Axel ignored the agents after that, making us fresh coffee and toast for breakfast with the meager supplies in the kitchen.

The two young agents huddled near the front door, murmuring to each other, giving up on the pretense of patrolling the house. They watched us, clearly put off by Axel's command of the situation, while we pretended they weren't there.

Axel seemed unconcerned, but I couldn't get comfortable while two strangers were watching me eat toast and whispering about me. I was relieved when the door opened less than ten minutes later and Agent Tierney entered.

The older of the two FBI agents he'd left on duty immediately started forward. Like a child eager to tattle, he burst into speech. "Mr. Sinclair said that he invited a visitor, Sir, but I assure you—"

Tierney waved his hand and interrupted, "It's fine, Agent Read." He sent a glare at Axel, one Axel ignored, and went on, "Evers Sinclair is cleared to visit. Against my better judgment, but—"

Axel cut him off. "If you want me to be your inside man with Harper, you'll let Evers watch over Emma. No Evers, no meeting with Harper."

Agent Tierney rolled his eyes and went to the kitchen, helping himself to a cup of the coffee we'd made. "We already had this conversation, Sinclair. I think you're being overly cautious.

"My agents and I are perfectly capable of protecting Emma. But if the only way I can get you to assist on the case is to let your brother in, I'll do it."

Axel shrugged as if saying he already knew this and he didn't need to be reminded. Tierney sent him another glare, one that faded from his eyes the second it looked like Axel might notice.

I found it interesting that while Agent Tierney liked to be in charge, he didn't seem comfortable bucking Axel's natural authority. Despite his threats of arresting Axel the night before, Agent Tierney didn't seem inclined to push Axel very far.

Before the two agents guarding us could relax, a quick triple rap sounded on the front door. Agent Tierney snapped to attention, and I sat straighter in my own seat, hoping it was Evers at the door and afraid that it wasn't. But who else would knock?

Axel answered the door himself, waving the agents back. He checked the door from a window in the dining room and then flipped back the deadbolt.

Evers entered, muttering something about Axel taking his time. He shouldered the door open, his hands filled with bags. I spotted several grocery bags, as well as two duffel bags.

Looking at me, Evers held up the hand with the duffel bags and said, "I brought some of your things from Axel's place. Figured you might want to change out of your clothes from last night."

Oh, did I. I took the duffel from Evers' hand and headed for the stairs. Then something occurred to me and I turned around. Looking at Axel, I said, "Don't leave until I get back."

He reached out and hugged me to him, laying a quick kiss on the tip of my nose. "I haven't even set the meeting with Harper yet. I was waiting for Evers to get here. I won't go anywhere until you come back down, okay?"

"Thank you," I said and left the men downstairs while I went to change.

It didn't take me very long to trade my cocktail dress for a pair of fine wale navy blue cords and another lightweight sweater, this one in dark green with a pretty shawl collar and embroidered sleeves.

Being a guy, Evers hadn't done a spectacular job of packing my makeup and hair stuff, but he'd gotten enough of it that I was able to get myself together.

I wasn't gone that long, but when I came back downstairs, Axel was on his feet and looked ready to leave. He came toward me as soon as I hit the bottom step.

"I'm heading out," he said. "Evers will be here until I get back. He tells you to do something, do it, understand?"

I nodded. Axel was careful to be neutral toward the three FBI agents, but I knew him well enough to see clearly that the only person in the room whom he trusted was his brother.

"Be careful," I said, smoothing his tie. Evers must have

brought him a change of clothes as well, because he'd traded the steel gray suit for one in a dark charcoal with almost imperceptible pin-stripes.

"I will," he said. "I promise."

I stepped back, prepared to let him go, knowing I had to trust him. He had one meeting and then he'd be back. I could hang on until then.

# CHAPTER THIRTY
## AXEL

I could think of a long list of things I'd rather be doing than having another meeting with William Harper. I've never had a problem playing a part. I'd had to do it often enough for different cases, and I'd always found it easy at worst and entertaining at best.

Pretending not to care what William Harper wanted with Emma was going to be a different story. After a tense negotiation with Tierney, we determined that I had two goals.

The first was to get William Harper to confess to as many of his crimes as possible while I was wearing a wire. Evers had brought our equipment with him. I'd refused to let Agent Tierney wire me himself. Until I figured out who was betraying us, I wasn't trusting anyone.

My second objective was to try to get Emma's laptop back from Harper. I didn't think we'd have much luck with that, but I'd prepared a scenario that might work. Harper's response to my proposal would tell me a lot about where he stood.

It didn't take me long to reach Harper's exclusive subdi-

IVY LAYNE

vision. He met me at the door, looking like a shadow of the man I'd seen the night I delivered Emma. Then, William Harper had been giddily triumphant. Now, he was pale and agitated, his eyes darting from side to side as he opened the door and let me in.

He closed it behind me more firmly than necessary, locking the door and setting the alarm. I followed him down the hall to his office.

He gestured at one of the heavy seats opposite his desk before sitting down himself. I sat, wondering if this was the chair he'd used to restrain Emma. The thought sent a flood of raw, aggressive rage through me.

I had to lock it down and push all thoughts of Emma as my girlfriend, my lover, out of my mind.

If I wanted her safe, I had to do my job, and at that moment, my job was to get this fuckwit talking, not to beat the shit out of him for hurting Emma. Already wanting to leave, I decided to skip the formalities and get the ball rolling.

"What can I do for you today, Mr. Harper?"

Harper shifted nervously in his seat. "It's odd, but I ran into a problem after you left the other night. Emma—Miss Wright— got away."

I decided to fuck with him just a little. "What do you mean, *she got away*? I thought you planned to call the police?"

"Yes, well, no. I decided I didn't want the publicity. I called a partner in to take her off my hands, you know, just to scare her a little, and, well, before he could get here, she got away."

"She was wearing handcuffs," I said, enjoying his discomfort a little too much. "Did you uncuff her?"

"No, no, but..." he trailed off, probably trying to figure

out how to explain what had happened without making himself look bad. "Apparently, a neighbor said they heard a scream. They called the police, and when the officer found her handcuffed, well, he took her with him."

"But you have the evidence, right? You still have her laptop, don't you?" I asked.

"I do, I do," he said. "But I needed to talk to her and find out if she'd done anything else, talked to anyone else. I have associates, and they're not comfortable with only the laptop.

"They—we—need to know more. We need to know everything she was up to. Who knows if what's on that laptop is the extent of her thievery? I need you to find her and bring her to me."

I resettled myself in my seat and studied him, watching him squirm under my level stare. "What are your plans if I find her and bring her back to you?" I asked. Harper looked away, but he didn't answer.

"Let's be honest with each other," I said, taking a risk that I could push him a little further. "You never intended to call the police on Emma, did you?"

Harper let out a gust of air as if he'd been holding his breath and got up from behind his desk. He crossed the room to pour himself a glass of whiskey from his bar.

He held the crystal decanter up, offering me a drink. I shook my head. The amount of whiskey Harper poured into the glass indicated that he was even more anxious and uncertain than I'd guessed.

He swallowed almost all of the whiskey in one gulp. Good. Once the alcohol hit his brain, he'd be less careful of what he said. I settled back in my seat and stretched my legs out in front of me, prepared to take a little time while the alcohol did my work for me.

"Have you had a chance to take a look at the laptop?" I asked casually.

Harper gave a jerky shrug of one shoulder. "It's in my safe, but no, not yet. I already know what's on it, anyway."

"Are you sure about that?" I asked. "Can you get into it on your own? She encrypted everything worth seeing," I commented, enjoying the way Harper's eyes flared in alarm.

"I didn't realize she would know how to do that," he said.

"Emma Wright was full of surprises," I said. "I can get into the laptop for you, if you need me to," I offered, hoping he would take the bait. He didn't.

"No, that's not necessary. I'm just going to destroy it."

"So, you don't want to know what she took?" I asked.

"I already know what she took," Harper said, and then continued cryptically, "it's more important that no one else knows what she took."

At first, his comment made no sense. Harper finished off the whiskey in his glass and went back for more while I sat in silence, letting his words filter through my brain.

If Harper was going to destroy the laptop, then it wasn't enough to have stopped it from getting to the FBI. Harper didn't want the FBI to have the information Emma had taken, but he also didn't want anyone else to know what was on the laptop either.

As soon as we got them, I needed to go through the files Emma had sent to her friend. Harper hadn't come straight out and admitted much yet, but my guess was that the laptop didn't just contain evidence against Harper.

It contained evidence that tied Harper to Tsepov. For Harper, the only thing more terrifying than the FBI getting that evidence would be Tsepov knowing it existed in the first place.

Evers had been right the day before. Tsepov did not have a forgiving reputation. I'd run into him in the past, and I knew he didn't tolerate incompetence in his employees or his associates. If he found out that William Harper had collected hard evidence tying them together, Harper was a dead man.

He must have thought his problems were solved when he had both Emma and the laptop, but with Emma running around loose, he was at risk again.

Judging by his slightly unsteady gait as he made his way back to his desk with a fresh whiskey, I decided to push a little harder. "Do you want me to find Emma and bring her back?"

"Yes. I need you to find Emma Wright and bring her to me so I can question her."

"I'd be happy to assist you with the questioning," I offered. "I and most of my team are well trained in interrogation. We'll probably be able to get more out of her than you could on your own."

"No, no. I can handle it. My... associate... will be able to get all the information that we need."

"And after you get the information you need?" I asked. "Will you need help dealing with Miss Wright when you're finished with her?" I wasn't sure he was drunk enough to take the bait, but the whiskey had done its work, and this time, he was.

"No, my associate will handle that. I can't have Miss Wright becoming a problem in the future."

"I completely understand," I said, my gut burning at the casual threat against Emma's life. "I'd feel more comfortable delivering the woman to you if I had some idea exactly whom I was dealing with. Who are your associates?"

Harper finished the rest of his second whiskey and

shifted uncomfortably in his chair, his eyes darting everywhere to avoid meeting mine.

"I don't know," he said haltingly. "I don't think... that is..."

"Harper," I interrupted, "Stop bullshitting me. Something you should know about me is that I don't ask questions to which I don't already know the answer. I know you're working with Sergey Tsepov."

The blood drained from William Harper's face as I said Tsepov's name out loud, as if by speaking his name I could conjure him from thin air. Harper's eyes darted around the room once more, his hand trembling where it rested on the desk.

"I don't know what you're talking about," he protested in a weak voice. I sat back in my chair and propped my ankle on my knee. Now that I had him scared, I could get him to talk.

"If you're not going to be straight with me, I don't have time for this," I said. "I'm not exactly desperate for the work, you know. I've had dealings with Tsepov before.

"I don't fuck around with him, so I need to know exactly what the situation is and what I'm dealing with before we go any further. If you won't talk, you're going to have to deal with Miss Wright on your own."

I crossed my arms over my chest and waited for Harper to break. It didn't take long. It was becoming clear that he needed to get Emma under his control before Tsepov lost patience with him, and without any resources of his own to accomplish this, he was desperate for my help.

"I... I am working with Sergey Tsepov, it's true. He, uh, contracts me to move... certain things," Harper said. He was weighing his words carefully, but the whiskey made his efforts useless. He'd just admitted to moving shipments for a known mob boss. Now I'd see if I could get him to admit what the shipments were.

"Tsepov's crew is known to deal in a lot of shit, Harper. What have you got your fingers in? Guns? Drugs? Women? Or all of it?"

Harper's back went straight at the direct question. He shook his head wildly, his thinning hair swaying with his jerky movements.

"I'm not... that is..." he stammered, not willing to give me an answer.

"There are things I'll touch, Harper," I said in a hard voice, "and things I won't. What are you into with Tsepov? Tell me, or I walk."

"All of it," Harper said, defeated. "Okay? All of it. I put my notes in a file in my desk so I could keep it all straight, and Emma stole the file for the FBI. You got it before they did, I think. I hope. I don't know exactly when she took it..."

Harper trailed off. I'd have to go back through the documentation once we got it from Emma's friend, but I was fairly sure that any hard copies had already been turned over to the FBI. The files I'd caught Emma with a few days before—it seemed like a lifetime ago—had all been digital.

Not letting Harper know he was screwed, I pressed further.

"And Emma Wright? You lost her, but she's not coming back to work, I assume."

Harper shook his head back and forth, his bloodshot eyes now fixed to the polished surface of his desk. I went on, "We got the files she was going to give to the FBI, so why do you need her?"

"She knows too much," Harper said, not taking his eyes from the desk. "She just knows too much. She has to go. I was going to give her to Tsepov to sell with the other girls, but now..." He trailed off.

"Why don't you just have Tsepov take care of the problem for you?" I asked, thinking about the shooter the night before. My guys had caught him, and they had him in our safe room, but he wasn't talking.

I doubted he was someone Harper had hired, because if Harper had those connections, he wouldn't have needed me to find Emma.

Harper was shaking his head. "No, no. I can't tell him yet. If he knows I fucked up like this... he can't find out."

This whole situation was one big clusterfuck. Someone had sent the shooter after Emma, and it hadn't been Harper. Harper thought he still had time to get Emma, and he didn't know where she was.

The only other person I could think of who would want Emma dead was Tsepov. Which meant the mole was working for him. I had work to do.

Harper had admitted more than enough for the FBI to use against him. I was done with him. Abruptly, I stood and said, "I'll take the job. I'll keep you posted on my progress. It shouldn't take me long to find her."

He just gave me a weak smile and said, "Thank you." Standing with obvious effort, he said, "I'll see you out."

Harper deactivated the alarm, unlocked the door and let me out in silence. As soon as I cleared the threshold, the door swung shut behind me, the deadbolt clicking into place.

Harper's paranoia was justified, but the alarm and deadbolt wouldn't do him any good if Tsepov decided he was expendable. Not my problem. I climbed into my SUV and called the office. Jamison picked up in the control room. "Got it, Boss."

"Good job. Get it backed up and send a copy to Agent Tierney. I'll be there in ten."

"I'm on it, Boss."

I drove back to the office. Tierney expected me at the safe house as soon as I was finished with Harper, but I had a few things to take care of first.

Harper was neutralized, between his hiring me to find Emma and admitting his guilt on record. He didn't have the resources to cause us any more trouble. But somewhere out there was Tsepov's mole.

I had a feeling we'd have to take the investigation away from the FBI if we wanted to stay alive. Since the FBI currently had Emma, I had to make some arrangements.

# CHAPTER THIRTY-ONE

## EMMA

I sat on the couch in the living room of the FBI safe house, waiting for Evers to make a move. Two playing cards lay facedown on the coffee table in front of me beside four other cards, these face-up. For the past hour and a half, we'd been playing Texas Hold 'em.

It was a good thing we weren't playing for real money, because Evers was kicking my ass. I was terrible. I'd never played much poker, and I'd learned that Evers played a lot.

The safe house didn't have cable, and I still didn't have my phone, so our options for entertainment were limited to cards or staring at the brown and yellow striped wallpaper in the living room.

Poker with Evers was much more entertaining than staring at the walls, and it helped me pretend that the atmosphere in the safe house wasn't quite so tense.

Agent Tierney paced around the kitchen like a caged animal, every so often stopping to have a hushed conversation on his cell phone. The two FBI agents from morning rotated through the house, keeping an eye out for any threat.

Agent Tierney seemed to make them nervous. Every time he paced close to them, they got stiff and hyper-alert, as if determined to show him what a good job they were doing.

I wondered why Tierney would have assigned two such junior agents. From what I'd learned so far, Tsepov was no one to mess with. The young agents gave the impression they'd drop their guns and run if a real threat showed up.

It didn't make sense, but then a lot about the situation didn't make sense. The day felt like it lasted forever, punctuated by seemingly endless rounds of poker, then war, then solitaire, which Evers and I played together, arguing over strategy the entire time. He liked to peek at the cards, and I said that was cheating.

Our bickering got on Agent Tierney's nerves and he snapped at us to *shut up* more than once, but we ignored him.

At one point, Evers got a text. He looked at his phone briefly, put it away and whispered to me, "Axel's out of the meeting. Everything's good. He's going to do a few more things, and then he'll be back."

A few minutes later, Tierney approached us and said to Evers, "You're staying until I can release your brother and Emma. I can't have you Sinclairs coming and going all the time, attracting attention. We should be able to make an arrest soon. Until then, you stay."

I expected Evers to argue, but he shrugged his shoulders and said, "Fine with me. You leaving?"

Tierney gave a short nod in response. "Axel sent me the audio from his meeting with Harper. I've got work to do. You two stay put. Axel should be back soon. I want everybody to hold tight until we bring Harper in."

"Will do," Evers said, his tone just sarcastic enough to

irritate Tierney, but not overt enough to give Tierney an excuse to get mad. I suppressed a smile.

The day had been so boring that I might have welcomed some drama, but I didn't want Evers to get into trouble. Since Tierney was the reason I was so mind-numbingly bored, I was happy to watch Evers poke at him.

Wisely choosing not to respond to Evers' taunt, Tierney grabbed his phone and keys off the kitchen counter, had a short word with the agents by the front door, and left, slamming the door behind him.

"I'm sorry you got tangled up in this," I said. "The safe house kind of sucks."

Evers tossed his head back and laughed, looking so much like Axel that my heart tightened in my chest. "It seriously does. I know the FBI's budget isn't huge, but this place is miserable. Or maybe I'm just spoiled. When Sinclair Security does a safe house, it's nothing like this."

After seeing Axel's lake house and his penthouse, I wondered what a safe house Axel designed would look like. I hoped I wasn't going to find out. We'd been here less than twenty-four hours, and I was already thoroughly sick of safe houses.

Evers looked at me and said, "Another game?"

I rolled my eyes. I was tired of card games. "Can you tell Axel to bring a book? Or a tablet? Something?"

"You're done playing cards with me?" Evers asked, raising his eyebrows in mock surprise.

"Not if it's the only thing to do," I said. "But anything else would be fun at this point."

"Obviously, you haven't been on many stakeouts," Evers said, shaking his head. "In this job, you get used to boredom."

"Tell me about your favorite case," I said, curious about the kind of thing they did at Sinclair Security.

"Our clients are confidential," Evers said. "But I can think of a few jobs I can share without giving too much away."

Evers proceeded to launch into a story about protecting the mistress of an extremely wealthy businessman who also wanted Sinclair Security to spy on said mistress, who he suspected was cheating.

She had been with his twin sons, who were working against him to conspire with the board of the family company to send the old man into an early retirement. Ouch.

After that, he told me about a hostage rescue in a South American country he refused to identify. It turned out that Sinclair Security had a hostage recovery team so respected that the FBI often consulted with them.

He was halfway through recounting a protection detail involving a starlet and her yappy Chihuahua when the front door opened.

I let out a breath I hadn't realized I'd been holding at the sight of Axel in the doorway. He'd changed from his suit into jeans and a dark gray sweater while he'd been gone. He looked hot in a suit, but I loved casual Axel just as much.

At the sight of the bag of take-out Chinese in his hand, I had the fleeting and useless wish that we were alone and none of the rest of this mess was happening.

I missed dating Axel, cooking with him and pretending to watch a movie while we made out on the couch. I liked Evers, but I wanted him—and the two FBI agents—gone.

More than that, I missed seeing Axel relaxed. I rose to meet him at the door. He pulled me in for a quick kiss, but his attention was on Evers. Evers gave him a slight nod and

Axel tipped his head forward. Their silent brother-speak was annoying.

I had no idea what they were saying to each other, but I could feel the tension in Axel's shoulders. He gave me a squeeze around the waist and let me go, saying only, "Let's eat while it's hot."

We ate dinner in silence, the FBI agents trading off, one eating while the other walked the perimeter of the house from the inside. With them sitting at the table, none of us wanted to discuss anything important.

Axel talked shop with Evers, discussing ongoing cases in shorthand to protect the clients, thus leaving me completely out of the conversation.

It was rude and frustrating. Axel usually had better manners than to shut someone out of a conversation, especially when that someone was me.

In another situation I would have confronted him about it, but I was feeling so off balance I let it go. I was cranky from being trapped in the little house, and I knew he wasn't feeling any more relaxed than I was.

We played cards again after dinner, though at that point I barely bothered to pay attention. Funny how boredom could erode fear. I was still scared, and I knew I was in danger, but the monotony of sitting in the same room for hours, waiting for something to happen, was almost as bad as being afraid.

Not long after nine o'clock, Axel stood and said, "Bedtime. I'm exhausted. Emma, you tired?"

It was the first thing he'd said to me in over an hour. He and Evers had been playing poker for the past two hours, locked in a battle for a pile of pennies they'd found in a drawer. Neither of them had noticed when I'd dropped out of the game.

I wasn't used to Axel ignoring me. Knowing that the house was probably bugged, I couldn't tell if he was really ignoring me or if it was a show for the agents or our eaves-droppers. Since I couldn't ask, I tried to relax and let it go, but with every minute that passed, the knot in my stomach got tighter.

I wanted my phone. I wanted to talk to Summer. I wanted to go home. Since none of that was going to happen anytime soon, and I *was* tired, though I'd done nothing all day, I got up and followed Axel to the second floor, with Evers behind me.

At the top of the stairs, Axel halted and leaned into his brother, pulling me close so I could hear his almost inaudible whisper.

"Keep your things in your bag, and sleep in your clothes. I want to be ready to move."

Evers raised an eyebrow at Axel. For a second, I thought he was going to question Axel's orders, but he didn't. He nodded his head and turned to the room opposite ours.

I followed Axel into the master bedroom and went straight into the bathroom, suddenly desperate to wash my face and get ready for bed.

Remembering Axel's orders, I carefully repacked my toiletries and makeup before I left the bathroom. Tucking the bags back into the duffel Evers had brought, I changed for bed, trading my cords and sweater for a long-sleeved t-shirt and yoga pants.

Axel sent a pointed look at the sneakers I'd left on the floor. I raised my eyebrows at him in disbelief. I got sleeping in our clothes, but he didn't want me to wear shoes to bed, did he?

He pointed at the shoes, then at my feet before he went to the bathroom. Fine, I'd wear the shoes to bed. I was annoyed with Axel, but if he wanted me to wear the shoes to bed, he must have a good reason. I put them on, tying the laces securely, and lay down on top of the covers. As tired as I was, I didn't think I'd be able to sleep.

Axel climbed into bed beside me. For a moment, I thought he was going to stay there on his side of the bed, leaving me on my own side, alone. The whole day had left me feeling unsettled, and Axel getting into bed without touching me just made it worse.

Tears blurred my vision as I stared at the shadowed ceiling. I felt weirdly homesick, the exact same hollow, lonely feeling in my chest I'd had the summer I'd gone to sleep-away camp when I was eight.

I'd missed my family with a desperation I'd never felt for the entire three weeks I was gone. Just then, lying beside Axel but not *with* him, I wanted my mom and dad, my brothers and little sister. I wanted my normal life back.

With a hard exhalation of breath, Axel reached over and rolled me into him, settling me half on top of him and tucking my head into his neck. He didn't say a word, but he stroked my hair back from my face, his fingers tugging lightly at my scalp, the gentle affection soothing my tension better than any words.

I drifted into an uneasy sleep, comforted by Axel's touch and the beat of his heart beneath my ear.

# CHAPTER THIRTY-TWO

## AXEL

Everything about this fucking mess had me on edge. It was bad enough that I'd had to listen to Harper basically say that he planned to kill Emma to get her out of the way, but being stuck in this ridiculous excuse for a safe house was grating on my last nerve.

Every instinct told me we needed to get out from under Tierney's control. The only thing that held me back was Emma. She was tied to the FBI, on record as their informant.

I could take care of myself, but until I was absolutely sure I could prove we had a good reason, I wasn't prepared to drag her into open defiance against Agent Tierney and the FBI.

So, we stayed in the little safe house, and every second that passed cranked my nerves tighter. I'd barely talked to her all night. I'd wanted to, but nothing I had to say could be said with the house bugged.

I'd settled for playing cards, then holding her close and feeling her fall asleep beside me.

I must have drifted off, though I'd intended to stay awake all night. A creak on the stairs woke me. Adrenaline slammed into my brain, washing away every vestige of sleep in an instant.

Suddenly alert, I rolled from the bed, gun in hand. Putting my back to the wall beside me, I waited. Across the hall, I heard the metallic sound of a door latch click, then a mechanical, racking, coughing sound—the sound of a suppressed weapon firing.

In the movies, silencers sounded like nothing more than *pft*, as if screwing in a silencer turned a gun into a blow dart. In real life, it didn't so much silence the sound of a gunshot as alter it and make it not quite as loud.

If a killer was truly concerned with being quiet, he used a blade or his hands. Whoever was here, they planned to take us all out and weren't overly worried we'd hear them coming.

Questions crowded my mind. What had happened to the two FBI agents we'd left downstairs? Had Evers been on the wrong end of the silenced bullet? Part of me wanted to check on him, but I knew better.

If Evers had been shot, I wouldn't do Emma any good if I got myself killed trying to find out. Evers was wearing body armor, and he was smart. I'd take care of him once the immediate threat was neutralized.

The door to the master bedroom swung open, inch by inch, and I raised my gun. The barrel of a weapon cleared the doorway, followed by a shadowed form dressed all in black, a balaclava covering the head, concealing everything but the eyes. Not Evers.

I put my gun to the intruder's temple, then saw a familiar weapon rise to press against the back of his head.

*That* was Evers. With my brother next to me, we had

246

the situation under control. The intruder whirled to face us, his gun raised. Before he could get off a shot, Evers and I both fired.

The intruder collapsed to the floor in a heap, his head thunking against the foot of the bed. Emma sat up, startled from sleep, her blue eyes wide and panicked.

"Axel?" She asked, scared, but aware enough to keep her voice low.

"Stay down," I said.

Emma rolled to her stomach and held her breath. I listened to the house. No movement. All was silent, as if we were the only ones there. That wasn't a good sign for the agents we'd left downstairs.

An hour before we'd come up to bed, the two agents from the night before had returned to relieve the agents who had been on duty all day. All four of them were no more than a year or two out of Quantico, and they had so little experience, I hadn't paid them much attention. I hoped they were still alive.

A whiff of smoke hit my nose. Fire, downstairs.

Leaving the body on the floor, I crossed to the bed in swift strides.

"Let's go," I said, helping Emma off the bed. I grabbed one duffel bag and handed Evers the other. If they got in the way we'd leave them, but they might come in handy. "Stay between us, Emma," I murmured. "If I tell you to do something, do it, no questions."

"Okay," she said, stepping behind me and tucking her tall frame against me as if trying to make herself as small a target as possible. I loved a lot of things about Emma Wright, and her intelligence was at the top of the list.

Evers moved into place behind her, using his body to shield hers as we moved to the top of the stairs. I didn't want to rush headlong into danger on the first floor, but every second that passed, the smoke filtering up the stairwell got thicker. I didn't think we had much time to waste.

Flames had already engulfed the back hall to the garage and most of the kitchen by the time we hit the bottom step. A body lay collapsed by the kitchen table, too close to the flames. One of the young FBI agents. Another body was facedown in the living room. The second agent.

From behind me, Evers said, "I'll check them; see if we're alone."

I shifted to tuck Emma into my side and made my way to the front door. We had backup in the neighborhood, but not much. Evers joined us at the front door, saying, "They're both dead. First floor is clear."

We had to get out of the house, but I took one more second to make a call.

"Status?" I asked when the phone was answered in our control room at Sinclair Security.

"No answer from Phillips," Billy said. "His line went dead ninety seconds ago. I've been trying to reconnect."

"We've got two agents down and a fire in the house," I said. "We've got to get out of here, even if we don't have any backup. Send a pickup. Look for my phone in the system in a minute."

"I'm on it," Billy said and hung up.

Quickly, I reactivated the GPS on my phone, shoved it in my pocket, and opened the front door, my gun raised, ready to shoot. The yard appeared deserted. I didn't like taking Emma out into the open without knowing who might be waiting for us. There was cover between the landscaping and the houses next door, but it still felt too exposed.

Evers left Emma's back again and disappeared into the night. With my arm around her, I ushered her across the yard to the side of the house and into the neighbor's backyard.

It was hard to see where we were going, but it was far less conspicuous than we would have been if we'd taken the sidewalk. Evers rejoined us two houses over.

"There were two more at the back of the house," he said. "Both out."

"Dead?" I asked, feeling Emma flinch at my side.

"Negative," Evers said. "Out cold. I didn't want to draw attention by firing outside."

"Billy's sending a pickup our way. Still no word from Phillips."

"The gazebo was empty," Evers said. "I took a quick look, but I couldn't find him."

I didn't like that. Phillips was one of my best guys, an excellent operative and a good man. If he'd been awake and functional, Phillips never would've left his post. I'd have to worry about it later.

For now, my job was to get Emma to safety. We kept to the shadows, using the darkness for cover as we crept through the silent neighborhood, waiting for the hum of an engine that would mean rescue.

# CHAPTER THIRTY-THREE

## EMMA

Chaos swirled around me, and I could barely keep up. We were in another safe house, this one belonging to Sinclair Security. It was the polar opposite of the FBI safe house we'd been in the day before.

This one was a newer apartment in a nondescript building in a suburb of Las Vegas—nothing special, a generic semi-upscale apartment building with a nice entry and a swimming pool out back.

Evers had told me that Sinclair Security owned the apartments on both sides, as well as those above and below, and had wired the building, unbeknownst to the other tenants. They'd know if a mouse squeaked anywhere near the apartment.

On the inside, it had a brand new, upgraded kitchen, a spacious living room, three bedrooms, and a TV—with cable—in every room. I would've loved to have been here the day before. Now, I didn't care.

Axel was pacing again and talking on the phone. They'd found their missing guy, Phillips, two houses away, with a severe concussion, a broken leg, and what they thought was a stab wound to one kidney. He was in the ICU, but he was hanging in there.

I wished I could do something to comfort Axel. Based on the way he gripped his phone and was wearing a groove in the carpet of the living room, I didn't think there was any way I could help.

He didn't look like he wanted a hug, and it didn't feel like the right time to drag him off to the bedroom for some stress relief. So far, he hadn't told me what we were doing next. It was obvious to all of us that the leak had to be with the FBI.

Evers had told me that Phillips had been the only one on Axel's team who knew precisely where we were. Until we'd needed a pickup, Axel and Evers had disabled tracking on their phones and hadn't told anyone at Sinclair Security where the FBI safe house was.

He'd been sure the leak hadn't come from his team, but Axel wasn't taking any chances.

Unless Phillips was playing a very deep game by hospitalizing himself, it was nearly impossible for anyone at Sinclair to be the mole. On the other hand, the FBI and everyone working with Agent Tierney knew exactly where we were.

Axel's phone had rung several times with calls from Agent Tierney, and Axel hadn't answered.

According to the police band, the fire at the safe house had been reported and the bodies discovered. I was sitting on the couch, clutching a cold mug of tea, waiting to see what was going to happen next.

Axel and Evers seemed to have a plan, but no one had bothered to fill me in. Across the room, Axel swore and tossed the phone down on the kitchen island.

"What?" Evers asked.

Axel turned to look at us, anger turning his dark brown eyes black. "I just got confirmation from Billy. The night we went to the Delecta, Tierney called into the control room looking for me, and Alan let our location slip."

My heart sank. I didn't like Agent Tierney very much, but I hadn't wanted him to be the bad guy. If Agent Tierney was the mole, it went against everything that I believed about the way the world should work.

I could accept that my boss—my former boss—was working with the Russian mob. It was a stretch, and it was crazy, but I'd seen the evidence, and he'd admitted it to me, so I could believe it was true.

It wasn't hard for me to accept the fact that the Russian mob was involved in dealing guns, drugs, and human beings. I didn't like it, but it fit with everything TV and the news had told me about the mob.

But to find out that the FBI agent I'd trusted with my life was the one selling me out? The one who'd set me up to be killed? Those men had broken into the safe house, killed two FBI agents, and put Axel's man in the hospital.

They would have killed Axel and Evers if they could have. Everyone near me had been marked for death. And then, as if murder weren't bad enough, they'd set the house on fire. All of that had happened because Agent Tierney of the FBI had told them where to find me.

Nausea rolled in my stomach, and I had the horrifying realization that I was going to throw up. Lurching to my feet, I raced to the bathroom, one hand clamped over my mouth. I got there just in time, hitting the marble floor with a jarring slam to my kneecaps, doubling over and losing every bite I'd eaten for dinner.

I heaved into the toilet until my stomach was empty. Then I heaved a little more, as if my body was so shocked it didn't care that there was nothing to throw up. It still wanted to empty me out.

When I was done, I laid my hot cheek on my arm and sat there, still slumped over the toilet seat, trying to catch my breath. A cold sweat had broken out on my forehead, and my mouth wouldn't stop watering.

In my rush to get to the toilet, I hadn't turned on the light. I sat in the dark, tears dripping down my cheeks, my stomach rolling, threatening to turn itself inside out again. A knock sounded on the bathroom door, then Axel's voice, muffled by the wood, asked, "You okay?"

I wasn't, and I did not want Axel to come in. As badly as I could use some comfort, I had just thrown up, and I felt disgusting. Not just gross, but sweaty, weak, and shaky.

I could handle this. I had to handle this. I couldn't lose it, not now. There was too much going on. It was dangerous for me to fall apart and be more of a burden than I already was.

Axel would take care of me. He'd proven over and over that he would go to any lengths to keep me safe, but I had to do my part. Being scared didn't mean I could afford to be weak.

Clearing my throat, I said, "I'm okay. I'll be right out."

When I was sure what was left in my stomach was going to stay put, I got to my feet, splashed water on my face, and rinsed the sour taste out of my mouth the best I could without a toothbrush. I left the bathroom and headed straight for the kitchen, wanting a glass of ice cold water.

Axel followed me. "You're sure you're okay?" he asked quietly.

"I'm fine," I said a little too brightly. "So, what now?"

"We're getting you out of Las Vegas," Axel said.

"We were going to leave anyway, right?" I asked,

remembering that we'd planned to go after Summer in a day or two. I was happy to get the hell away from Harper and Tsepov—the sooner the better.

"We were," Axel said carefully. "But plans have changed."

I was confused. "I thought we were leaving," I said, getting nervous when he looked down at his phone, avoiding my eyes.

"We were. Then I got this." He showed me the screen of his phone.

*I don't want a war with you. Give me the girl, and your assurances that you'll stay out of my business, and I'll let this go. Let's meet. Tomorrow.*

"Who is that?" I asked, already knowing the answer. "Is it him?"

"It's Tsepov," Axel confirmed. "He knows you're with me. If I stay with you, he'll use me, and Sinclair Security, to track you. I can't keep you safe while he's watching me."

"So, you're sending me away? Alone?" I knew I sounded pathetic, and the tears spilling down my cheeks didn't help. I couldn't stop it, though. Axel had become my rock. How could he send me away?

He set his jaw and shoved his phone back in his pocket. "It's all been arranged. We have a friend in Atlanta who will watch over you. He isn't associated with Sinclair Security in any way, but he's an old friend. We did his system, and his place is as secure as one of our own. You'll be safe with Jacob."

"So that's it? I don't get a say?"

"Emma," Axel growled, "I'm trying to keep you alive. Sergey Tsepov wants to meet with me, face to face. I can't afford to have you anywhere nearby when that happens. I need you gone."

I tried not to feel like Axel had stabbed me through the heart. I wanted to believe he meant that he wanted me safe and away from any threat. I was sure that was what he meant. But his words scored my heart. *I need you gone.*

I wasn't a fool. If Axel thought I needed to get out of town, I'd go. I wanted to stay alive, with or without Axel at my side.

An hour later, I was boarding a small plane, a duffel bag in each hand, with the sun rising in the sky at my back. To my surprise, Griffen was waiting for me, a can of soda in his hand. He pulled the door closed and pushed me in the direction of a seat, taking my bags and stowing them in the back of the plane.

"Put your chair back and get some sleep, Emma," he said. "Everything is going to be okay."

I didn't believe him. Without Axel, nothing was okay.

# CHAPTER THIRTY-FOUR

## EMMA

I would have sworn that there was no way I could fall asleep on the plane as we taxied down the runway and lifted off into the air, leaving the bright lights of Las Vegas behind.

Leaving Axel behind. I was too keyed up. My chest was tight with anxiety, a sour knot was lodged in my stomach, and I was off-balance without Axel by my side.

Having Griffen there was a comfort, but as nice as he was, it wasn't the same as being with Axel. Once we were in the air, Griffen got up, went to the front of the plane, and came back with a drink. Handing it to me, he said, "Rum and Coke. You need to relax. It's going to be a long flight."

I didn't protest. A rum and Coke wouldn't have been my drink of choice at that moment, but I didn't argue, and I drank it down in one shot. Griffen had mixed a strong drink. Not too long after I finished it, with the alcohol to relax me, my eyelids began to droop.

Griffen took a blanket down from a storage compartment and handed it to me, saying, "Get some sleep."

"What will happen when we get there?" I asked,

unfolding the blanket and wrapping it around my body, tucking myself into the plush seat.

"What did Axel tell you?" Griffen asked.

"Just that he needed to get me out of town and that it wasn't safe to be near him now that Tsepov was paying him so much attention. He said he was sending me to a friend. I can't remember his name."

"Jacob Winters."

"Is he related to Summer? She's never mentioned having any family in Atlanta. Do you know him?" The way Griffen had said his name felt more businesslike than someone talking about a friend.

"I have no idea if he's related to your friend, but I'm sure Evers and Axel are checking it out," Griffen said wryly.

"And I know him only by reputation, but I do know he went to school with the Sinclairs, and they've all known each other practically since the cradle. Jacob is in real estate. From what I've heard, he owns a good chunk of Atlanta, on top of developments all over the southeast.

"Sinclair Security set up his building, which is also where he lives, and it's one of the most secure places in Atlanta outside of the Sinclair properties.

"It's known that Jacob is friends with the Sinclairs, but he's not a business associate. He's not in security or protection, so it's unlikely that Tsepov or the FBI will look for you there. Sending you to Jacob is the safest Axel can make you right now."

"Okay," I said. It wasn't okay. I didn't want to go to Jacob Winters, whoever he was. I wanted to be with Axel. But I wasn't a child, and I knew by now that I couldn't always have my way. Axel wanted me safe. This was the best way he thought he could protect me, and I wouldn't argue about it.

That didn't mean I had to like it. More than going to a stranger, what I really hated was leaving Axel behind with Tsepov. The thought of Axel—my Axel—sitting down with a killer and playing a game with him, when everything I'd heard about Sergey Tsepov was that you didn't play games with that man, froze my heart.

If something happened to Axel, I didn't think I could stand it, especially if it happened because he was protecting me. The thought of Axel close to the Russian mobster had my stomach rolling.

I took a deep breath, grasping for calm. I had to hold it together. I had to be strong. When all of this was over, I was going to curl up and have a big, long cry. But not yet. Not until everyone I loved was safe.

Even after a strong rum and Coke, I didn't think I could fall asleep. I must have, because I opened my eyes what felt like days later to the sound of voices—Griffen's familiar voice, and another, a man who spoke in clipped sentences, his voice smooth and deep.

I felt a hand on my shoulder and heard Griffen say, "I have to go, Emma. Jacob's here. He'll take care of you. Listen to what he says and be careful."

He was gone before I could force my eyes open. I struggled to sit up, tangled in the blanket. When I pushed it down to my waist and opened my eyes, I was confronted with the sight of a stranger. He sat in the seat opposite mine with his elbows braced on his knees, studying my face with arresting silver eyes framed with thick, black lashes.

I blinked the sleep out of my eyes, trying to take in his sudden appearance. Now that I was alert, or at least conscious, he rose out of his leaning position and held out a hand.

"Jacob Winters," he said. "It's nice to meet you, Emma Wright."

He was polite but not flirtatious, and I was head over heels for Axel Sinclair. Still, as Jacob Winters shook my hand, I felt myself blush.

There was something overwhelming about him. I could tell from the way he filled the airplane seat that he was tall, with broad shoulders and a body that looked fit beneath his perfectly-cut charcoal suit.

His eyes were a shade that could only be called silver. Too light to be gray and without a hint of blue, they were magnetic. His hair was dark, almost black, and he wore it a little too long, curling around his ears and the back of his neck. A chunk fell down over his forehead, and I wanted to brush it back.

Idly, with my brain still waking up, I wondered how many women had that same urge. Taking in Jacob Winters' confidence and self-assurance, I bet all of them. He looked like a man who was used to handling the attention of women.

I broke eye contact and stood up, folding the blanket to keep my hands busy as I asked, "So what do we do now? Axel didn't tell me much."

Jacob followed my lead and stood up as well, bending forward a little in the compact airplane cabin. "I'm going to take you back to my place," he said.

"I can bring you in through the underground garage—I had the cameras temporarily shut down. No one will know where you are. No one will see you come in, and there won't be a record of your entering the building.

"You'll stay in my penthouse until Axel gives us the all-clear. We'll let Axel and Evers do what they have to do, and hopefully, you won't be under house arrest for too long."

"All right," I said. None of it was really all right, but I didn't have a better suggestion. I was a human resources director. I wasn't going to try to out-think the security experts.

I followed Jacob to the door of the plane. A small flight of stairs led from the airplane door down to the tarmac.

Just in front of the base of the stairs, I saw a cargo van, the kind used for deliveries, though this one had no writing or logo on the side. It was newish and clean, plain white, with nothing to distinguish itself—completely generic and unnoticeable.

Jacob gave me a hand as I climbed in the back. I was surprised to see carpeted benches along the walls. They didn't look comfortable, but they were better than sitting on the floor. My two bags were already waiting for me. At the sight of those duffel bags, familiar and reminding me of Axel, my eyes teared up.

I missed him. Jacob seemed nice enough, and if I weren't already Axel's, I would probably be panting after him. He was ridiculously attractive, and he had an air of power I could recognize as seductive, even though I had no interest in being seduced by him. The childish part of me wanted Jacob to go away and to bring back Axel.

Again, I reminded myself that I was going to have to deal with the situation as it was until things could work themselves out.

I took a seat on the side of the van as Jacob closed the doors. He gave a single rap on the plywood wall separating us from the driver before he sat on the bench opposite me. A moment later, the van started up and began to move.

Jacob didn't make conversation on the ride into the city, for which I was grateful. Another time, silence with a stranger might have bothered me, but while still trying to get used to being most of the country away from Axel, I was happier left alone with my thoughts.

I distracted myself with thoughts of the vacation I wanted to take with Axel when all this was over. A luxury cruise? A private island somewhere? Or a cabin in the mountains with a hot tub? I didn't really care as long as I could be alone with Axel, just the two of us, with all of this mess and trouble behind us.

It was a fantasy. Real life had thrown us some major roadblocks in the form of a dirty FBI agent and the Russian mob, not to mention my former boss asking Axel to find me so he could have me killed—but I couldn't do anything about all of that.

Focusing on our vacation was more relaxing than stressing over all the things that were out of my control.

I never thought I would miss gathering evidence for the FBI. Every moment of it has been nerve-racking, but at least I'd been doing something positive by moving the case forward. Now, with my part in the case done, all I could do was wait and follow orders.

I didn't want to be an operative or whatever it was that the people who worked for Sinclair Security called themselves. My brief stint as an FBI informant had been enough to tell me it was not the life for me. That didn't mean I was happy being passive.

After a half hour or so, the van took a sharp turn and began to drive downward. Based on our speed and direction, I guessed we were in the parking garage. Good. I was ready to get where we were going and try to settle into yet another strange place.

The van parked, but Jacob stayed where he was, holding up a hand to indicate that I should do the same. A few minutes later, a double knock sounded on the cargo door and Jacob stood, holding out his hand for mine.

He helped me out of the back of the van, grabbing my two duffel bags with one hand, and led me to an elevator that, like the entry to Axel's office, operated with a hand scanner. The doors to the elevator slid open and Jacob ushered me through.

The inside was a marked contrast to the sophisticated electronics and sleek metal of the exterior. With dark polished wood, gleaming brass buttons, and brass detailing on the chair rail, it had an old world elegance I hadn't expected, complete with an oil painting on the back wall. I guess I'd thought it would look more like the brushed steel and black leather of Axel's offices.

Jacob pressed a button marked with a barely noticeable *P*. The elevator doors silently slid shut, and the elevator carried us to the top floor of the building.

It opened directly into Jacob's foyer, revealing a polished hardwood floor and smooth, creamy walls, with heavy crown molding in a soft white. Oil paintings like the one in the elevator were scattered on the walls.

A narrow table sat against one wall with a stack of mail on top beside a set of keys. A long hall lined with white wainscoting led us to the rest of the penthouse.

I followed Jacob and found myself in a wide-open space with the kitchen and breakfast area on one side, and a huge sitting room complete with comfortable looking leather couches and an oversized television on the other.

The rooms were filled with polished antiques—except for the television—yet the penthouse managed to be as welcoming as it was elegant and refined.

"I'll show you to your room," Jacob said. I followed him as he turned down another hallway, this one also lined with creamy white wainscoting and oil paintings and the same heavy crown moldings around the ceiling.

We passed what looked like a dining room on one side and an office with glass French doors on the other. We turned once more, and Jacob opened a door.

"This room is yours for as long as you need it," Jacob said.

The room was spacious, dominated by an enormous black canopy bed covered with a snow-white duvet and masses of matching white pillows. I'd slept for most of the plane ride, so I wasn't tired anymore, but that bed made me want to crawl in and take a nap. It also made me think of Axel. Then again, these days, most beds made me think of Axel.

Jacob dropped my duffel bags on the floor and turned to face me. "I need to get to work," he said.

"There's no phone and no computer. Axel said he's more comfortable if you don't have access to the outside world for now. If you need anything, hit the green button next to the elevator. I'll get the message and come right up. I've got cable, and there are books in the library. Feel free to help yourself."

"Thank you," I said. "I appreciate your helping us out like this."

"Axel is like a brother," he said. "I've known him since before I could walk. There's nothing I wouldn't do to help him—or his woman—out of a jam." He winked at me, and my knees went a little weak.

Griffen had said that Jacob had gone to school with Axel and his brothers. Recalling that Evers was pretty hot himself, I had a moment of both envy and pity for the girls at their high school. These men were lethally attractive, and they knew it. When they were sixteen, they must have been every girl's dream and nightmare rolled into one.

Jacob headed for the door, saying over his shoulder, "I'll bring something back for dinner, but if you get hungry, there's plenty of food in the fridge. Help yourself." At that, he was gone.

I picked up my bags and decided to unpack. With that chore done and with nothing else to do, I thought I might as well take a shower. A peek in the bathroom revealed what looked like acres of white marble, a gigantic shower, a garden tub, and a long marble counter highlighting the custom glass sink in a delicate sky blue. Gorgeous.

I organized my toiletries and decided that the tub was calling my name. At least it would give me something to do while I waited for my life to work itself out.

# CHAPTER THIRTY-FIVE
## AXEL

The air in the car was heavy as we drove down the two-lane road into the desert. Meeting with Sergey Tsepov was dangerous enough. There was no way I was going to do it on his turf or on his terms.

As he'd felt the same way about meeting with me, we'd decided on the desert, like an old mob movie from the 60s. I drove, with Evers in the passenger seat beside me and two of my men in the SUV behind us.

As if it were a chess match, both of us calculating our moves with care, Tsepov and I had agreed to no more than three backups, guns allowed but not drawn. If we could get through this without any of them being fired, I'd consider it a win.

Of all the things we'd done since I'd gotten involved in the situation with Emma, this meeting with Tsepov was by far the most dangerous.

William Harper had been a pain in my ass, but he was mostly a joke. Tsepov was anything but. The man was dangerous and willing to do anything to get what he wanted, and in the last few months, I'd seen evidence of cracks in his organization.

First, he'd been betrayed by one of his own, who'd tried to kill Nolan, Sam's fiancé's brother. Now he was doing business with someone as unreliable as William Harper. It wasn't a good sign. When a man like Tsepov made stupid mistakes, people died. I didn't have any intention of being one of them.

We turned down a sandy road to reach the appointed meeting place and discovered that Tsepov and his men were already there. Unsurprisingly, he had three vehicles to our two and five men as backup to my three, despite our arrangement.

It might have bothered me, but I'd expected him to try to get one over on me, and he might have had more muscle, but I could guarantee that my men were better trained.

Evers had been a marksman in the military, and all my people knew how to handle a weapon. They also knew how to keep a cool head—when to fire and when to hold tight. I was going to try to keep this short and to the point to minimize the chance that things would go haywire.

We parked about 20 feet away from Tsepov's vehicles. Evers and I left the car at the same time. He hung back, leaning against the hood of my SUV, his arms loose at his sides. He looked relaxed, but I knew he could have his gun in his hand before I could blink if he thought he needed it.

I picked a spot between the two sets of vehicles and waited. The door of a black Cadillac opened, and Sergey Tsepov unfolded from the vehicle.

He looked good for an older man, though his black suit and starched white shirt were out of place surrounded by desert and scrub brush. From what I knew of him, I doubted Sergey Tsepov ever dressed down.

He was in his late 60s, but his posture was firm and upright, his shoulders broad, his torso lean. The silver at his temples gave his strong features a refined elegance that women loved. I thought it made him all the more creepy, knowing what he was on the inside.

This was the man who'd planned to pay Emma back for her whistle-blowing by selling her as a sex slave on the black market. This was a man who dealt in weapons, drugs, and human lives without a thought or care for the implications of his actions. This man was evil.

"Axel Sinclair," he said, his tone relaxed, as if we'd run into each other at an art opening or charity ball instead of a clandestine meeting in the middle of the desert. "It's been a long time. I can't say that I'm pleased to see you, under the circumstances."

"Neither can I," I said. "It seems like we need to resolve some business."

"Indeed, we do. My information tells me that you've been with Emma Wright. She is a problem. I need her else-where. Is she under your protection?"

"Emma Wright was a job," I said, using all of my acting ability keep my voice level and emotionless. "I met with William Harper yesterday and he asked me to find her and bring her in. He implied that he wanted me to deliver her to you. Is that correct?"

"William Harper is no longer of concern," Tsepov said smoothly. "I believe you'll find, in gathering further informa-tion, that any contract or arrangement you had with William Harper is now dissolved. If you're in the business of collecting Emma Wright and delivering her to anyone, you can deliver her to me."

Shit. I was pretty sure that meant that William Harper was dead. I couldn't muster up much in the way of concern for

Harper. He'd hired me to deliver Emma for execution, so I was more than happy to have him out of the way. However, if it meant that Tsepov was cleaning house, we were all in trouble.

"You want me to bring Emma to you," I said, both buying some time and feeling him out. "I assume I shouldn't ask what you're going to do with her."

"I've always said that you are intelligent. I'm gratified to be proven right. Emma Wright has created problems for me. I'd like to talk to her personally about the best way we can work together to end those problems. I heard a rumor that she was under your protection and in your bed."

"Just part of the job," I said, hating the sound of the words coming out of my mouth. "Sex is the best way to get a woman to do what she's told."

"That's what I suspected." He gave a casual shrug and said, "I hoped that was the case, because if you are prepared to keep Emma Wright from me, I don't think you would appreciate the consequences."

"Consequences? Are you threatening me?" I asked. I was shooting for an air of mild concern, but I wasn't sure I pulled it off.

He gave another negligent shrug and said, "Do I have to? I'd prefer not to issue threats against you and your family. It would be a shame if any of the Sinclairs were forced to suffer for Emma Wright's bad judgment. If you deliver her to me in twenty-four hours, consider us even and your contract with William Harper discharged."

"I don't have Emma Wright and I don't know where she is. I can find her, but it's going to take me longer than twenty-four hours. I'll need at least three days."

"Unacceptable. Three days is a ridiculous amount time. No more than two."

"Three days," I said again. "No less."

We needed at least three days for Summer to get back from her trip so we could collect the evidence.

Depending on what we found, we might need more time to deal with the evidence in a way that would keep Emma safe and, hopefully, bring Tsepov down. Allowing Tsepov to set a deadline any tighter was just setting us up for failure and his promised consequences.

"No more than three days," Tsepov agreed rigidly. "Not a second longer. I'll be watching you, and yours, very carefully."

"Understood," I said.

Tsepov took a step toward his Cadillac, apparently ready to conclude our meeting. His closest bodyguard followed suit, but he set his foot wrong in the loose, sandy gravel and stumbled. The bodyguard cried out in surprise, and around me, bodies flowed into movement, guns appearing out of nowhere.

"Stand down," I shouted. "Everything's good, stand down."

None of my men, Evers included, lowered their guns. Neither did Tsepov's. I fought the urge to roll my eyes. If someone weren't willing to drop his weapon, we could stand there all day, ready to shoot for no reason other than paranoia.

With an irritated sigh, Tsepov said, "Lower your weapons, gentlemen."

Slowly, the bodyguard whose slip had started the standoff let his gun fall to his side. The other guards did the same, along with Evers and my men behind him.

Relieved, I let out a breath. I was confident we were better shooters, but without the cover of the vehicles, I didn't want to test my theory. That could have gone bad way too fast.

Ready to leave, I nodded my head at Tsepov and said, "I'll be in touch."

"Don't disappoint me, Axel Sinclair," he said. "I have no desire to go to war with you, but if you don't deliver Emma Wright, I will do what I have to do."

"I'm as eager to end this as you are," I said and turned to get in my car.

Evers got in on the passenger side and we pulled out, heading back to the highway. Neither of us spoke. I knew Evers, like me, would want a little time to digest the meeting before we started analyzing Tsepov, his threats, and what he wanted with Emma.

She'd only left me a few hours before, and I already felt a gnawing need to be with her. I hated leaving her side, no matter how well protected she was with Jacob in Atlanta. I had to wrap this up and get back to her side where I belonged.

Evers and I split up when we got back to the office. Evers went to the temporary office he'd been borrowing, muttering something about checking in on a few leads.

I went back to my own office and got behind my desk, running through my options. I wanted to call Emma, but while it was extremely unlikely anyone had ears on Jacob's phone, I couldn't take the chance.

I'd have to be patient. Normally, patience wasn't a problem—except when it came to Emma. Tsepov's threat against my family pissed me off, but it didn't scare me.

I didn't have to talk to my brothers to know that they'd have my back. That's what family was. At least, that's what my family was. We gave each other shit, but we always backed each other up.

A cryptic text from Jacob said, *all clear*. It was enough to make me relax just a fraction with the confirmation that Emma was safe at Jacob's. Evers gave a quick double rap on my office door and came in, shutting it firmly behind him. He sat in the chair opposite my desk and propped one ankle on his knee.

"We're going to have to make calls," he said. "Emma's Agent Tierney is dirty. Filthy dirty. As far as I can tell, he's the only one in his office who knew you two would be at the Delecta. On top of that, Emma's previous contact at the FBI, Agent Harold Jensen, has been missing since shortly before Tierney took over the case."

"That's more than a little suspicious," I said. "We have any hard evidence or just a theory?

"Nothing that would hold up in court," Evers said. "I think we need to call a few people in Atlanta and get some backup from within the Bureau," he said. "There are a few agents I work with at home who have the clout to help us out with Tierney."

"Matt Holley?" I asked, thinking of the SAC—Special Agent in Charge—we'd worked with before.

"For a start," Evers confirmed.

"That sounds good," I said. "And if Tierney is working for Tsepov, I don't think we should stick around Las Vegas."

My office phone beeped, signaling a call from Billy at the front desk. I picked up the phone and said, "What is it, Billy?"

"Thought you'd want to know William Harper was found dead in his home early this morning. A single gunshot to the forehead, execution-style."

It wasn't a surprise, but still, it was. It's always a surprise when someone you know is murdered, even in a situation like this. I said, "Thanks, Billy," and hung up the phone.

"What?" asked Evers. I told him.

"We need to wrap this up before it gets messy."

"I agree," I said. "I need you to find Emma's friend, Summer."

"Not a problem. Full name and location?"

"First and last is Summer Winters, no middle."

"Seriously?" Evers asked, laughing a little.

"According to Emma, her parents were hippies. And she doesn't like to be teased about her name."

"Any relation to Jacob? I don't believe in coincidence," Evers said.

"I don't know, I haven't had a chance to check her out. But finding her is the first priority. We can figure out who she is later."

"Where is she?"

"At a conference in Houston. You need to locate her and make sure she's back in Atlanta by Friday night, with all the evidence Emma has sent her. As far as we know, she's completely off the radar, but I want her to have protection, and I need her at Jacob's, where we can keep everyone on lockdown. Doesn't hurt to be cautious."

"I'm on it," Evers said, standing up. "I'll get to Houston, track her down, and keep an eye on her until it's time to bring her in. You stay safe."

That was the plan. Stay alive and get this mess cleared up so I could go get my girl.

# CHAPTER THIRTY-SIX

## EMMA

I wandered through Jacob's penthouse, feeling like a ghost. I wasn't used to this much time completely on my own. Jacob, as promised, had delivered dinner the night before, but he'd left immediately after, saying he had a business dinner he had to attend. That was fine.

He'd opened his house to a complete stranger to help out his friends. He didn't need to rearrange his schedule to keep me entertained.

At first, I'd sat down on the couch to watch TV. After the stress of the past week and shuffling through the FBI's safe house, then Sinclair Security's safe house, it was something of a relief to just chill out, knowing I was secure and that I didn't have to make any life-changing decisions for the next day or two.

I spent the first day resting, watching the best cable television had to offer after a long, hot bubble bath. I'd gone to bed early, telling myself that I didn't feel unbearably lonely without Axel.

Maybe it was the lack of danger or the feeling of isolation alone in Jacob's penthouse, but I fell asleep as soon as my head hit the pillow and was out for a solid ten hours.

I woke the next morning to a note from Jacob, telling me to help myself to breakfast, and that he'd see me later. I did as he suggested, but it wasn't long before the television got boring and I was itching for something else to do.

I wasn't usually nosy, but I ended up exploring Jacob's house. I didn't go in his bedroom. That seemed too rude, even as bored as I was. Instead, I poked around the living room, not seeing much that was personal.

Pictures of him with an older couple who looked enough like Jacob that I assumed they were his parents. A picture of him with a guy who wasn't Axel or Evers, but who had to be another Sinclair.

Another few pictures of him with a group of male friends, all in tuxedos, looking like they were posing for a spread in a men's fashion magazine. Interestingly, there wasn't a single photograph of Jacob with a woman, if you didn't count the one of him with his mother.

There was no evidence of a girlfriend anywhere that I could see. I'd wondered briefly if Jacob could be gay, but, though he'd never hit on me, the appreciative way he'd looked at me made me think he wasn't into men.

He was probably one of those guys who plowed through women in a series of one-night stands, never making a connection or letting one stick around long enough for her to make an impression on his home. I wanted to ask, but while Jacob had been kind, there was a formality to him that didn't invite prying.

On the afternoon of my first full day in Jacob's place, I ended up in his office, looking for something to read. Jacob's taste ran less toward mysteries and romance—my preference—and more toward books on real estate law and finance. He did have a few weighty treatises on American history during the Civil War. Not what I was looking for.

I ended up choosing a well-worn copy of Hemingway's Farewell to Arms off the shelf. I remembered finding it kind of depressing the first time I read it, but beggars couldn't be choosers, and if I had to watch one more minute of daytime television, I thought my head might explode.

I considered looking for a pen and paper so I could start making lists of places to look for a new job, but Jacob didn't seem to have any notebooks or loose paper lying around his office.

He had a few pens in the top center drawer of his desk, as well as something intriguing—a woman's earring, a good-sized pearl dangling from a diamond-encrusted ball. Both delicate and feminine, it was a very expensive piece of jewelry. The woman who'd lost it probably wanted it back. Why was it in Jacob's desk?

Had she left the earring in an attempt to get Jacob's attention when she returned to collect it? No, Jacob didn't strike me as a jerk. He would have returned the earring if he hadn't wanted it, though he might have used the mail or a courier if he wanted to avoid an over-eager former lover.

What really caught my imagination was the way he'd carefully placed the earring in the drawer. It hadn't been casually tossed on top of a bunch of paperclips or rubber bands.

He'd set it carefully beside a Mont Blanc Pen in a compartment of its own as if he'd wanted to take care that it wouldn't get lost or damaged. It could have been his mother's, or maybe he had a sister who'd come over and left it by accident.

But something about the way he'd tucked the earring beside the expensive pen, somewhere he'd see it every time he opened his desk drawer, made me think that maybe, possibly, Jacob had a sweetheart.

I would have to live with my curiosity, because I knew I'd never work up the nerve to ask. Jacob came home for dinner that night, bringing a pizza that he said was from a local restaurant that made the best pizza he'd ever had, and I agreed. It was fantastic.

Jacob was charming and funny, telling me stories about Axel when they were teenagers together, his open tone making it clear that he considered me part of the family rather than a temporary girlfriend.

I hadn't heard a word from Axel since I'd left him at the Sinclair Security safe house. I knew I shouldn't let it bother me. Axel was doing everything he could to keep me safe and end this whole mess.

I wasn't going to get angry about that. I just hated knowing that he was most of the way across the country and had met with Tsepov the day before. Not knowing what had happened was killing me. Someone would have told me if anything had gone wrong, but that was a weak reassurance.

Over pizza, I asked Jacob if he knew how Axel was, but he only shook his head and said, "No contact. I haven't heard from any of the Sinclairs, especially not Axel or Evers. They'll get here when they can. Until then, you just have to let them do their jobs."

"I know," I said. "It's just frustrating to be so out of the loop. I hate not being able to do anything."

Jacob's silver eyes softened on my face and he said, "It sounds to me like you've already done plenty. Axel said that the whole case hung on the files you got for the FBI."

"Maybe. But now it doesn't feel like much. I just want all of this to be over."

"It will be, soon enough," Jacob said. He watched me with appreciation, but he never flirted or indicated any interest, not even for fun, like Griffen had. His manner, respectful and kind but nothing more, made me like him even more.

His loyalty told me more about who he was than my snooping. After dinner, we watched a movie. It must not have been that interesting, because I woke up in the middle of the night on the couch, covered with a warm blanket.

I'd made my way back to the guest room through the dark, silent penthouse and passed out again in the big bed beneath the fluffy white duvet. I dreamed of Axel—that he'd come to me in the night and held me close. I dreamed that I felt his arms around me, his heat against my back, and his lips on my neck.

I woke in the morning alone, feeling bereft after the memory of my dream Axel. The waiting was worse than the boredom. I hated feeling ineffectual, and I hated missing Axel so much. I refused to consider that something could have happened to him. He was coming for me. I just had to be patient.

I wanted to go home and start our lives, to find a new job and go back to dating Axel the way we had when I thought he was Adam, this time without any lies between us.

I got out of bed, took a shower, and got dressed, dreading another long day with nothing to do. By lunch time, I thought I was going to go nuts. I would've killed for a laptop, tablet, or phone. With any of those, I could've downloaded a book or streamed a yoga video. Something. With only the TV for company, I was bored beyond belief.

Shortly after I'd eaten a turkey sandwich and washed the single dish I'd used, I heard the elevator doors slide open. Eager for diversion, I left the kitchen and went to the end of the hall to see who it was.

At the sight of Summer's curly blonde head, I shrieked and took off at a run. She met me halfway, her arms wide open, closing around me in one of her trademark tight hugs, rocking me from side to side and whispering, "What have you gotten yourself into, Emma girl?"

Summer gave the best hugs in the world, and I burrowed into her for a long minute, soaking up her love before I stepped back and saw Evers standing behind her, looking at once amused and annoyed. "Evers," I said in surprise. "Did you bring Summer here?"

In answer, Evers said, "Axel owes me one." He walked past us down the hall and headed for the kitchen. Not used to seeing Evers cranky, I looked at Summer and raised an eyebrow.

"Tell me what's going on," Summer demanded.

"What do you mean? You don't know? Evers didn't tell you anything?"

"No," Summer said, linking her arm through mine and leading me down the hall to the kitchen as if she knew exactly where she was going. That was Summer, never hesitant, always ready to forge her way forward.

"Your Evers showed up in the last few hours of my conference this morning, told me just enough to convince me that he knew you and that you were in trouble, then he drove me back home, made me get all my mail plus the packages you sent me, and dragged me here.

"He refused to let me call you. Actually, now that I'm telling you this, I can't believe that I went with him at all. He was very convincing. And very rude."

"Rude?" I asked. That didn't sound like Evers. He stood in the kitchen, drinking beer from a bottle, still looking annoyed. I whispered to Summer, "I haven't known Evers long, but I've never seen him be rude."

Summer put her hands on her curvy hips, tossed her curls over her shoulder, and said, "He keeps calling me Winters. My name is Summer. He seems to think it's funny." She skewered him with her dark blue eyes. "It's not funny."

"Maybe if you were less of a pain in the ass," Evers said, lowering his beer, "I would call you by your given name."

"I am *not* a pain in the ass," Summer protested, her eyes narrowed on Evers. "You can't just show up out of nowhere, tell me what to do, tell me my best friend is in danger, not let me call her, and expect that I just follow your orders."

Evers raised an eyebrow at her as if to say, *Why not? Everyone else does.* As if reading his mind, Summer said, "Everyone else does what you tell them to, don't they?"

"I think it's a Sinclair thing," I said. "Axel tells me what to do all the time."

"I can't imagine that goes over well," Summer said briskly. I bit my lip and flushed, looking at my toes as a laugh erupted from Evers. Summer looked between us, then grinned at me.

"Oh, it's like that, is it?" she asked.

"Axel's very... compelling," I said. "You know I don't like doing what I'm told, but he looks at me and..." I bit my lip again. I wasn't going to get into this with Evers standing right next to me. That was way too embarrassing.

"So, now that I'm here, is anyone going to tell me what's going on?" Summer asked.

I looked to Evers for guidance and he shrugged.

"Now that we're here," he said, "you might as well. I

have everything you sent to her. We need to start going through it."

"So?" Summer asked again.

"Grab a drink in the kitchen. We can sit down, and I'll tell you everything."

# CHAPTER THIRTY-SEVEN

## EMMA

I fell asleep late that night feeling better than I had since I'd arrived in Atlanta. Not that Jacob wasn't a good host, but there was nothing quite like having Summer around to make me feel better. I still missed Axel, but I'd been dying to talk to Summer ever since I'd discovered that Adam wasn't Adam.

I'd filled her in on the case in front of Evers, but when we were done with business, I'd stood up, made us two rum and Cokes, grabbed Summer's arm, and excused us, dragging her to my bedroom. It was a little rude, leaving Evers on his own, but I figured that, unlike Summer and me, *he* still had his phone.

Then, like we had when we'd been roommates in college, Summer and I curled up on my bed and giggled about boys. Well, I don't think you could call Evers and Axel *boys*. Still, some things never change.

Like most of the women I knew, myself included, Summer didn't have the best luck in picking her boyfriends. Unlike most of the women I knew, Summer always gave great advice.

I told her everything that had happened: how Adam had become Axel and the confusion that had followed, not hiding anything from her. I never would have been so honest with anyone else, but with Summer, I always told the truth. She didn't judge, and she loved me.

I told her how Axel could be controlling, how he'd turned me over to William Harper, despite my pleas for him to listen. I also told her of all the ways he'd protected me since.

I didn't go into too much detail about Axel's skills in the bedroom—as much as I loved Summer, some things were private—but she got a pretty clear picture of what Axel had to offer in that area.

She listened quietly, absorbing every word, interrupting only when she wanted more detail or to clarify a point. When I was done, she finished what was left of her drink and set her glass on my bedside table. Looking at me, she said, "You want to know what I think?"

"Of course, I want to know what you think, Summer. Why else would I have told you all of that?" Bracing myself, I finished the rest of my drink and put my empty glass on the table beside Summer's.

She said, "I think that you are a very lucky woman, and if Axel is anywhere near as hot as his brother, you should hold on tight and not let go."

"Oh, Axel is hotter than Evers. At least, *I* think he is. But do you really think I should just forgive him for all the other stuff, for lying to me and then not listening to me?"

Summer gave me a long, measuring look and said, "Sweetie, you know what's out there. You've dated the same kind of guys I have, and it sounds like your Axel made a mistake. Everyone makes mistakes.

"What's more important than any mistake he might

have made in the beginning—when he didn't know you as well and still thought you were a job—is the way he's treating you now. You're not his client now, right?"

"No. I mean, I'm not paying him. I hope I'm not paying him, because I'm unemployed, and I don't think I can afford Axel," I said, mostly joking.

"Exactly. It's not just that he's put his life on hold to help you, but he's put himself and his company at risk by turning on a client and going up against the FBI. It sounds like he's doing everything he can to get you clear of this mess.

"And the whole time, he's doing his best to show you how he feels about you. To me, that's what's important. That's what matters."

"He hasn't called since I've been here," I whispered. "I know it's not safe and he shouldn't. I don't want him to call if it's not safe, but I hate being apart from him like this.

"I know I should be more independent. Not so scared. I just want him to come home." I said the last part so quietly that I could barely hear myself. Summer heard, and she pulled me into a hug.

"I'm so glad you found a good man, Emma," she said. "I love you so much, and you're such a good person. You deserve everything. I can't wait to meet your Axel."

I lay my head on her shoulder and said, "You're going to like him."

"I already do. As long as he's not as annoying as Evers."

I sat up, pulling out of Summer's arms, and gave her a sharp look. I'd sensed some tension there when they'd come in, but I'd been so focused on getting alone time with my best friend, I hadn't stopped to find out what was going on. There was no time like the present.

"What's up with that? Evers likes to pick on Axel—I

think it's a family sport with the Sinclair brothers—but otherwise he's been really nice. Was he teasing you about your name?"

Summer scowled. She was pretty laid back, but she didn't like being teased about her name. Her hippie parents had been in love with the idea of naming her for two opposing seasons, believing that it would give her balance and perspective.

She *was* one of the most balanced people I knew, and she had a fantastic perspective, so maybe they were right. Summer, who was more of a businesswoman than a hippie, had always found her name annoying.

"He seems to think it's hysterical, and even funnier that I have the same name as Jacob," she said, her eyes narrowing at the memory of Evers' teasing.

"That is weird," I interrupted. "Are you related to Jacob?"

"No," she said, but her eyes slid to the side, not meeting mine. Definitely weird, but I'd let it go for now.

Changing the subject back to Evers, she said, "We didn't get along very well at first because he was incredibly bossy and he couldn't *prove* that you'd sent him, then he wanted everything you'd mailed to me after you'd told me not to give it to anyone but you—"

"I'm sorry about that," I interrupted. "I had no way to let you know what was going on. I didn't even know that Evers was coming to get you. I thought they would wait until you came home. I guess he and Axel planned that part without me.

"Everything happened so fast when I left Las Vegas that there wasn't time for them to lay out the logistics for me. How *did* Evers talk you into giving him all of the evidence and then coming with him?" I asked.

Summer was not gullible, and Evers hadn't had anything from me to use to convince her to go with him. Her cheeks flushed, and she looked away.

"I don't know," she said, sounding both annoyed and frustrated. "It wasn't like me at all. He was so bossy and authoritative—it was annoying—but I believed he was helping you and that I needed to come with him to find you. What if he hadn't been?" She asked, looking horrified by the thought. I leaned over and gave her a quick hug of reassurance.

"It's okay, Summer. You believed him because he was telling the truth. And you're here now, which everyone tells me is the safest place we can be. I know Axel is working hard to get this all cleared up. Maybe by the end of the weekend, it'll be over, and we can go back to our normal lives."

I hoped that was true. I wasn't sure I believed it.

"So," I teased. "You think Evers is hot?"

Summer blushed again. This time, her cheeks turned brick red in embarrassment. She shook her head but said, "I'm not blind."

I giggled. "Wait until you meet Jacob," I said, fanning myself. "I am *very* taken, but I have to say that Jacob is easily as hot as Axel and Evers—in his own way, maybe hotter." I thought about it, then amended my statement. "Well, not hotter than Axel, but he might be a little hotter than Evers."

"No way," Summer protested. "I don't believe you."

"You'll see," I promised. "He said he's coming back for dinner tonight."

Jacob did come back for dinner, and I had the amused satisfaction of seeing Summers' jaw drop when she laid eyes on him. Then, even better: Jacob, who had been nothing but respectful to me, proceeded to flirt with my best friend all through the meal until she was alternately blushing and giggling.

The best part was seeing Evers' reaction to Jacob's flirting with Summer. There was something between Evers and Summer. She didn't usually get irritated with people. She was too relaxed for that, believing that it wasn't worth wasting her energy getting annoyed unless she absolutely had to, but Evers seemed to get under her skin effortlessly.

Watching his eyes narrow as Summer laughed at something Jacob said, I knew that Summer had gotten under his skin as well. This could be interesting.

Evers was a good man, and Summer, my best friend in the whole world, the best friend I could ever have wished for, deserved a good man. Watching Summer pointedly ignore Evers, I had a feeling that if he was interested, he was going to have to work for it.

I joined in the conversation during dinner, joked around with Summer, and asked Jacob and Evers more about their work, but the entire time I was thinking about Axel—missing him, hoping he was okay, reminding myself that his meeting with Tsepov had to have gone okay, because if there were anything wrong with Axel, Evers would have told me.

Even if Jacob could have kept it from me, I knew that Evers wouldn't be sitting here in the middle of a social dinner if something was wrong with his brother.

I reminded myself over and over that everything was going to be okay, and Axel and I would be together soon, but by the time dinner was over, I was exhausted from the pretense and just wanted to go to sleep.

I excused myself, giving Summer a goodnight hug and thanking her for not being mad that she'd been pulled into this whole mess before disappearing down the hall to my bedroom. I pulled a strappy silk and lace nightgown over my head, washed my face, and crawled into the big bed, wishing with all my heart that I wasn't alone.

Playing my favorite game to distract myself from missing Axel, I fell asleep imagining where we would go on our vacation. Fiji? I could buy a new bathing suit for Fiji, but with my pale skin, the sun wasn't a great idea.

I fell asleep imagining taking a week off and spending it at Axel's lake house, curled up in front of the fire, just the two of us.

I had the dream again, the dream that I was with Axel. We were in bed together, his arms around me, his body heat against my back, warming me as he held me close. His lips kissed the nape of my neck, feather light as they moved, touching the back of my ear and nuzzling my throat. I rolled over, still mostly asleep, reaching for my dream Axel.

My eyes flew open as my hands encountered a hard, bare chest. Axel's dark eyes gleamed at me in the shadows, turning my muddled world right-side up.

"You're here," I said a little too loudly.

Axel's fingers landed over my lips and he said, "Shhh. Everyone is sleeping. I let myself in, and I don't want to wake anyone up."

That was fine with me. I didn't want to wake anyone up either. Not when I finally had Axel all to myself.

"Is everything okay? How did the meeting go? I hated not being able to talk to you."

Axel kissed me, his lips gentle, lingering on mine. He pulled back only to answer my question, saying first, "I missed you too. I hated sending you away, and I really hated not being able to call you. We're not doing that again."

A quiet laugh of relief escaped me. "No, we're not. Was the meeting with Tsepov okay?"

"About as okay as a meeting with a mob boss can be," Axel said. "We got confirmation that Tierney's dirty."

"But what are we—"

Axel laid his finger over my lips, and I fell silent. "Let's talk about this tomorrow. I promise you that we have things under control, okay? I promise," he repeated when I opened my mouth to protest. "For now, I just want to be with you and not talk about the case. Just for a little while."

I was fine with that. Instead of answering with words, I wrapped my arms around Axel's neck and pressed my body into his. "That sounds good to me," I said.

# CHAPTER THIRTY-EIGHT

## EMMA

Axel rolled me onto my back and settled between my spread legs, kissing me hard, his mouth hungry and demanding. We'd only been apart for a few days, but it felt like years. Something had happened in my heart while we'd been separated. All of my doubts and fears about Axel had dissolved under the weight of how deeply I'd missed him.

I didn't like that he'd lied to me about how we'd met. It would take some time before the shock of discovering the truth about 'Adam' would fade, but in the past few days, it seemed to matter far less. Axel was what mattered.

I kissed him back, as eager for his touch as he was for mine. With one hand on the back of his neck, I scrambled with the other to pull off my nightgown. I wanted nothing between us, not even the filmy silk.

All I wanted was Axel, his heat and strength against me. He tore his mouth from mine and reared back, taking the nightgown in both hands and tearing it down the center. Lace and silk split and fell to the sides, leaving my body exposed to his heated gaze.

"I missed you," he said, staring down at me. "I missed everything about you. I missed holding you. I missed kissing you. And I missed fucking you."

That was so Axel—sweet and crude at the same time. His blunt words thrilled me.

"I missed everything about you, too," I said, reaching to pull him down to me. I didn't want any space between us. "I missed everything, but I definitely missed you fucking me." I felt heat bloom in my cheeks at the last part. I had no idea how I could still blush after some of the things we'd done together.

Axel's fingers dipped between my legs and he stroked over my folds, slick and ready for him. Dipping one finger inside, he murmured into my mouth, "I love your pussy— always wet for me, so hot and tight."

Proving his point, he worked two fingers in, letting me feel the stretch as he opened me. I pulled my knees back, inviting him into my body, desperate for him. I didn't want to be teased tonight. I didn't want to wait. It felt like years since he'd touched me.

I wanted all of Axel, and I wanted it right away. As always, he knew how to give me what I needed. His fingers slid away, curling around the back of my thigh to hitch my leg higher as the head of his cock pushed inside me.

It was heaven, even the little pinch of pain a jolt of bliss. I rocked my hips up into him, taking him deeper, needing to feel him inside me to the hilt.

With a hard thrust, Axel gave me every inch, filling me, pinning me to the mattress. He stayed where he was, his strong body covering me, his dark eyes intent on my face.

"I'm never leaving you again," he said, his gaze locked on mine. "As soon as this is over, we're going home where we can start fresh. You and me."

I wrapped my legs around Axel's waist, the shift tipping my hips so that I took his thick cock even deeper. I reached up to trace a finger over his sharp cheekbone, feeling tears well in my eyes. "I don't want to start fresh. I don't want to forget the way we met. It's part of us."

"I love you," he said, dropping his mouth to take mine in a slow, sweet kiss. Hot tears slipped from my eyes, gliding down my cheeks as his words struck my heart.

"I love you, too," I whispered, my words choked.

Axel gave a short growl. "You'd better. If you didn't, I'd tie you to the bed and keep you here until you changed your mind."

"You can keep me here anyway," I said, kissing his jaw and squeezing his hips with my thighs. "I want to stay right where I am for the rest of the weekend."

Axel answered me with a shallow thrust of his cock. After that, we stopped talking. He fucked me hard the first time, taking me with his cock as if claiming me, driving me to orgasm faster than usual.

I barely had time to catch my breath before he started all over again, his mouth and hands making a feast of my body, tasting and touching every inch of me until I was begging him to take me again. He did, not making me wait. I had no problem believing that he'd missed me as much as I'd missed him.

We passed out, exhausted, sometime before dawn. I woke draped across Axel's chest, a little sore and more content than I'd ever been in my life. Axel's hand ran down my spine, and I realized he must have already been awake.

"We need to get moving," he said. "It's after ten, and we have to figure out our next move."

"You mean you don't already have that planned out?" I

teased, not believing for a second that he was entirely without a strategy.

"I've got some ideas. But I need to talk to Evers and take a look at the data your friend brought with her."

Giving my ass a smack, he sat up, taking me with him, and carried me to the shower. We did get ready for the day, but it was close to eleven before we managed to get our clothes on.

Emerging from the hallway into the main room, we found three smirking faces waiting for us. I would have thought Jacob too elegant and reserved to smirk, but I would have been wrong.

"Did you two get a good night's sleep?" Summer asked, her voice sweet and her deep blue eyes amused. Trying for dignity, I pretended that they weren't all laughing at us.

"I did. Axel got in late, so he might need a nap later." At the lascivious glance I gave Axel, Summer burst out laughing.

"Yeah, well, you two lovebirds will have to wait," Evers said. "I've been going through the files Emma sent to Summer, and I think I found what Tierney and Tsepov wanted so badly."

"That sounds promising," Axel said. He gave me a squeeze around my shoulders and then dropped his arm, preparing to go join his brother at the dining room table, where it looked like they'd printed and spread out all of the files I'd sent to Summer since the case had begun.

"You want me to get you some coffee and food?" I quietly asked Axel.

"Thanks, sweet Emma." He left me with a kiss on the cheek, and I headed straight for the kitchen, my stomach growling, suddenly dying for coffee. Summer left the men to pore over the paperwork and joined me.

"You were right," she said in a low voice. "He *is* as hot as Evers."

"Hotter," I said firmly. Evers Sinclair was one good looking man, but seeing him standing next to Axel, there was no contest.

"So, everything is good?" Summer asked, concern evident in her teasing tone. That was my girl, always looking out for me.

I didn't hide my smile when I said, "Everything's great. Did Evers really find what we need? I collected all those files, but half the time, Agent Tierney and Agent Jensen just told me what to get. I don't really understand the relevance of half of it."

I poured coffee for Axel and myself and put together a plate with bagels, cream cheese, and smoked salmon. We joined the others at the table, where they were flipping through papers and murmuring to each other. I looked at Jacob, who was standing to the side, mostly watching, a curious expression on his face.

"What are they looking at?" I asked after I'd put the food and coffee in front of Axel.

Jacob shrugged one shoulder and said, "I'm not exactly sure. I deal with real estate finance. Forensic accounting isn't my area of expertise, but I think your boss kept a second set of books for the work he did with Tsepov, including detailed notes on the jobs, dates, and locations." Jacob's distinctive silver eyes narrowed in disdain. "Your boss sounds like a complete idiot."

"Former boss," I corrected, "and he kind of was."

Axel looked up and caught my eyes, a gravity in his dark ones that made my stomach hitch in apprehension. "What?" I asked.

Axel made a face and said, "William Harper is dead. It looks like Tsepov had him executed."

I let out a breath and sank into a chair at the table, wrapping my hands around my hot coffee mug, stunned. I shouldn't have been so shocked. We'd said more than once that Tsepov was not known for his forgiveness. Harper had messed up big time.

When you worked for the mob, it was never as simple as just getting fired. I didn't want to know, but I had to ask. "What happened? How did he die?"

"Single gunshot to the head," Axel said. "It was quick, Emma. He didn't suffer."

Maybe not physically, but I'd bet he'd been terrified. Part of me was horrified that someone I'd known had died so badly. But the part of me that vividly remembered Harper punching me while I was tied to the chair and his threats to rape me before he sold me—that part of me didn't feel bad at all.

I didn't know many people who deserved a single gunshot to the head, but William Harper was on the list. Right along with Sergey Tsepov.

"Are we sure Agent Tierney was the leak? That he's working for Tsepov?"

Evers and Axel both looked grim. "We're as sure as we can be without catching him red-handed," Axel said.

"I have an idea," Evers said, looking at his brother and raising one eyebrow. Axel narrowed his eyebrows, reading his brother's face. They were doing that brother-speak thing again, having entire conversations without ever opening their mouths. It was both cute and annoying.

"What are they doing?" Summer whispered to me, loud enough that everyone heard her.

In the same tone, I said back, "I think it's some sort of Sinclair telepathy. They do this all the time."

She crossed her arms over her chest and glowered at Evers. He glared back. I shouldn't enjoy seeing my best friend so thrown by a guy, but I couldn't deny that it was funny, especially since she seemed to be enjoying her irritation with him, though she'd never admit it.

"So, what's the idea?" I asked.

Axel answered, "We have a contact, an SAC—Special Agent in Charge—in the Atlanta FBI office who we've worked with a lot. We've known him for years, and I would bet my life that he's completely clean.

"I think we need to call him in, showing what we have, and explain the situation. If he agrees to have our backs, the best thing we can do at this point is to set a trap for Tierney and see if he takes the bait."

I was intrigued. "Trap?" I asked.

Axel shook his head. "First things first. Evers, can you call Agent Holley?"

Evers pulled out his phone and hit a few buttons. One short, cryptic conversation later, he hung up and said, "Holley's on his way." Things moved quickly after that.

Agent Holley, a tall, lanky man wearing a suit on a Saturday, arrived at Jacob's place twenty minutes later. After less than a half-hour of going through the files, he interviewed me about the case, then Axel, and disappeared into Jacob's office to make some phone calls.

Waiting for him to come back made me nervous, but Axel seemed completely relaxed, confident that things were finally moving in the right direction, and I trusted him. I tried to relax. I wanted so badly for all of this to be over, to go back to our normal lives without having to be afraid.

Special Agent in Charge Matthew Holley came back

into the room almost an hour later and gave Axel and Evers a brisk, affirmative nod. "Everything is in order. An agent will accompany Evers back to Las Vegas. Axel, you and Emma will stay in Atlanta until the arrests have been made. It shouldn't take long to bring them in, if all goes to plan."

*If all goes to plan.* Famous last words, but delivered with Agent Holley's authority, they comforted me nonetheless.

## CHAPTER THIRTY-NINE
### EMMA

The day had passed in a flash. I'd been so worried about what was going to happen that I hadn't realized how long Axel and I had spent with Agent Holley until he'd left, Evers in tow.

Summer had also gone, giving me a tight hug and a kiss on the cheek, telling me she was coming out to Vegas for a long weekend soon so she could check out Axel's lake house and get to know him a little bit better. I thought that sounded like a great idea. I was only sorry that she had to go so soon.

I thought that Jacob would stay with us, but he left shortly after Summer, saying, "I'd love to be your third wheel, but I have a socialite dying to be my arm candy and a god-awful, boring art opening to attend."

"Can you skip it?" Axel asked. Despite his humor, Jacob didn't look all that excited about his plans for his date.

"No, I promised I'd go."

Axel studied Jacob for a moment, then he said, "Someone there you want to see?"

I thought it was an uncharacteristically nosy question,

but Axel knew his friend well. Jacob's face closed down and he said, "Of course not. Just an art opening I said I'd go to. Then I have something tomorrow. I won't be back for the rest of the weekend."

He was gone a few minutes later. Surprised by Jacob's abrupt change of mood, I said to Axel, "I think you made him mad. Why did you ask him that?"

"I don't know," Axel said. "He had a look in his eye when he mentioned the art opening that I thought was interesting. I was curious."

Thinking about the pearl and diamond earring I'd found in his desk, I said, "He doesn't have a girlfriend?"

Axel burst out laughing. "There are about a hundred women who would kill each other for the chance to be his girlfriend, but he never dates any of them for very long. I don't think he's built that way. Jacob doesn't do love."

I told Axel about the earring I'd discovered in Jacob's desk, and Axel looked thoughtful for a moment before shaking his head.

"I wouldn't spin any romantic dreams about Jacob Winters falling in love with some woman. I'd be happy as hell for him if he found someone he cared about enough to settle down, but I don't see it happening. He's just not that kind of guy."

"You never know," I said. "People can change."

Axel turned and drew me into his arms. I was suddenly acutely aware that we were alone in the penthouse and likely to remain that way for at least twenty-four hours. I lost all interest in dinner.

"No, they don't. Not really," Axel said, interrupting my thoughts.

"What?" I asked. Distracted at the thought of being alone with Axel, I'd lost track of the conversation.

"People don't really change," Axel said. "Things about them might change, surface things or goals, dreams. People themselves don't really change. I was never a one-woman man until I met you," he said. "But I always hoped that one day I would be. I just wasn't willing to settle down until I met the right woman."

I reveled in the thrill his words sent through me. I loved that Axel didn't feel the need to hide that he was in love with me. "Are you saying you don't think Jacob is capable of falling in love?" I asked.

"I could be wrong," Axel said. "If anyone I know has hidden depths, it's Jacob Winters. But he's never struck me as a guy waiting for the right woman. He makes me look completely laid-back. And I've heard rumors that he's into some kinky stuff in the bedroom.

"My best guess would be that if Jacob were looking for a committed relationship, it would have nothing to do with love and everything to do with sex, but who knows? Maybe someday he'll surprise me."

I liked Jacob. He'd proven that he was a good friend, and he'd been more than welcoming to me during a time of extreme stress and uncertainty. I liked that he'd come to Axel's aid without question. I'd also liked him even more when he'd flirted with Summer the night before just to irritate Evers.

The idea that he might never find the right woman and fall in love was a little sad, but to each his own. I was too happy, and too in love with Axel, too thrilled to know that Axel was in love with me, to get depressed about Jacob. Pushing him from my mind, I leaned into Axel and rested my head on his chest.

"Now that we're alone, what do you want to do?" I

asked, teasing him. In answer, he picked me up, swinging me into his arms, and carried me off to bed.

We didn't come up for air until late that night, emerging from the bedroom to scrounge for food in the kitchen, me in a robe and Axel in a pair of boxer briefs that made my mouth water. Someone had made a huge grocery run, because the fridge was packed with tasty treats. We settled on reheated mushroom ravioli and key lime pie.

While we ate, perched on stools at the kitchen counter, I asked Axel, "So what *was* the plan? Who went back to Vegas with Evers, and what are they doing?"

"Evers, an agent who looks a lot like you, and Agent Holley went to Vegas, though Holley only went to hook Evers and the other agent up with the FBI contact who would help arrest Tierney. Holley should be on his way back here by now."

"Why did they need an agent who looks like me?" I asked.

Axel popped a bite of tart, sweet pie between my lips and said, "Because we want to see what he'll do if he has the opportunity to get to you. You're a loose end. If he's really working for Tsepov, then he'll want you taken out of the picture. You've seen the evidence Harper collected. You know too much."

"So, the agent who looks like me is going to set up a meeting with Tierney?" I asked, dismayed at the thought that he would harm me. I knew Agent Tierney was the bad guy, but it still bugged me.

"Nothing that overt. She's going to send a text from your phone saying that you got away from me and you have back-up evidence that you want to deliver. We think he'll try to kill you—or really, her—when he realizes you still have the files. Either way, we'll know if he's truly dirty or not."

That made sense. It might have been wrong, but part of me hoped the plan didn't work and that Agent Tierney showed up to collect the evidence like he should. I didn't like him, but if he was working for Tsepov, it made me doubt my own judgment even more.

I told Axel as much, and he said, "Emma, that's not fair. You're not a trained operative, and you had every reason to expect that an FBI agent was trust-worthy. When you're predisposed to assume someone is honest—someone in a position of authority like an FBI agent—it's very hard to know that they're up to something unless you catch them in a direct lie."

"I still feel stupid."

"Well, don't. You're not stupid. You managed to get all those files and collect what the FBI needs to arrest Tsepov with no training and very little guidance from Jensen or Tierney. I'd say that you're not only smart, but you're resourceful."

I loved Axel's compliments. He could have said something empty and clichéd to soothe my worries, but instead he gave me logic, logic that gave my flagging confidence a boost. I thought about saying *thank you*, but that didn't seem good enough. So I jumped him.

It was a good thing Jacob wasn't coming home that night. I ended up on my knees between Axel's legs with the can of whipped cream we'd grabbed for the pie in my hand. Axel's cock tasted great on its own, but everything was better with whipped cream on top.

By the time we were done, the can was empty and Axel was coming in my mouth, his hands buried in my hair, calling out my name as he gasped for breath.

He paid me back with the fudge sauce we found in the pantry, laying me out over Jacob's huge dining room table and drizzling the thick, sweet chocolate over my body and licking it off. He took his time, painting my nipples and licking them clean more than once before making swirls of chocolate over my pussy and sucking it off.

I came twice, then begged him to fuck me. Jacob's table was the perfect height. After my third orgasm, I made a mental note to try out the table in Axel's penthouse. I liked table sex with Axel.

We passed out in bed, our bodies wrung dry and exhausted. I woke deep in the night to hear Axel on the phone, his voice too low to decipher his words. He hung up and I asked, "Who was that? What time is it?"

"It's just after 2 A.M. It was Evers. Tierney took the bait. He set a meeting with the agent he thought was you and tried to kill her."

I sat up in bed, sleep forgotten. "What? How?"

Axel pulled me down and tucked me under the covers, pressing my head to his chest and stroking strong fingers down my spine.

"He set the meeting for a dark parking lot, then he tried to shoot her. She's fine. She was wearing a vest. He was taken into custody, and everything is okay."

"What if he'd aimed for her head? She could have been killed," I protested, freaked out that this woman I didn't even know had risked her life pretending to be me. And—to be honest—a little more freaked that Agent Tierney had tried to murder me.

"It's her job," Axel reassured me. "There's always a risk, but she had plenty of cover. Evers said that they're picking up Tsepov tonight. He's headed back here on an early flight, and we're going to take the plane back to Vegas in the morning, after we get some sleep."

I tried, but I couldn't relax after Evers' phone call. Axel eventually gave up on the back rub and cradled me in his arms, pulling my leg over his hip and sliding inside me.

We took each other slowly, whispering insensible words of love as we moved together. My orgasm, cresting in a wave that built bit by bit and fell away just as gradually, seemed to last forever. I didn't remember falling asleep.

I woke to the sound of birds singing and Axel's smile, as bright and magnetic as the morning sun. Our troubles were finally over. It was time to go home.

# CHAPTER FORTY

## EMMA

I napped through most of the flight home. I still didn't have a phone or tablet. We'd flown out of a private airstrip, so I hadn't been able to grab so much as a magazine. And I was tired. We'd gone to bed late, then woken in the middle of the night—not that I was complaining about all the orgasms.

I was *really* not complaining.

The plane was the same one that Griffen and I had taken a few days before, with the same plush, spacious seats. This time, Axel sat beside me and raised the armrest between us.

He pulled me against him, tucked my head into his shoulder, and draped a blanket over us both. Of course, the first place my head went was all the trouble we could get up to underneath a blanket, but a few minutes later, I was out cold.

We didn't eat on the flight and were met at the airport by one of Axel's guys in another of Sinclair Security's ubiquitous black SUVs. I don't think I'd seen any of them drive anything else.

On the way back to Axel's penthouse, we stopped and went grocery shopping, the most normal thing Axel and I had done together since the night he'd taken me in hand-cuffs to William Harper.

I knew as time went on that something as mundane as grocery shopping would be a chore, but just then, grocery shopping with Axel was the most fun I thought I'd ever had. We bickered good-naturedly over how ripe the fruit was and tried to decide what we wanted to cook for dinner that night or if we wanted to cook at all.

We ended up choosing something in between: eggs, potatoes, asparagus, and brownies—ready-made. We'd be cooking, but it wouldn't take much effort. After everything that had happened, I just wanted to relax with my man.

I had to find a new job, and eventually, I supposed I had to go back to my apartment. There would be time to face all of that later.

We went back to Axel's place, where I found a brand-new cellphone, tablet, and laptop waiting for me. Axel just shrugged and said, "You needed upgrades, and I'm the one who took your laptop, so I should replace it."

He'd replaced all of my things at a much higher quality, but at this point, I knew better than to complain. The money wasn't a big deal to him, and I appreciated that he thought to spend some of it on me.

I played with my new toys for a while, downloading some books to read, setting up my phone, and generally chilling out. I was tempted to look at the want ads or work on my resumé, but I didn't bother. Job hunting would stress me out, and I'd had enough stress to last me for a lifetime.

Axel was in his office, catching up on business he'd missed while he was dealing with my situation. There was something homey and comforting about lying on the couch in his modern living room, listening to him on his computer on the other side of the penthouse.

Looking around, I wondered if he'd let me redecorate a little. I liked aspects of his penthouse—it was modern, expensive, sleek, and a little dangerous. And cold. I didn't like that part. Axel was tough, and sometimes he was even scary. He was never cold.

I'd ask him later. So much had changed in the last week, and I knew men could be funny about women coming in and changing their stuff around. Maybe I'd wait for him to offer. Later that afternoon, after we'd eaten lunch, I wandered into Axel's office.

"You think we could run by my place?" I asked. "All the stuff that Lola got me is great, but I would love to have my own makeup, hair stuff, and everything..." I trailed off, suddenly not sure if I should assume I was supposed to stay. "Or if you want, I could just stay there and—"

Axel was out from behind his desk in a flash, his face hard. "You want to go back to your place? You need some time?"

"No," I said uncertainly. This was a first for me. I had no desire to have any time away from Axel, but I didn't want to crowd him. All of a sudden, I wasn't at all sure where we stood.

"If you don't care either way," Axel said evenly, "I'd rather have you here. We can go get your things. I was gonna give you a couple of days before I brought this up, but if you feel like it's not too soon, I'd like you to move in with me."

He spit the last part out in a rush as if he were nervous. His brief lapse into uncertainty reassured me. Axel was always so in control. It made me feel better to know that he was a little at sea as well.

"I want to be with you," I said, "and I'm not that attached to my apartment, but are you sure you're okay with me moving in? It's a big step. You might get sick of having me under your feet all the time."

Axel's eyes heated and he gave me a lecherous grin. "You won't be under my *feet*, Emma," he said, pulling me in for a hot, slow kiss.

I was moving in with Axel Sinclair. We'd come a long way since I'd worried that I'd never seen Adam's apartment. Axel reached into his desk and opened the top drawer, pulling out a gun. At the sight of it, the dark black metal, so foreign in his hand, I stiffened.

"Do you need that?" I asked. "I thought everything was fine now."

"I carry a gun most of the time," Axel said. "Partly out of habit, and partly because it's my job. I wouldn't have brought you home if I wasn't sure you were safe, but with everything that's happened, I'd rather be prepared."

"Okay," I said, not willing to argue about it. I wasn't anti-gun, which was probably a good thing, considering who I was about to move in with. We took the elevator down to the garage, and Axel said, "We'll go into the office tomorrow, and I'll get your prints and palm recorded so you can control the elevator."

That was pretty cool. Axel pulled into the parking garage at my apartment building and circled twice before choosing a spot. Everything looked normal enough to me, and we went up to my apartment, me in front, Axel taking the rear.

It was weird to be back at my place after a week. My house plants were a little wilted, but otherwise, everything looked normal, not as if my life had been turned upside down. Everything but the door to my bedroom. That was still torn from its hinges, on its side in the hallway. Looking at it, I said, "I don't think I'm getting my security deposit back."

Axel's eyes darkened at the sight of the damage. "I'll have it taken care of. Just get as much of your stuff as you want, and I'll have movers come in and take care of the rest. Do you want your furniture?"

My things were on the shabby side of shabby chic. They'd look awful at Axel's place. "I don't think my furniture would look right in your place, Axel," I said.

He gave me a level look and said, "I don't give a fuck. If you want it, we'll redecorate."

Hmm, that gave me a lot to think about. I packed my clothes and makeup, considering what, if anything, I wanted to take with me. In the end, I said, "I don't think any of this stuff is worth moving to your place. I've been carting it around since college, and most of it is ready to fall apart. But maybe we could redecorate a little."

Axel pressed a kiss to my forehead and said, "Whatever you want, Emma. Whatever you want."

I leaned into him, wondering if we had enough time to make out. For once, we didn't have anything pressing to do. No work, no appointments with the FBI or running from the mob. Life was about to get blissfully boring. I couldn't wait.

I wound my arms around Axel's neck, burying my fingers in his silky hair as I drew him down for a long, slow kiss. His hands dipped below my waist, cupping my ass and pulling me into his hard, thick length.

We had plenty of time and nothing more important to do than to be together. With that in mind, my hands went to the buttons on Axel's shirt, and I got to work.

I had most of them undone when I heard it—the distinctive squeak of the hinges on my front door. I'd always meant to take care of those, but I kept forgetting. Who would have guessed they might save my life?

I stepped back to see who was at the door as Axel whirled and shoved me behind him, his gun raised. I caught a glimpse of a tall, distinguished-looking older man at the door, and the flash of a gun in his hand, before the room exploded around me.

Gunshots. I thought that's what they were, though they sounded different than the shots I'd heard at the safe house. These were more like the attack in the parking garage. Three of them. One from Axel, two from the man at the door.

"Get down. Take cover behind the bed," Axel hissed at me, not taking his eyes off the threat down the hall. I dropped to my knees and scrambled to the side of the bed, drawing my knees to my chest to make myself the smallest target possible.

Axel stood in the doorway, his eyes and gun trained on the intruder, leaning to the side to minimize his exposure. It took me a minute to spot the blood trickling down his left arm, staining the sleeve of his button-down a muddy red.

"Axel," I said, staring at his arm. He didn't turn, but gestured at me with his free hand, telling me to be quiet. "He shot you," I whispered.

He waved his hand at me again, reminding me to be quiet. I pressed my lips together, telling myself to think. It had been a stupid thing to say. *He shot you.*

Axel probably knew he'd been shot. Duh. But I was in shock, too overwhelmed at the shift from kissing to dodging bullets to come up with something more intelligent to say. Since I didn't have anything useful to contribute, I'd huddle on the floor and keep my mouth shut.

Digging his hand into his pocket, Axel tossed his phone to me and said, under his breath, "Text Evers and tell him Tsepov is here and shots have been fired. Then call 911 and tell them the same thing."

Relieved to have something useful to do, something that would take my mind off the fact that the man I loved was bleeding, had been shot and was holding off an armed gunman, I sent a quick text to Evers and called emergency services.

I wondered if they'd been looking for Tsepov, because when I identified who had broken into my place, the operator became far more alert. She directed me to stay on the line and assured me that the police and an ambulance were on the way.

The police had an ETA of five minutes, the ambulance a little longer. I knew that was a fast response time, but cowering on my floor, watching blood drip from Axel's arm to stain my carpet, five minutes felt like an eternity.

"The police are already on their way, Tsepov," Axel said. "Drop the gun."

"Why?" Tsepov responded. "You betrayed me, sent the FBI to me, and let your whore sell me out. I said I didn't want war, but you've forced my hand. I'll kill you both and be gone before the law gets here. Then I'll go after every Sinclair I can find until you're all dead."

Axel fired his gun down the hall. I flinched at the sound, reporting what had happened to the frantic 911 operator. For a moment, I thought Axel could hold Tsepov off until the cavalry arrived. Then Tsepov fired, not down the hall, but through the wall of my bedroom.

I stared at the little round hole that appeared in the wall, the puff of drywall dust, and watched in horror as Axel dropped to his knees, a red stain spreading rapidly across the right side of his chest. In slow motion, he hit the floor, his gun tumbling from his hand.

I dropped the phone and lunged for Axel, grabbing the gun as I moved. I didn't know how to shoot—not beyond pointing and pulling the trigger—but I wasn't going to let Tsepov take us both without a fight. Not if I could help it. I scrambled behind Axel, cradling his head in my lap and lifting the gun to point it at the door. It was surprisingly heavy.

"Good girl," Axel whispered. I started to look down at him, but he said, "No, eyes on the door, Emma. I'm okay. Shot was high. Keep that gun on the door and shoot anything that moves. Got it?"

"Got it," I whispered back, my hand shaking from fear and the strain of holding the weapon up, aimed at the open doorway.

"Fucking got both arms, the bastard," Axel whispered. "You have most of a clip, Emma. Don't be afraid to shoot."

"I'm not," I lied, holding my breath, waiting for Tsepov to come for us. The apartment was silent except for the rasp of Axel's breath.

He'd said he was okay, but as the seconds passed, his breathing became louder, strained and thick, as if he were breathing through water. I didn't allow myself to think about what that might mean. All that mattered was staying alive until the police got here.

I wanted to beg the 911 operator to tell the ambulance to hurry, that Axel needed help, but I stayed silent. The phone was a few feet away on the carpet, and I didn't think it was a good idea to announce to Tsepov that Axel was hurt.

My ears strained for the sound of movement. Nothing. Either Tsepov was waiting for us to come out, or he was

314

really good at sneaking around. A few seconds later, I spotted the edge of his sleeve at the doorway.

My finger tightened on the trigger, but I didn't fire. Not yet. I didn't want him to know I was ready while he still had time to duck out of the way.

With my whole arm shaking from the strain of holding up the gun, I eased my other hand away from Axel's head and used it to brace the hand holding the gun like I'd seen on the cop shows I watched on TV.

Instantly, the gun steadied, and I felt more in control. When Tsepov took a step into the doorway, I fired. The gun lurched back at me and I almost dropped it. I didn't remember seeing *that* on TV.

Tsepov stumbled to the side, but he caught himself and raised his gun again, pointing it right at me. I thought that I'd hit him, but if I had, it wasn't enough to stop him. Remembering what Axel had said, I braced my arms to shoot and pulled the trigger again. And again.

I pulled it over and over, unloading the whole clip into Tsepov, numbly watching the bullets slam into his body— and the wall behind him—until the gun stopped firing and made useless clicking sounds.

I dropped it on the floor beside me, looking at Tsepov only long enough to be sure that he wasn't moving. Crawling to the phone, I snatched it up and shouted to the operator that we needed an ambulance before I went back to Axel. His eyes were closed, but he said, his voice almost inaudible, "Did you get him?"

"I think he's dead," I said, afraid to ask Axel if he was going to follow Tsepov into the dark. Axel's shirt was red with blood, his breath a hollow rattle in his chest.

"That's my girl," Axel said, closing his eyes, a tiny smile stretching across his lips. "Love you, Emma."

"I love you, too," I said, my voice wobbly with tears as I pressed a wad of blanket into his wound, trying to stop the bleeding while we waited for the ambulance. "If you die on me, I'm going to kick your ass, Axel Sinclair," I muttered, knowing I wasn't making any sense.

By that point, I was more than a little hysterical. Axel's eyes remained shut, and he didn't say anything, but the little smile remained on his face. He turned his head into my open hand as if to reassure me that everything was going to be all right.

Despite the blood and his labored breathing, his skin was warm against my palm. Something eased in my chest, and I knew he'd be okay. He had to be. I'd finally found my true love, and I would fight death itself to keep him. Axel was mine, and I wasn't going to let him go. Ever.

# EPILOGUE

## AXEL

Getting shot sucks. Big time. A collapsed lung is no picnic either. Between two bullet wounds and the lung, I was stuck in the hospital for almost a week. Emma refused to leave my side the entire time.

My girl was amazing, first shooting Tsepov, then putting pressure on the worst of my wounds while she calmly waited for help to arrive.

She told me later she'd been so scared that most of it was a blur, a normal response for a civilian with no experience in combat. The important part was that she'd held it together under pressure and saved both of our lives. If I hadn't already been in love with her, that would have done it.

Sergey Tsepov had walked out of FBI custody over something as mundane as a paperwork error and a clerk too new to know that he should have double-checked the release order.

Tsepov's lawyer had taken quick advantage of the

mistake, and Tsepov had come straight for Emma, knowing he was operating on borrowed time. We still didn't know why no one had thought to warn either of us that Tsepov was free.

Emma had killed Sergey Tsepov. Of the thirteen shots she'd fired, three had struck Tsepov and ten had buried themselves in her drywall. She was many things, but my girl was not a crack shot. I was going to remedy that.

Hopefully, she'd never again have cause to fire a weapon, but if she did, I would make sure she could do it well. *If* she agreed to pick up a gun again.

She'd said she was okay with Tsepov's death, but I'd urged her to see a counselor anyway. Taking a life, even when you had no other choice, wasn't a simple matter. She would suffer for it.

It burned, knowing she'd had to shoot my gun for me. I should have been the one to kill him. But he'd nailed me in the left shoulder, making my arm go numb, then he hit my right side, the bullet going through the top of my lung and my bicep.

He'd shot me right through the wall—fucking lucky bastard—though it helped that the walls in Emma's apartment were paper thin. Maybe I could have held up my gun long enough to shoot him, but it wasn't likely. Without Emma's bravery, we both would have been killed.

My girl was a tiger. The ICU nurses tried to throw her out more than once, but she'd refused to be moved, telling them she was my fiancée and she wasn't leaving. By the third day, most of them had given up on arguing with her.

Evers never left the airport in Atlanta. He'd gotten back on a plane and arrived in Vegas less than twenty-four hours after he'd left. His presence had gone a long way toward helping Emma make her stand.

He'd brought her clean clothes and stood guard while she'd snuck a shower or some food, going above and beyond to make sure she never had to leave me. By the end of my hospital stay, the nurses loved her.

It would be an understatement to say that I was a terrible patient. Emma ran interference, cajoling me into the ten thousandth blood test or vitals check when I would have snarled at the nurses on my own.

My other brothers came as well, Cooper and Knox, along with my mother. By the time they brought me home, Emma had been securely adopted into the Sinclair fold. It was a good thing, since she'd be marrying me as soon as I could manage a wedding.

She'd told the nurses she was my fiancée, thinking it was an expedient lie. When I'd called her on it, she'd turned a deep red and apologized, but I'd assured her I wasn't bothered. She'd let the subject drop, probably thinking that was the end of it.

Not for me. The first full day I was out of the hospital, I'd had Knox sneak me out of my place so I could pick out a ring while my mother kept Emma occupied with moving her things. I'd worried I wouldn't find the right one. It had to be perfect—unique, special, and exactly right.

Vegas had a ton of jewelry stores, but there was only one Emma Wright, soon to be Emma Sinclair. It must have been fate, because I found it at the second store, a two-and-a-half karat pear-shaped diamond surrounded by smaller bead diamonds. The ring sparkled, its curved shape and brilliant fire warm instead of cold. The perfect ring for my Emma.

I didn't wait to give it to her. Before Tsepov and my stay in the hospital, I'd toyed with half-formed plans for an elaborate proposal and a big wedding. Instead, I kicked my family out, sending them to bug Dylan and Leigha at the Delecta.

I took Emma to bed, though she'd refused to have sex with me—some bullshit about the doctor recommending we wait another week—but I'd managed to kiss her senseless, making her come with my mouth and my hands after promising not to pull any of my stitches.

I'd emerged unscathed—barely—and slid the ring on her finger while she was still gasping for breath after her second orgasm. Maybe it wasn't the most romantic proposal, but watching her passion-dazed eyes register the sparkle of the ring, her pale skin still flushed with pleasure, was one of the best moments of my life.

"Marry me," I'd said, a clutch in my stomach as I waited for her answer. I knew she was going to say yes. Of course, she'd say yes.

Instead, she said, "Really?"

I shook my head in half-frustrated amusement. Could she still question how much I loved her? "Yes, really," I said. "Forever. Be mine forever, Emma."

"Yes," she finally said, with tears spilling over her cheeks and her blue eyes shining with love as they went from the ring to my face and back again. "Yes, yes, yes."

I married her two days later. I didn't want to wait, and fortunately, Emma didn't put up a fight. I hadn't come close to dying, but knowing that Tsepov's loaded gun had been aimed at Emma had changed things for me.

I'd already known I loved her, already planned to marry her, but before she'd had to kill Tsepov, I'd been content to wait. No more. After I got out of the hospital, all I wanted was to make Emma mine.

With my family already in town and hers only a plane

ride away, I got the ball rolling as soon as she agreed. Lola sent over a selection of wedding gowns, and Emma chose the right one with Summer, her younger sister, and both of our mothers at her side.

We had the wedding—family only except for Dylan, Leigha, Sam, Chloe, and Summer—at my lake house, then we kicked everyone out for the honeymoon.

Two glorious weeks of just Emma and me, alone in a house with five bedrooms. Though the weather was good, we only made it out on the boat twice. The rest of the time we spent in various states of undress, rarely more than a few inches apart.

The outside world threatened to interfere a few times in the form of annoyed calls from Summer about something Evers had said or done at the wedding, and, oddly, the same complaints from Evers about Summer.

After the fourth such call, I'd confiscated Emma's phone and told the two of them to work out their issues on their own time. As long as we were on our honeymoon, Emma was all mine.

Watching her lounge on the couch, her blue eyes fixed on the view of the lake and her luscious curves wrapped in a creamy silk robe, I knew Emma had been right. I couldn't regret a single moment that had led to this one.

We hadn't needed to start over. Every step we'd taken, the good and the bad, had brought us to this, the first moment of the rest of our lives.

I joined her on the couch and pulled her into my arms, holding her close. I'd told her the truth at Jacob's. I'd never been a one-woman man before, but I'd always hoped that someday I would be.

I'd just been waiting for the right woman.

I'd been waiting for Emma.

**Turn the page for a sneak peek of The Winters family saga, as well as Evers & Summer's story!**

# THE WINTERS SAGA

## BY IVY LAYNE

**The Winters family had it all.**

Unimaginable wealth.
Power.
Love.
Until scandal and death stole the fairy tale.

Now, they're cursed by unrelenting media attention,
haunted by loss, and still searching for the mysterious
villain who destroyed their family.
Read *The Billionaire's Secret Heart* and see how the saga
begins.
Keep reading for a sneak peek!

# THE BILLIONAIRE'S SECRET HEART

## EXCERPT

### *Josephine*

I turned my head, and my eyes fell on the most beautiful man I'd ever seen. He was sitting on the end of the couch closest to me, his full lips quirked in amusement.

"Good one," he said, his low voice washing over me like warm honey. Dark eyes traveled my body slowly, making no effort to hide his appraisal. Unlike Stuart's leer, this man's look was all admiration. I crossed my legs, startled by the rush of heat between them.

"Excuse me?" I asked, watching him from the corner of my eye while keeping my face turned in Stuart's direction. The stranger gave a soft laugh.

"Please tell me this is a first date," he said, his voice quiet enough to avoid Stuart's attention. "You look way too smart to go out with this guy a second time."

I stifled a laugh and risked a quick turn of my head to meet his eyes, whispering, "Blind date. I almost left him at dinner when we split the check and he tried to stiff the waitress, but he had a VIP invite, and I've never been here before . . ." I trailed off, biting my lip.

I was constitutionally incapable of being cool. Oh, well. I was never one for pretending to be what I wasn't. Cool, at least the VIP level of cool, was beyond me. I shifted in my seat, angling my body toward the hot stranger as I turned my face back to Stuart. He was still rambling on about his dissertation and slurping at his drink, unaware I was talking to another man.

"Ouch," the stranger said. "How did a guy like that get a date with a woman like you? You're way out of his league."

I blushed. Feeling the heat in my cheeks, I blushed harder. I cleaned up well, but the make up and the short skirt weren't really me.

This man was gorgeous. I'd bet he'd be gorgeous the morning after a bender, with no sleep, hungover. I took another quick look, one that ended up lingering as I took in his bladed cheekbones, deep brown eyes, and shining, thick hair the color of espresso.

I couldn't see much of his body, but the length of his legs and the breadth of his shoulders hinted it would be worth getting a closer look.

The stranger beside me wasn't just some guy. He was a man. He lounged on the couch as if he owned the place, both commanding and at ease. I shifted in my seat as he tilted his head closer to mine, his warm breath on my cheek sending a pulse of need straight between my legs.

I'd never reacted to a man like this, my body jumping to 'Go' before I knew his name. But as I mentioned, the man beside me was no 'guy'. He was more potent than any male I'd ever spoken to before. It was no wonder my body was overwhelmed.

His lips grazed my ear as he said, "Do you want to come sit over here?"

My jaw must have dropped. I *did* want to go sit over there. Could I? Just stand up and abandon my lackluster blind date? Before I could respond, I felt the stranger beside me shake his head. "No," he said. "Never mind. Let's just get out of here. I want to show you something."

I was still trying to catch up when he stood. Taking the step from his seating area to mine, he stopped before me, his hand extended. I stared up at him dumbly.

I'd been right. His body was well worth a closer look. Looming above me, he filled my vision. I didn't think about it. I just put my hand in his larger one and let him pull me to my feet.

Off in the distance, through the buzzing in my ears, I heard a laugh and a female gasp, then caught the sound of Stuart sputtering a protest. The stranger had me caught in a spell, his dark gaze hot as he scanned my face, dipping only briefly to my exposed cleavage before locking on my eyes.

Pulling me closer, he said, "I know it's crazy, and completely inappropriate, but I've been wanting to do this since you walked in the door."

A sharp tug on my hand and I fell forward, closing the inches between us, my breasts pillowing against his hard chest. Startled, I looked up to see his face draw closer until his mouth came down on mine.

I'd been kissed before—not a ton, but more than a few times. I'd never been kissed like this. His arm wrapped around my waist, pressing my body to his, turning me until my legs straddled his thigh. His hand closed over my hip with a possessive grip.

He didn't start slow. His lips hit mine, opening my mouth to him, his tongue stroking, teasing me, claiming me.

If I'd thought about it, I'm sure I would have done something—backed away, protested, something.

Anything other than what I did. I curled my fingers around his shoulders and held on for dear life while a complete stranger ravaged me with the kiss of a lifetime.

I'd stepped out of my boring blind date and into a dream. I'd never seen a man this hot in real life, much less been kissed by one. I didn't have it in me to shut him down.

Maybe it was the margaritas at dinner or the pathetic excuse for a date. Maybe the stranger kissing me was just that hot. I didn't care. I kissed him back with everything I had, holding on tight, relishing the scrape of his stubble on my cheek and the heat of his lips moving on mine.

When he finally broke the kiss, I was panting. I may have been whimpering, just a little. His lips dropped to my ear, nipping the lobe for a second before he said, "Do you want to get out of here?"

Want More?
Read *The Billionaire's Secret Heart* Now!

# SNEAK PEEK: UNRAVELED
# (EVERS & SUMMER)
## CHAPTER ONE: SUMMER

The knock at the door startled me so badly I almost dropped my curling iron. I wasn't that late, was I? I wasn't supposed to be downstairs for another...

Oh, crap. I *was* that late.

Unplugging the curling iron and giving my lashes a quick swipe of mascara, I rushed to the door, swung it open, and froze.

It wasn't Julie, here to pick me up for a girls' night out.

No, standing in the door was my very own, personal Achilles' heel.

The devil come to tempt me.

Eve with the Apple.

Okay, bad analogy. Evers Sinclair could be a devil, but he was no Eve.

Evers Sinclair was male temptation incarnate, and I'd never been able to resist him.

He smiled at me, lips curved into a grin seasoned with mischief and filled with promise.

That grin always got me, even when I'd resolved to resist him.

Especially when I'd resolved to resist him.

He leaned in my doorway, one arm braced against the frame, his ice-blue eyes doing a slow perusal from my head to my toes, heating as they took in my deliberately-tumbled blonde curls, little black cocktail dress, and mile-high spike heels.

"Going somewhere?"

His voice was all flirtation, but his eyes said something else. Something I couldn't quite read.

Annoyance?

Irritation?

That couldn't be worry, could it?

Giving an internal shrug, I stepped back to let him in. I'd given up on understanding Evers Sinclair. Evers walked in as if he belonged in my apartment, dropping his over-stuffed briefcase on the chair by the front door before heading into the kitchen to help himself to a beer.

Popping the cap off the bottle, he turned and leaned against the counter, taking a long swig.

"I like the dress," he said, lids heavy over those cool blue eyes, gaze smoldering.

Ignoring the flash of heat at the look in his eyes, I rolled my own. "It's new," I said.

"You didn't answer my question," he said smoothly, his gaze tracing the V-shaped neckline of my dress and the generous display of cleavage framed by black silk.

His eyes peeled the dress off my shoulders, stripped me naked. It had been three weeks since I'd seen him, and I'd felt his absence every day.

The heat growing in my belly kicked up a notch. I gritted my teeth and pushed it back. I did not have time for this. My body didn't care. It never did where Evers Sinclair was concerned.

He showed up, smoldered at me, and my body was ready to go.

"Which question?" I shot back, always ready to play the game with Evers, even against my better judgment.

Since the moment we'd met, he'd been getting under my skin. As hard as I tried, I couldn't quite work him back out.

"Are you going somewhere? If it's a bad time I can leave."

I stopped, the quick retort frozen on my tongue. I took another look at Evers, seeing past his distinctive eyes, his broad shoulders and sharp cheekbones, past the beauty to the man beneath.

He was tired, I realized with surprise. More than tired, he looked exhausted. His face was drawn, lines bracketing his mouth, purple-gray smudges beneath his eyes.

I had no idea what he'd been doing since the last time he'd shown up at my door, but whatever it was, he looked like he needed nothing more than a good meal and a solid night's sleep.

I bit back the sarcastic retort on the tip of my tongue and told him the truth. "I am. I'm sorry, I didn't know you'd be coming by and—"

"Hot date?"

I wasn't imagining the edge in his voice. I debated how to answer.

It wasn't any of his business if I did have a hot date. We had a thing, yeah. A thing neither of us had ever bothered to define. A thing that was definitely not exclusive.

I didn't know who he was with when he wasn't with me. I could never bring myself to ask. That way lay heartbreak.

Evers Sinclair was a player.

He was not a one-woman man, and he never would be.

I'd known from the start I had a choice. Take what he was willing to give or walk away.

It had never occurred to me that he would care if I saw other people, but the way he'd asked *hot date?* didn't sound nonchalant.

Again, I went with the truth.

"Not tonight. You know my friend Julie?" Evers nodded. I'd mentioned Julie before. She and I had known each other since college. "She and Frank broke up."

"That was a long time coming," Evers commented.

He'd never met Julie, but he'd heard me bitch about her boyfriend more than once. Frank was an asshole who didn't deserve my sweet, funny friend, and she'd finally figured it out. Hallelujah.

"I know. She caught him flirting with the waitress when they were out to dinner, which would have been bad enough, but when he disappeared to the bathroom for a little too long and she went looking for him—"

"Let me guess, she walked in on him in the back hall with his hand up the waitress' skirt," Evers said dryly.

I shrugged a shoulder. "Close enough. The waitress smacked him—apparently, she had better asshole radar then Julie—and then Julie kicked him in the nuts and walked out."

"Good for her," Evers said.

That was the thing about Evers. He was a player and a flirt, but he was honest about it. He'd never once made me a promise he couldn't keep. Never once implied that he could give me more and let me down.

He was a player, but he wasn't a liar.

That was the only reason I could make this crazy arrangement work. Well, that and the sex.

The sex was amazing.

Fucking fantastic.

Fantastic fucking.

Hell, however you wanted to put it, getting in bed with Evers Sinclair was worth the dangerous game we were playing.

I was going to end up getting hurt.

I knew it, but I couldn't seem to stop myself. He was dangerous, but he was Evers.

Just like the second piece of chocolate cake. I kept telling myself *only one more bite* and found myself going back for more.

Over and over.

Eventually, I was going to work up the willpower to give him up completely.

Eventually. But not tonight.

I picked up my purse from the kitchen counter, removing lip gloss, wallet, and emergency cash, transferring them to the small black purse that matched my dress.

"Julie's finally past the sappy movie and ice cream stage and she wants to go out. Get dressed up, you know, have a little fun and discover a new, post-Frank world."

"And you're playing wing-woman?" Evers asked, taking another pull on the beer, his eyes lingering on the short hem of my dress.

"Something like that," I said, the trail of his gaze heating my skin. I found myself wondering if I could bail. I wasn't the only one going out with Julie and—no.

No.

I was not bailing on a girlfriend for Evers.

No way.

This was Julie's night. Ditching her for hot sex, even stupendously hot sex, was not cool. I pressed my thighs together, willing my body to stand down.

I swear, one look at Evers and my hormones leapt into overdrive.

He took another pull on the beer and didn't say anything. Something in the line of his neck, the tilt of his jaw made me think he didn't like the idea of me being Julie's wing-woman.

I fought back the urge to make an excuse, to explain that I wasn't going to pick anybody up, I was just there to support a friend.

It wasn't any of his business what I did.

That wasn't what we were.

I didn't know what the hell we were, but I knew it wasn't that. It wasn't explanations and promises.

It was moments of time.

It was the present, not the future.

I knew that. So why did I find myself saying, "I won't be late. If you want to hang out, I have leftover Chinese in the fridge from last night. Orange beef, your favorite, and some egg rolls. You can eat dinner, watch the game until I get home."

My stomach lurched.

*Why did I say that?*

Evers had never been in my apartment without me. He'd never spent the night. We'd fallen asleep together, too exhausted to move after a marathon of sex, muscles wrung out, nerves fried with pleasure. In the morning, he was always gone.

Why had I offered him my leftover take-out, my couch, and my TV? And why did he look relieved?

My phone chimed with a text. Julie, downstairs waiting. I didn't have time to figure out the mystery of Evers Sinclair.

"That's Julie. I've got to run. Do you want to stay?"

Evers set his beer on the counter and prowled toward

me, cool blue eyes intent on mine. "Come here," he growled, reaching out to pull me into his arms. His mouth landed on my neck just below my ear, sending sparks through every nerve in my body.

Evers could play my body like an instrument, and he did. Moving his lips down the cord of my neck, his strong arms absorbed my shivers, his leg nudging between mine, hand dropping to cup my ass, urging me closer until I ground against him, shuddering under his mouth, the caress of his lips, the heat of his tongue on my skin.

Lifting his mouth, he nipped my earlobe before whispering, his breath hot in my ear, "Have fun. Stay out of trouble. When you get back I'll fuck you until you can't walk."

I thought *promises, promises,* but the words remained unspoken, short-circuiting between my brain and my mouth. All I could do was gasp as his teeth nipped my jaw and his mouth fell on mine.

Evers Sinclair knew how to kiss. Like, he really knew how to kiss. I wrapped my arms around his neck and held on for dear life, his lips opening mine, tongue stroking, his hands everywhere.

A heartbeat later I was flushed with heat, hips rolling into his, every inch of me wound tight.

Desperate. For him.

My phone chimed again, the high-pitched sound cutting through the haze. Reluctantly, I eased away, sliding my hips out of his grip, dropping my hands from his neck, breaking the contact between our mouths.

I had to go.

I had to go, but I didn't want to end that kiss.

I already knew I was a mess, hair all over the place, cheeks flushed, lip gloss smeared across my cheek.

I didn't expect the flags of red on Evers' cheekbones, the

335

tight set of his jaw, the glitter in his eyes. His hands flexed at his sides as if he wanted to reach out. To drag me back.

On shaky legs, I stepped away, hiding the roil of my emotions, lust, and want. Longing.

"I have to go," I said inanely. He already knew I had to go. Why wasn't I leaving?

"Go then. I'll be here when you get back."

His words sounded suspiciously like a promise. *They aren't*, I told myself as I considered one more kiss, then thought better of it.

If I kissed him again, I'd never leave my apartment, and Julie was waiting.

Grabbing my purse, I headed for the door without another word. Standing at the elevator, I lectured myself.

*Be sensible.*

*This is Evers Sinclair.*

*He might get bored and wander off before you even get home.*

*Don't count on him being there.*

*Don't count on him for anything.*

I warned myself, but I didn't listen. I never had where Evers was concerned.

I had no idea what I was doing with him. We were a total mismatch.

From the moment we'd met we hadn't gotten along.

He was bossy, autocratic, arrogant, and an incorrigible flirt. Evers wasn't my type in so many ways. I favored serious guys, usually cute, but not hot. Guys with normal jobs and normal lives.

I sound exciting, don't I? But that's the thing, I'm not exciting. I'm a perfectly normal girl with a perfectly normal life. A least I was, until the day Evers swept in and turned everything upside down.

I was at a conference in Houston, kind of bored, kind of having fun, looking forward to the weekend when I was expecting a visit from my best friend, Emma.

Evers had appeared out of nowhere, claiming that Emma was in danger and she needed my help. If I'd heard that line from anyone else I would have laughed him out of town. Especially since he refused to tell me what the trouble was or how she needed my help.

I'd known, the way best friends always know, that Emma was involved in something, but that didn't mean I trusted Evers. Still, I'd gone with him, all the way to Atlanta, bickering the whole time.

I couldn't help myself. He was so high-handed. He strolled in and expected me to do his bidding just because he said so.

It hadn't helped that every time I looked at him, my knees went weak.

Back then he'd worn his hair almost military short, and it left every inch of that chiseled face on display, from his dark brows to his ice-blue eyes, his sharp cheekbones and full lower lip.

His face is enough to make a girl swoon. His body kicks the whole package up a notch. I didn't have to see beneath the suits to know that Evers Sinclair was sex on a stick.

So out of my league. So very much out of my league.

We'd bickered and flirted, and that had been it.

Until Emma's wedding.

A little too much champagne, an argument over the wedding cake, and before I knew it, I was backed into a wall behind an arrangement of potted plants, Evers' hand on my ass under my bridesmaid's dress.

I could blame the champagne for falling into bed with Evers, but that would be a flat-out lie. It had nothing to do with the champagne and everything to do with Evers Sinclair.

Damn, that man knew how to use his hands. And his mouth. And everything else.

We'd spent Emma's wedding night locked up in my hotel room. And the night after. And the night after that.

Then I'd flown home, he'd left town on a job, and I wrote off Evers Sinclair as a wedding insanity mistake.

Maybe not a mistake.

It's hard to call sex that good a mistake.

And what's wrong with having a fling every once in a while? Every girl should have a fling. Except I was a serial dater. I didn't fling. One-night stands seemed like too much work for not enough payoff.

With Evers, it was all payoff and no work. When I bumped into him again a year later at a client's party, my body went on full alert the second my eyes met his.

I'd convinced myself I'd forgotten Evers, but my body hadn't. Not for one red-hot second.

Evers had his own gravity, a magnetic pull that drew me across the room, demanding my attention even when I was in the middle of a client's party. At the end of the night, he'd been there, lounging against my car, waiting.

I'd invited him home, we fell into bed, and our non-relationship was born.

He showed up every once in a while, knocking on my door with no notice, and I always let him in. Every now and then, I'd text, and he'd come. I'd never been to his place and wasn't exactly sure where he lived. Somewhere in Atlanta.

I was in Marietta, northwest of the city. Close enough that we could have seen each other more often, but neither of us offered or asked for more.

I didn't ask because I knew I wouldn't get it, and Evers because he didn't do more. More wasn't his thing.

Julie was waiting in front of my building, the car running, music blaring through the open windows. She was ready to party, but she didn't miss a thing. A grin bloomed on her face when she saw me.

I snapped my seatbelt into place as she said, "Your lip gloss is smudged."

"I still have lip gloss?" I lifted a hand to wipe my lips. I'd have been shocked if Evers hadn't kissed every speck off my lips. I pressed my knees together at the thought.

*Down girl, tonight's not about you. Not until you get home. If he's still there.*

Julie stared at me for a minute before her eyes flared wide and she glanced at my building. "Is he up there? Did he come by tonight?"

She thought my weird thing with Evers Sinclair was the stuff of fairytales. Evers Sinclair of the Atlanta Sinclairs. She imagined he'd fall in love with me, and we'd live happily ever after in a little mansion in Buckhead.

I gave a mental snort. Not likely.

I couldn't see Evers settling down, and if he did, it wouldn't be with someone like me. Someone normal. Average.

He'd find some society princess or a former model. An actress. Somebody with flash. With flair. Someone exciting enough to fit into his life.

Evers Sinclair came from a long line of Atlanta Sinclairs who, a few generations back, had founded the premier security agency in the country.

They protected royalty. Celebrities.

Designed security systems that put Fort Knox to shame.

He was James Bond come to life, from the perfectly-

SNEAK PEEK: UNRAVELED (EVERS & SUMMER)

tailored suit to the Aston Martin. I wasn't the first to get caught in his orbit, and I wouldn't be the last. I was just enjoying the ride.

I shook my head at Julie. "He's up there, but don't worry about it. Tonight is about you."

Julie hesitated before putting the car in gear. "Are you sure? I mean, we can go out any night. He hasn't come by in a few weeks, and—"

"I'm sure," I insisted, irritated that even Julie thought the world should stop for Evers Sinclair. "If he wanted to know if I was free, he could have called. He shows up, he takes what he gets. Tonight is for you. He can wait."

Julie leaned over and threw her arms around me in an awkward hug, considering our seatbelts. "You're the best friend, Summer. Most girls would have ditched me for a hottie like Evers Sinclair."

My libido bitched at me when I said, "I'm not most girls, and he'll be there when I get home."

I hoped.

I really, really hoped he'd be there when I got home.

**Read *Unraveled* Now!**

# ALSO BY IVY LAYNE

**Don't Miss Out on New Releases, Exclusive Giveaways, and More!!**

Join Ivy's Readers Group @ ivylayne.com/readers-group

## THE HEARTS OF SAWYERS BEND

Stolen Heart

Sweet Heart

Scheming Heart

Rebel Heart

## THE UNTANGLED SERIES

Unraveled

Undone

Uncovered

## THE WINTERS SAGA

The Billionaire's Secret Heart (Novella)

The Billionaire's Secret Love (Novella)

The Billionaire's Pet

The Billionaire's Promise

The Rebel Billionaire

The Billionaire's Secret Kiss (Novella)

The Billionaire's Angel

Engaging the Billionaire

Compromising the Billionaire

The Counterfeit Billionaire

## THE BILLIONAIRE CLUB

The Wedding Rescue

The Courtship Maneuver

The Temptation Trap

## ABOUT IVY LAYNE

Ivy Layne has had her nose stuck in a book since she first learned to decipher the English language. Sometime in her early teens, she stumbled across her first Romance, and the die was cast. Though she pretended to pay attention to her creative writing professors, she dreamed of writing steamy romance instead of literary fiction. These days, she's neck deep in alpha heroes and the smart, sexy women who love them.

Married to her very own alpha hero (who rubs her back after a long day of typing, but also leaves his socks on the floor). Ivy lives in the mountains of North Carolina where she and her other half are having a blast raising two energetic little boys. Aside from her family, Ivy's greatest loves are coffee and chocolate, preferably together.

### VISIT IVY
Facebook.com/AuthorIvyLayne
Instagram.com/authorivylayne/
www.ivylayne.com
books@ivylayne.com

Made in the USA
Middletown, DE
14 November 2024

64602552R00197